Kate Finn grew up on the South Boston docks idolizing her commercial fisherman father, Seamus Finn and his friends. Now she's a marine biologist working for the FDA who still spends as much time as she can on the docks near this salty crew. That is, until one misty morning when she discovers her father's best friend, Sammy, dead there. All signs point toward Seamus and he is arrested and accused of the murder.

At the bail hearing Kate learns a family secret—her father killed a man in self-defense when her mother was pregnant with Kate. Acquitted then, this time he's sent to prison to await trial. Raised with the fierce loyalties of South Boston in her blood, Kate vows to clear his name. Soon Kate accepts a job that violates all of her family legacy. She goes to work for Colin Greely at Greely Seafood Labs where fish are genetically engineered. Kate will use her scientific training to investigate the murder of Sammy and save her family.

Turns out she has some distractions. Another fisherman is attacked on the docks. Now who can she trust? Greely? His right-hand-man Ed McGann? Detective Rich Madley? Her mentor, Dr. Zion? Her old love interest Pierre Gosselin? Or, are they all in league against the Finns? Kate learns that *circumstances are not always as they appear.*

D1564294

PRAISE FOR THE DOCKS
***

Joanne Carota weaves a tale of suspense through the gritty lives of South Boston fishermen, marine biologists working to save the environment, and the greedy fat cats who rule the seafood distribution industry. Carota's Kate Finn is thrown headlong into these murky waters and struggles to stay afloat as she hunts for a killer.
— **James Potter**, longtime Boston editor

***

Set in and around the Boston Fish Pier, Joanne Carota's *The Docks* is a shaft of light on a storied but fading district of one of America's most interesting and infamous cities. The men and women who "go down to the sea in ships" to bring back a precious catch are the characters who bring vibrant life to Carota's novel. Salty to be sure and Irish to the core, they are a plenitude of good and evil, right and wrong, fierce passions and long-held secrets. This tautly plotted story moves with speed but does not neglect weight—its powerful themes are those universal struggles between generations, between the old ways and the inevitability of change, and between those who cut corners for profit and those who hew to the law even when the statute books can't keep pace with corrupt science and the cops are not always on the up and up. The Fish Pier has its ways and its language, and *The Docks* captures both, the latter a symphony of Irish Boston and the sea — **Sterling Watson** is the acclaimed author of eight novels including: *The Committee*, *Suitcase City*, *Fighting in the Shade*, and *The Calling*. He is the Peter Meinke Professor Emeritus of Creative Writing and Literature at Eckerd College and co-founder with Dennis Lehane of the Eckerd College Writers' Conference, Writers in Paradise.

continued ...

***

The Docks is a fast-paced and atmospheric mystery with an intelligently flawed and engaging female protagonist. Joanne Carota is adept at creating believable characters intertwined with fascinating scientific marine details and daily life among the commercial fisherman and inside the fishing industry of Boston. In the best tradition of mysteries, the setting is evoked with a quiet mastery that draws the reader into a new world. *The Docks* is a distinguished debut. — **James Anderson**, author of *The Never-Open Desert Diner* and *Lullaby Road*

***

Rich with the unique flavor of the South Boston waterfront and the pulse of the shifting Boston underworld, *The Docks* is filled with family saga, murder, mystery, corporate intrigue, and even romance. Brace yourself as the young marine biologist, Kate Finn, is pulled deeper and deeper into a frightening and twisted web of Frankenfish, false alliances, and treachery. Carota captures the psyche of this area and reveals the inner-workings of the shady seafood industry while telling a hair-raising tale that will keep you turning pages past your bedtime. — **Alison L. McLennan** author of *Falling for Johnny*, *Ophelia's War*, and *Dangerous Mercy*

***

The Docks, at once gritty and charming, brings together Boston's salty watermen with modern environmental mobsters. Carota jigs from the chilling sea, where things first seem fishy, to the family "pahlah," where she wraps us in warm Irish wool, hooking and holding us through every last tantalizing page. It's a wicked pissah! — **Terese Schlachter**, author and Emmy-winning documentary producer

continued …

***

The Docks is a well done mystery with a strong and highly contemporary spine (the conflicts — including murder, blackmail, and corporate spying — are tossed up by the need to make commercial fishing sustainable), and a thoroughly likeable marine biologist heroine who has the requisite touch of vulnerability, as well as an appealing appreciation of where she's come from. Indeed, all the characters are well drawn and thoroughly fleshed out, and the locale intriguing. *The Docks* takes place largely on the Boston waterfront, and Carota gives us plenty of verisimilitude--both the grit of Southie, and the scene that attracts the sophisticates of academia and cutting-edge business. — **Beverly Swerling**, international author of book series including: *City of Glory*, *Bristol House* and *City of God*

***

The piers, pubs, and laboratories of Joanne Carota's New England are filled with secrets and a web of conspiracies that lead to catastrophic choices as characters pierce through the façade of the fishing industry. A suspenseful mystery filled with poignant family history, an acute sense of place, and disturbing discoveries.

— **Marjan Kamali**, award-winning author of *Together Tea* and *The Stationery Shop*

THE DOCKS

JOANNE CAROTA

THE DOCKS

Copyright © 2019 by Joanne Carota

Neptune Books

For more information, address: jmc3160@gmail.com

Book designer/editor James Potter

Book cover art by Robert Simonson and Paul Keaney

Cover photo by pexels.com, back cover photo by Ricardo Resende, unsplash.com

Copyeditor Kate Victory Hannisian

Neptune Books Logo Joanne Kenyon

ISBN: 978-1-7331069-0-0 (paperback)

ISBN: 978-1-7331069-1-7 (ebook)

For Mark, with love.

Acknowledgements

I am grateful to my parents, Bernard and Frances Sheehy. Dad lifted words onto trucks at the docks of Houghton Mifflin. Though he had no time to read books, he provided us a home stocked with good reads. Ma encouraged education and the arts while she modeled how to be a good wife and working mother. Somehow, they successfully launched all 10 of their children. From the top, thank you for my siblings: Bernie F. Sheehy, Patty Colella, Tommy Sheehy, Rosemary Lind, Elizabeth Gillis, Stephen Sheehy, Priscilla Arbuckle, Brian Sheehy, Caroline Cote and yours truly. Also, to spouses, children, and grandchildren. We are a lucky family.

With deep gratitude to all members of my family: the Sheehys, the Carotas, the Kopaczes.

Thank you to my niece, Sarah Colella, for marrying Joe Daly at Anthony's Pier 4 in November of 2006 when this story took hold inside of me the morning after at Fish Pier.

Thanks to:
Readers Marjan Kamali, James Anderson, Lisa Mahoney, Jen Gentile, Mae Capriole, and Holly Gonsalves, my beautiful daughter, who has believed from the beginning - Bermie Bears and all. You are generous and astute reviewers.

The Solstice MFA community led by Meg Kearney.

Sterling Watson, my mentor and friend. A distinguished writer, professor, gentleman and Southern ambassador of Legal Seafoods, thanks for your refreshing approachability and generous advice.

Mentors David Yoo, Steve Huff, and Sandra Scofield. Craft masters, indeed!

Students Alison McClellan, a first residency redeemer. Sorry for prematurely snarking your cat story (so good, really!). Kassie Rubico for introducing me to Solstice and your joyful presence. Lisa Mahoney for your good nature and smart, tireless reads. William (Buffy) Hastings whose writing I admire. James Anderson, you write beyond and still help the novice. Heather Christie - a talent. Sabra Benedict, we are waiting for your next book. Terese Schatler and Jen Grant looking forward to our next writing retreat. Lee Hope for Solstice Lit Magazine and lunch meetings at Nordstrom.

Rivier University support from Larry Maness, Sister Lucille, Brad Stull and Tim Doherty, advisor, writer, professor, and reader of sophisticated tastes. You embody your mission of teaching with empathy. Thank you for your continued support.

UMass Lowell where I have the good fortune to be an alumna and now teach part time in the English Department.

The Java Room's Candy and her entire staff who welcome all of us. Creative endeavors thrive at Java. Laura Marshall and all the indie authors of SIPA, who meet at Java on Fridays.

Copyeditor Kate Hannisian, a pleasure to work with such a professional.

Steven Holler, Massachusetts lobster fisherman, for sharing

your lobster story on a windy May 2013 day at the Cardinal Medeiros Dock.

The entire commercial fishing community and all who labor.

Joanne Kenyon for your talent and expert advice on the logo.

Robert Simonson and Paul Keaney for your cover artistry. Go raibh míle maith agat.

A special thanks to James Potter who took *The Docks* from doc to print. Jim, consummate editor, researcher, fact-checker, proofer, designer, layout expert, reader, and neighbor. A skilled journalist who sees Boston from the inside, invaluable. Also, thanks Sue and Jim Potter for your kindness and all you do to make our community a good place to live. You throw some Christmas party!

To the A-team of Mark, Matt, Holly and Tim your unconditional family love and support are everything.

There was a young fellow named Fisher,
Who was fishing for fish in a fissure,
When a cod with a grin
Pulled the fisherman in…
Now they're fishing the fissure for Fisher.
--Anonymous

Prologue

At 5:30 a.m. the brass bell clanged, a signal to open the auction on Fish Pier in South Boston. Kate loved the auction. At four years old, she'd wake up before the sun rose, creep into her parents' room and shake her father. "C'mon Poppy, time to go to Fis' Pier."

Seamus Finn drove them in his silver Ford F-150 truck with an extended cab, the car seat properly reinforced, checked more than once. Sometimes he'd buckle her too tight. When she complained, he insisted that she needed to be legally strapped in for their short drive because they couldn't take a chance of getting pulled over by the Massachusetts Dock Police (MDP).

"Mommy's a cop so we'll never get in trouble," Kate continually claimed.

Each time he'd correct her.

"Mommy's a crossing guard. And trouble will find anyone."

On the drive Seamus recited limericks. While Kate didn't fully understand them, she liked the rhyming patterns—giggling and repeating them over and over. Whenever they did see an MDP car, a signature white Camry with the outline of a codfish skeleton on the driver's door, her father's voice sank to a murmur.

"Skeleys."

Chapter One

K ate Finn liked Sunday mornings on the South Boston docks because the harbor was alive with spirits. Symphonic squeals from wooden piers echoed into the horizon; buoys melodically clanged; foghorns blasted vibrations into the harbor's thick, smoky atmosphere, and seagulls descended in search of fish droppings. Putrid smells of decomposing fish weren't offensive to Kate because she'd grown up here.

Kate pulled the sleeves of her hooded Aran cardigan over her hands and sipped her morning cup of coffee. Her small feet led her along Fish Pier's creaky planks while Neptune, god of the seas, peered from his perch on the stone conference building at the end of the pier. Kate looked down through the cracks at the salt water. No more dubbed Boston's Harbor of Shame, this former sewage container and site of 1773's Boston Tea Party had cleaned up nicely. These days blue chip companies, tech startups, luxury hotels, multi-million-dollar condos, and restaurants flooded Boston's Seaport District. Even the shrine Our Lady of Good Voyage, also known as Our Lady of the Last Minute for Catholics who delayed attending Mass until Sunday evening, had gone corporate when the Boston Archdiocese cut a slick deal with investors for a new shrine.

"In with the new; out with us oldies," Kate's Pop, Seamus Finn, often said.

Yet, through these changes, one of her favorite dock rituals remained. Without fail, at ten o'clock every morning, Uilleann bagpipes blasted "Love That Dirty Water," Dropkick Murphys-style, through outdoor speakers on Fish Pier—Kate's cue to jig and the Hub's signal to serve alcohol.

In Finn family folklore, Kate and her younger brother Michael, practically her Irish twin, jigged before they walked. Coffee cup in hand, she danced up the main dock facing East Boston wearing boat shoes and wishing she had on ghillies to properly flex her arches. Lift, hop. Count two. Turn and skip. Her auburn hair swung back and forth between her petite shoulder blades. Lift, hop. Turn, skip. Repeat. Butterfly. Birdie midair, interrupted by the loud thumping of a boat against the pilings.

Milady was tied up on the right side of the pier, where the fishing boats unloaded their daily catch. Kate shifted out of her step dance.

"Sammy," she called out. "What's up?"

No response. Kate approached the rocking vessel.

"Captain Robbins. You don't fish on Sundays."

He was slouched in his high-back captain's seat.

"Hey! You asleep?"

She climbed down the dock ladder onto Sammy Robbins' boat,

clenching her cup, coffee sloshing over the rim.

"Wake up, Captain."

Still nothing. He had on his usual cool-weather gear, head-to-ankle yellow Mariner rain slickers and black rubber boots. His eyes were open, vacant, staring east. Kate shivered at his shark eyes.

She reached out and shook his shoulder.

Leaden!

She backed away in horror while the boat slapped against the pilings, off-rhythm with her racing heartbeat. The unsynchronized movements made her unsteady.

Gasping for air, she fumbled inside her windbreaker for her phone but realized she'd left it on her desk. Tilted off-balance, she tripped toward his body, hoping he would miraculously respond.

Sammy's face was pallid, his lifeless lips a fluorescent green.

And there was something else. A protrusion from his chest area.

The heartbeat in her eardrums violently vibrated while she pulled the slicker's zipper halfway. A giant codfish sprawled across Sammy's enormous chest.

Its cheeks had been removed.

She splayed Sammy's jacket open. A chunk of cod cheek fell into his lap.

The fish was tinted fluorescent green, like Sammy's lips.

As if compelled by scientific rote, she tossed the remaining coffee, picked up the chunk of fish with her thumb and forefinger, which became slightly green-tinted as well, and placed it inside her coffee mug. She covered the mug with her palm and gripped the edges.

The Spirit of Boston cruised mid-harbor. Milady absorbed its wake and Kate's world started to spin. At center aft, she vomited into the harbor before clambering off the boat up to her office.

Inside her office on the pier overlooking Sammy on Milady, she scurried over to the horizontal freezer and opened the top. It was full of pink Hostess Sno Balls. She shut it, placed the fish sample in her desk drawer, reconsidered, then covered the mug with paper towels and stuffed it out of sight behind binders in her bookcase.

Chapter Two

Once Kate had called the police she walked back down to the docks and stood watch over Sammy, slumped lower in his captain's seat. It was the least she could do for her father's best friend.

Growing up, Sammy used to let Kate sit behind Milady's wheel while the boat was in port. Because she got seasick easily, going out on the water didn't really interest her, but dock activities did. And though Mom claimed the docks were no place for a young girl, Kate nagged and Pop defended, usually convincing Mom to let Kate accompany him and visit with Sammy. Sammy loved children although he had none of his own. He sang Irish tunes like "Danny Boy" without any apparent self-consciousness. Kate joined in when she knew the lyrics, often offering her hand to Sammy for a dance. Those were happy times on the docks, when Pop would sing and jig along, too.

That was a long time ago. These days she worked on the docks as an independent contractor for the Food and Drug Administration, assuring that consumers could continue to eat fish without fear of accidental poisoning. Fish paid her a living. But things were changing in the Seaport—local fishing was being rapidly replaced by global distribution companies, like Greely Labs, Groundfish Partners, Common Ground, Flippin' Fish, and AgaCulture, that all undermined the prices of daily catches by local fishermen.

"It's criminal" was the mantra of the fishermen whose return on investment got lower each year.

"Miss Katherine Finn?"

The voice startled her. Kate nodded to the man in a dark raincoat.

"I'm Detective Rich Madley, Massachusetts Dock Police."

She inspected him. She'd never really dealt with the police and Pop had especially steered her away from skeleys. She remembered his mantra: "Skeleys are not real cops. No one respects them." He was like that—crystal-clear about his opinions.

"It is Miss?" he asked.

"Actually, it's Doctor."

"MD or PhD?"

"Marine Biologist. PhD."

"Right."

She shook the detective's hand. It was cold and crushing.

"Kate is fine."

"Miss Finn, I'm sorry for your recent situation."

"Why? Was it your fault?" Her voice sounded as if it were coming through a tunnel and she wished she could rephrase her defensive response. But she couldn't clear her thoughts or even her vision. Brain fog. Everything looked tilted, a crooked house. And she found him arrogant, with his insistence on calling her "Miss."

He pulled out a notepad and pen.

Kate recited her name, address, and contact numbers, adding, "You guys still use pen and paper?"

"Some of us. Why?"

"Well, it is the twenty-first century and we are in the Innovation District."

He flipped through his notepad and continued.

"Witness: Katherine Finn. Slim woman." He chuckled. "Freckles, red hair, sparkling green eyes."

She sent her steely gaze straight through him. "Auburn hair."

"How tall?" He cocked his head. "Five feet?"

"Five-three." People who underestimated her height irked her. "Are these personal details really necessary?"

"Age?"

"Twenty-seven."

Madley's head dipped.

"Problem?" she asked.

"You just look much younger. Must be the freckles."

"Well, I'm not. Can we get to Sammy?"

"You knew the deceased?"

She was exasperated. "Yes. The deceased is my father's friend, Sammy Robbins."

Madley cleared his throat like he had a nervous tic. "As you know, this is Massport property, but MDP has jurisdiction, not the staties or BPD." He grinned. "Though they're both always trying to take back the docks. No way, we got the docks and we'll keep them." He cleared his throat. "Nevertheless they have been contacted and understand that the area where the body was found has been secured during the preliminary investigation. The body stays put until we get things settled here."

Why was he telling her all this? He sounded like a madman. Pop was right; skeleys were an odd lot. She felt disoriented.

"Do you need something?" he asked. "You look pale."

"Please, let's just get this over with."

Meanwhile sirens whined, and marked and unmarked vehicles pulled up to the docks. Madley remained in position.

"We'll proceed. How did you find the body?"

"I got up this morning and took my coffee down to the docks."

"Got up where?"

She bowed toward her building. "Over there."

Madley took in the implication. "You work over there? The first building? The corner office facing the Fishery Exchange Building? You slept in your office last night?"

Kate felt like she was sinking in his barrage of questions. "I work odd hours. Get more done at night in the lab. I was saying, I walked up to the edge of the dock and I found Sammy." She felt a lump in her throat. "Dead." The scene was still surreal to her, but when she said "Sammy" and "dead" together it started to feel real.

"I'm surprised you didn't see anything. Did you see anyone coming or going off the docks?"

Kate felt tense. What was he getting at? "No. I didn't."

"What's your job here?"

8

"I contract for the FDA, in HACCP. I test fish samples for levels of toxins and bacteria and provide traceability through serialization of approved lots."

Madley looked confused. He stopped writing and stared directly at Kate.

She continued, "Hazard Analysis Critical Control Program. I'm certified in the quality assurance area."

"Impressive."

Kate rolled her eyes. She was forming an opinion of Madley and it was not complimentary. He was stiff, robotic. A real chump. "Ever hear of the National Oceanic and Atmospheric Administration? NOAA?"

"Of course," he said. "Who hasn't?"

"Well, they started the whole program."

"Let's go up to your office."

Kate led the way into the building and up the stairs to her third-floor office. Her face was flushed. She couldn't remember if she had picked up her personal items after she hid the chunk of Sammy's fish. Maybe she made a mistake; maybe she shouldn't have taken the fish.

At twelve feet by twelve feet, Kate's office was perfectly square with cream-colored walls, nautical maps, marine biology posters, and FDA standards hanging from the bulletin board adjacent to the window overlooking Boston Harbor. Her cot was propped up against the farthest wall, looking out over the window. She usually put it away in the closet on the weekdays. Madley looked around and took notes. He reached inside his raincoat and pulled out a small pocket camera and took some photos.

"If I knew you were going to come up, I would have been more prepared. My office is a bit scrambled."

"No problem," he said. "Best nothing has been touched."

Gradually she realized she was under investigation. It occurred to her that maybe she should call a lawyer and then stubbornly pushed the thought out of her mind. This hack could not possibly think she was involved on any level with the death of Sammy. He was a family friend. She was being paranoid.

"Nice setup."

"Thanks. It's home." She scurried to her cot and scooped up the jumble of her day-old jeans and sweater, her red bra and panties streaming out from the sides of the pile. She shoved the undergarments under the sweater and put the clothes under the cot's pillow.

Madley opened the blinds. Now the light exposed her. She had the same feeling as in her recurring naked dream, in which she walked around public places in front of fully clothed people trying to assure herself it was perfectly normal. Then panic set in when he moved to the bookcase.

Kate mindlessly neatened the papers on her desk.

"Please don't move anything yet," he reiterated.

The bookcase displayed many personal memories. One was a photo of her at age ten with Mom, Pop and her brother Michael, nine at the time, standing on the docks. Her father looked so proud of his family. They had posed for the photo in the same spot where she'd found Sammy dead this morning. Until today this had been her favorite family photo.

"Is this your family? Your father is a big guy."

"He's six-three, same as my brother."

"Fisherman?"

"Nah. Never took to the docks. He works over the bridge in finance."

Madley looked over at the vent next to the bookcase. "Why is it so loud?" The pictures pulsed. "The thing is rattling."

Kate rushed over, kneeled and tapped the grates. She could see behind the bookcase. The vibration had moved her cup away from the folders. The fish-cup was stuck between the wall and the shelf. Her body quivered as well. There was no way she could discreetly push it back.

"Damn thing. Maintenance was just here on Friday. I'll have them check it again tomorrow."

"You should do that." Madley picked up another picture.

"Who is this guy with your father?"

"That's," her voice cracked and she cleared it. "Sammy."

Madley took a note. Kate felt more uncomfortable. Did he think it was suspicious for her to have a picture of her father and his friend in her office?

"He looks different with pink lips."

Kate was speechless. How could he be so callous?

Madley's eyes swept the office. He gripped his notepad under his right arm, turned, faced each wall, and with his left hand, snapped photos.

"Who is Mr. Robbins's next of kin?"

"A brother in Florida. That's it."

He moved around the room. "Freezing fish for dinner?" He opened the freezer's horizontal door. "Holy God. How many Sno Balls do you have in here?"

"Actually I'm down. Got to get over to the new Hostess distributor."

"Why?"

"Seriously? You haven't heard about the Hostess scare? They went belly-up for a while, stopped making everything, Twinkies, everything! Anyway, I've loved these cakes all my life and now I stock up on them." She understood this kind of blathering sounded nonsensical and cleared her throat. "Just in case."

He added another note.

"Can we go to the lab area you mentioned?"

"Down the end of the hall," she said. "Are we done in here?"

He covered his nose with his sleeve. "I hope so."

"Industry hazard." She pointed toward the harbor.

"Make sure you don't move anything," he warned her.

Kate's body shook with fear as she locked her office door and guided Madley down to what she called her lab. She would need to get back to her office and move the fish. The curious detective was too curious for her taste.

In the lab, she pointed out her FDA testing equipment and explained that her role in HACCP was as the first line of defense in the system-based approach aimed at reducing occurrences of food poisoning. She told him that since they had started collecting and tracking daily samples from each commercial vessel's catch, the accidental food poisonings had been significantly reduced.

He shook his head. "Ciguatera and scombroid poisoning. A deadly couple."

She persisted, "The fishermen are less than thrilled with the program because it cuts into their profits."

"I bet!" Madley retorted. "Good stuff you're doing. I got food poisoning at Jimbo's when I was a kid from baked stuffed haddock. It was brutal. I haven't eaten haddock since."

Kate smirked. "A New Englander who doesn't eat haddock, how odd." But she remembered Sammy's cod and wondered if she would ever be able to eat codfish again.

"Detective, what happens to Sammy now?"

"An autopsy will have to be performed on Mr. Robbins."

"When?"

"I couldn't say right now. It depends on how in-depth the coroner has to go to determine cause of death. If the first indications appear to be natural causes, then the timetable will be shorter."

He was looking at a printed report on Kate's workstation. Other FDA offices shared this lab for their own testing and analysis. She had access to all the testing equipment and results, but she was confined to a small worktop where she did her reviews unless she wanted to run back and forth between the lab and her office. The fishermen pushed to get their results ASAP to know what was saleable.

"How do I read this? It looks to me like Mr. Robbins had consistently good catches, some at one hundred percent approval. Is that possible?" Madley asked.

"I admit it seems like a super-clean catch, especially compared to the other fishermen's' fallout—a high percentage of bacteria has been showing up in their catches lately due to contaminated waters. As much as twenty percent of their catches has to be dumped, if my testing finds issues. But Sammy was hitting some good luck."

"So others lost ten to twenty percent of their catch while Sambo reaped one hundred! How long had his good luck been running?"

"Sammy. His name is Sammy." Then Kate stammered, "It was last summer sometime."

"Be specific. It's April now. How many months?"

"Um. July?" Kate scowled at him.

He shook his head and made a note.

Kate reflected on when Sammy's numbers had changed. It was in July. There was typically some minor fallout in her sampling, even in good batches. Too many microbes. But Sammy was beating the odds and Pop stood in awe of Sammy's luck, dubbing him the Codfather.

"His numbers started their upswing in the summer. Around July," she reasserted.

"Long trend." He handed the reports back to her. "I want to see his numbers for the last year and compare them to the rest of the fishermen. And, um, fisherwomen."

"There are no commercial fisherwomen at this port," she said. "There are barely any fishermen. This area has become a shipping exchange—mostly distributors."

"Your father is one of a dying breed."

She smarted from his insensitive comment.

"Sorry," he muttered. "Let's hope not, for your family's sake. I'm going to seal this area until I can subpoena all the data. By the way, there is a lobsterwoman over on Cardinal Medeiros Dock. Know her?"

On occasion, she'd heard some of Pop's crew crooning over a "sexy lobsterwoman," but then Kate never paid much attention to guy talk. "Can't say I do."

"Really?" he pushed.

"I don't hang out at D Street." She was curt.

Madley palmed his radio. His glance was stern. "Let's go down to the scene and go through your morning."

"Again?"

"Bear with me." He spoke with authority. "Important for the record."

"Oh, so you can see if my story lines up. I'm starting to feel uncomfortable. Maybe I should have a lawyer here."

"Up to you."

Kate and Madley looked at each other in a standoff. His eyes flickered with amusement then quickly retreated back to police intensity.

"Forget it. I have nothing to hide." She was anxious to get outside the building, away from her stashed fish.

Yellow police tape roped off the scene while skeleys, staties, Boston cops, firefighters, and EMTs milled around. The sight made Kate choke back tears. Sammy had been in good spirits on Friday and had given her a warm smile when she gave him the okay on his catch. She wrestled with how a man could be happily fishing in his boat one day and dead in it two days later.

She looked up at Madley while he wrote in his notepad, balancing his raincoat, which was draped over his arm. A leftie with no wedding ring on his finger. For the first time, she noticed he was a good-looking guy. He had dark brown hair. The light hit his blue eyes, revealing fiery speckles that momentarily shapeshifted into red rays. He was clean-cut and fastidiously dressed in tan khakis and a black cashmere sports jacket. Did all skeleys have style when out of their navy white uniforms or just this dock detective? She looked down at her own substandard dress of dark blue chinos with deck shoes and the cable-stitched Irish sweater her mother had knitted for her. When she looked up, she noticed he had caught her checking herself out. She blushed.

A disheveled man yelled over to Madley.

"Rich, can we take the stiff now?"

Madley gave two thumbs up. "Go for it."

Kate looked at him with disgust.

"Coroner." Madley shrugged.

A town car with a vanity plate, letters GSL, slinked alongside the yellow tape.

"What's going on here?"

Kate recognized the driver from newspaper photos. Colin Greely. Nemesis of the old guard. Pop and the rest of the fishermen fumed about Greely's success in the Seaport.

"This is a crime scene, sir. Police only. Please be on your way."

Greely puckered his brow at them, then closed the window and slowly drove off.

"Guy thinks he owns the docks." Madley's tone was overtly hostile, as he shoved his notes inside his coat.

"One final question, Miss, I mean Doctor Finn. Was anyone with you this morning?"

"I beg your pardon?"

"Well, it seems odd for a young woman to hang out at the docks alone."

"That's really none of your business. I told you how I work."

"Well, I didn't mean to imply anything," he said.

Kate was incensed but caught herself. "We are done here. Right, Detective?"

"A Southie, eh? There's a certain cadence."

His assumption and misuse of Southie angered her. "Southie is a place not a people." She turned from him and walked toward her car.

He called after her, "I'll be in touch, Doctor!"

She peeled out of the parking lot away from the tall warehouses, away from the site of the fish auction, away from Sammy, toward home, less than a mile away.

Chapter Three

The best part of Kate Finn's day was when Pop came to the pier with his catch and she inspected it. Pop's takes were usually clean with small fallouts. He and Sammy used to run neck-and-neck until Sammy became the Codfather. When asked how he did it, Sammy would respond, "My magic fishing hole!" Fishing holes were sacred secrets and the other fishermen were envious. Some claimed even Kate's tests were bogus. She posted all test results on the bulletin board in the main building of Fish Pier. The numbers didn't lie. Still, there was resentment.

Today she had to tell Pop that his best friend was dead and this made her feel guilty. Her guilt ran deep like that of most Irish Catholics, even the non-practicing. Because she had found the body, somehow this would be an indictment of her, her piece of the tragedy. Undoubtedly, her parents would harp on her about looking for another job away from the docks. They always did because they allied on everything, including their provincial views. They continually rebelled against political correctness and terms like "diversity." Pop often said, "Diversity! Those mugs want to see diversity? I'll show them a real working neighborhood. Ha! No handouts for ours. No siree!"

"Amen to that." Mom's finale to all Pop's political rants.

But they were only bigots in theory because they treated everyone equally, which made Kate proud of their actions at least, since she had no tolerance for the mugs either—those touting airtight inclusivity and diversity values while they attended private schools and vacationed in elite style. Still, she found her parents' bigoted talk ugly and offensive. After years of trying to make them see the fault of their ways, there was no other solution for familial peace but to accept and limit conversation to benign topics like food and the weather. But today would be different. Today it was personal.

Kate walked toward the cement stairs to the lime green vinyl-sided house on O Street. The home Pop was so proud of. He was an only child who had come to Southie with his parents at age two from County Cork with nothing in hand but the American dream. Pop grew up in their rented third-floor tenement one street over on N Street. When he could buy his own house, he felt he had achieved his parents' dream. But by then they'd already passed.

The Burke woman—that's how her parents referred to neighbors, "the" fill-in-the-blank woman, man, or kid—was walking into her house with groceries. She shouted over a cheerful "good afternoon" and Kate responded in kind. Mrs. Burke was always in high spirits. Kate wouldn't burden her with their latest troubles because long ago, Mom taught Kate to keep her business to herself. "Do not air your thoughts in public."

She entered the house through the side door, careful not to let the door hit the hooks behind it hosting various jackets and her mother's reflective orange crossing guard vest. Inside, the mudroom was cluttered by two washing machines. One for fishing clothes. One for the rest of the laundry. Kate smelled the scent, soft remains of fish mixed with soap, that signaled she was home. Mom had few rules for Pop but did insist that he strip off his daily fishing clothes, toss them into the "fisherman's washer" and douse them with homemade borax detergent. Some days, usually after a few beers, Pop crossed the threshold into the kitchen and swung Mom into his arms, singing the "Irish Fishing Ballad," insisting his Peggy loved her man's fish smell—the smell of money. Kate adored their dance. They had some moves. Though Mom initially resisted, she'd eventually join in the Celtic waltz, which inevitably ended in a full dip and hard kiss on the lips.

Today, Pop sat at the kitchen table, shoulders hunched. His curly salt-and-pepper hair was matted down and the skin surrounding his blue eyes had crevices. His giant hands were anchored to his personalized POP coffee mug, given to him by Kate and Michael when they were much younger.

"You heard?" Kate asked.

"Rob called." He responded in the matter-of-fact way that was Pop's trademark when dealing with dramatic events. His Irish stoic nature. "Was on the police scanner so Rob went down but the Pier was all cordoned off."

"He looked so helpless, it made me sick."

"Stop." He slammed his coffee mug on the table. "Just stop,

please."

Kate was startled and hurt. "Okay. I'm sorry."

"I'm sorry, too." Pop put his head down.

It was rare for him to apologize and her guilt mounted.

"Can't believe you had to be the one to find Sammy." He shook his head. "So wrong."

"A skeley, Detective Madley, kept me for questioning."

"I don't get you. Why are you down there on a Sunday? Bad enough you're there all week."

"What did Rob say, Pop?"

"Said rumor is, Sammy had a heart attack." He took a large swig of coffee and stared out the back window. "I don't know, the guys have been noticing weird stuff with him lately."

Rob Fitzpatrick still worked as a deckhand. All the men on the docks watched out for each other. This June, Pop, Sammy, Rob and Louie turned sixty. In years past they cited their birthday month as a reason to celebrate over a few more beers than usual, their gathering laced with rough language and innocuous sparring about their fishing prowess. Pop never swore at home so it embarrassed him if Kate overheard what he considered "dock talk."

Pop continued, "He was breaking away from us. You know we're a protective lot about our fishing spots. Sammy was getting withdrawn, more and more. He stopped having beers with us on Fridays in the parking lot after docking."

He ran his hands through his thick, curly hair. "I shouldn't even be saying this, but some heavy guys have been down on the docks talking to him after the inspections."

"Who?" Kate asked.

"The suits. Greely's buyers."

"Sammy hates those guys, Pop. He has his own customers." She felt somewhat disingenuous. She, too, had seen Sammy talking to the men in suits. Even now she shrank from what she still saw as her father's domain. She decided not to tell him about the fish she'd stashed.

Pop was still reciting his soliloquy about the struggles of fishermen. "Times are tough for the small guys. A lot of people are doing things out of character."

And then he stopped talking, got up from the table and walked into the living room to watch his shows, sitting down in his brown leather recliner that had seen better years. He was an avid game show fan—he said the programs relaxed him by using his mind and releasing his body from his daily labor. Lately, Kate could see that most days he was wrung out.

The bellowing quiet left in the kitchen, the face-to-face silence with her mother, made Kate uncomfortable. "Sounds like he's making this my fault." The lump in her throat swelled.

"Don't be ridiculous. Not your fault." She pushed a long auburn lock pasted with gray off her forehead. "Your father is just sick over losing his best friend. Can you imagine how that must feel?"

"I'm pretty sure I can. I found the body, remember? That was no picnic at sea." Kate's voice receded. She didn't yell when she was mad. Her voice sank from its generally clear, crisp pitch to baritone.

"Aw-right, aw-right! Let's just calm down."

Kate collapsed into the kitchen chair and pressed her head into folded arms. She could hear her mother weeding through the cupboards, crinkling something. When she picked her head up, there was a single Sno Ball packet in front of her.

"Singles?"

"They had a special at the Stop and Shop."

"Cool." She devoured the treat.

Mom knew when Kate had reached her breaking point. But her mother didn't even hug Kate. Theirs was an awkward relationship. They'd been closer when she was young, when Mom got a kick out of her science obsession. On her sixth birthday, she asked for a chemistry kit and recruited her mother as her lab assistant. The kitchen was their laboratory. Together they would create homemade volcanoes with baking soda, vinegar, and dish detergent; green slime with food coloring and laundry detergent; and rock candy with string, water, and sugar. Kate had placed in every science fair from middle school through high school. Now, even though they physically resembled each other, they had little in common.

Mom yanked another brown mug out of the white metal cupboard to the left of the sink, framed by a bump out window with plants inside and a bird feeder outside, all facing the small back yard.

Finn coffee was mud and Kate shuddered at the thought of its bitter taste, especially after the sweetness of the chocolate, marshmallow and coconut cake. She usually passed but she didn't want to rock the boat today. Still, caffeine was the last thing she needed.

She stood up and glanced out the window. The old shed where Pop kept his fishing equipment was getting tired-looking; small holes in the siding let rodents inside. Squirrels were running across the pitched roof, tearing at the weathered shingles. The door flew open. "Pop still hasn't fixed the shed door?"

"What? I fixed that dammed thing." He ran outside in fury. Without a jacket!

"Mom. He's out of control. It's just a shed."

"He fiddled with that thing all last Sunday. 'Tighter than Fort Knox,' he said."

"In that case the country's gold is at huge risk."

Mom poured the silt into the rugged twelve-ounce mug. "Sit down and tell me what happened."

Kate relayed how she'd found Sammy dead in his boat, leaving out her hijinks of stashing the piece of codfish. She described the crime scene in detail, including Detective Madley and his endless questions. When she finished, she thumped her coffee cup down on the table. "Mom, I have a funny feeling."

"Feelings usually mean trouble."

Once again Kate shook off her mother's stoic manner. "You heard what Pop said. Sammy was acting weird."

"What are you talking about? Rob told Pop he'd been fishing. Most likely a heart attack or a stroke. Prime age for these guys," Mom said.

"That's not logical. Sammy never fished on Sundays. You know that. Trust me. I have a feeling about this. More than a feeling."

She was glad she hadn't told either of her parents about the piece of codfish she took from the scene.

"You keep your feelings to yourself. Your father is in enough pain. He worries about you, and now you're spieling this prattle. Let the law take over now."

Kate knew Mom was a force to be reckoned with, particularly when it came to Pop. He was her world, had been since they had met at the Boat and Titling Registry on Causeway years ago when Mom processed applications there. Gruffly handsome but shy and respectful, Pop made up excuses to come back to the registry with paperwork questions. Finally, she asked him to go out on a date. Since then she was his "true light," which he compounded into the name of his boat, Truelight. She "preferred dry land, thank you very much," and was content to walk down the block to her school crossing guard job rather than be anywhere near boats or docks.

Kate couldn't stand to sit with her mother any longer. She glanced up at the wall clock shaped like a teapot. "It's late. I'm supposed to meet Erica. Tell Pop sorry, again."

She waved her off. "Go meet, Erica. But, you need to come home every night. It's dangerous out there. Time to settle down, you know, you're not a student anymore." She was in her proselytization pose. "I'm just telling ya."

The lecture was coming and Kate would avoid it. I'm telling ya, the battle cry of every Bostonian, usually followed by general knowledge, empty advice. She poured her coffee down the drain and waved goodbye to her mother.

Kate felt released from the staleness of her parents' house. She knew she should get her own apartment; she could certainly afford it on her salary. But why should she pay rent when she preferred sleeping in her office and touching base at her parents' house from time to time?

The Dingle Pub and Grille was three blocks away. Locals called it Dingles. In Southie, every name morphed into a shorter version with an s at the end. Dingles grounded Kate. It wasn't so much that she drank a lot, more that she felt good in the place.

The Sullivans managed Dingles. Erica Kelly had attended kindergarten through high school with Kate, then married William Sullivan, her high school boyfriend. They lived in an apartment over the bar.

Kate took a deep breath, walked up the two granite steps, opened the heavy teak door and entered the small, dark pub.

"Kate! What's up?" Erica came from behind the bar and hurried over to give her a bear hug. Erica was an attractive hefty, tall, big-haired blonde with an acerbic veneer.

Kate hugged Erica back, just as tight. She felt more comfortable hugging Erica than hugging her own parents. Rarely did the Finns hug, and when they did it was structural, two stiff boards. When possible, hugs were avoided. After a couple of drinks, Finns were customarily affectionate, before the tipping point when they cried in their beer.

"Bad day," Kate said.

Erica motioned for her to sit at a small table in front of the mahogany bar, backlit with etched mirrors outlined by fluorescent bar lights.

"Wow, you're all gloom and doom. You fit right in with the regulars. What happened, did your UMass Boston friend show up?

Have she and Pierre spawned?"

"No, Erica. Haley didn't show up. I don't think she's come back here since she graduated. And she wouldn't come here without Pierre." Kate had studied with Pierre Gosselin at Woods Hole Oceanographic Institute, WHOI. And she fell hard for him. Three years older than Kate, Pierre had a trim, muscular body with curly, dirty-blond hair and deep-set, root-beer-colored eyes. His manner of speech and tone could melt chocolate. Originally from Chestnut Hill, the tony section of Brookline, he studied at Phillips in Andover, then Yale. Now Pierre was a top scientist at the up-and-coming Nobska Fisheries, a spin-off founded by Woods Hole senior technical staff. "Please, stop," Kate said. "They're my friends."

"Yes, she's a great one, stealing your man. Typical New Yorker. Can't believe you befriended a Yankees fan." Erica smirked.

"Sammy is dead, Southern Connecticut, and she never even knew I had a thing for Pierre."

"Sammy Robbins?" Will transported a draft glass of Murphy's Stout to Kate. A strapping Irish-American, Will appreciated beer and his physique showed it.

"Yes, Sammy Robbins, and I found him."

Will kissed Kate on the head. "Rough."

"I feel pretty numb. Where's your wife's?"

Erica put her hand up. "None for me."

"Since when?"

"Cute. Continue with your story," Erica said.

Kate drank her Murphy's and told Will and Erica about the events leading up to her visit. She told them how the day had started out normally—until she found herself standing in her office with her underclothes hanging over her arms while talking to a dock detective.

"And what an ass." She wiped beer from her upper lip with the back of her hand. "After he questioned me at length he asked me why I hung around the docks by myself."

Kate caught Will and Erica's smug expressions.

"What? I'm busy. Why don't people understand that when you have a job with my kind of responsibilities . . ."

"Here we go," Will chided. "The critical job."

Erica added, "We just want to see you with someone who shares your interests. I know you really liked Pierre but it never got off the ground. You should act when you are attracted to someone. Life will pass you by otherwise."

"Please. All I meet are schmucks around here."

Erica's tone shifted. "Really? I know I didn't go to college and maybe our schmuck life seems trite to you, but there is more to life than work."

The stuffing was all out of Kate. "Not you guys. Erica, I don't consider anything about your life trite." She took a big breath. "I want to have a nice guy like Will someday, just not now."

She smiled graciously at Erica and her friend responded with a grateful grin. "Hey, look at that guy over there. He's handsome."

Kate leaned her head under her left arm, which held the beer steady, and quickly turned back. "I'm leaving, now."

"What? No good?"

"He's the dock detective I told you about. Madley. Detective

Richard Madley." Kate downed her beer and reached for her pocketbook. "I'll call you."

Will wouldn't let her off the hook. "He's a dick? His name is Richard? Hey, Dick for short! Dick, Dick."

Kate and Erica burst out laughing as Kate choked out her beer and it sprayed all over Erica's white linen shirt. Kate tried to make amends by wiping the shirt with cocktail napkins. Madley walked over to the commotion. "What brings you to Dingles tonight, Doctor?"

Kate was cornered.

"Friends, Detective. Friends. Let me introduce you, sir. This is Erica and Will Sullivan."

"What a coincidence seeing you here tonight. I'm off duty. May I sit down?"

"I'm leaving soon," Kate said.

"You two sit and talk," Erica said to Madley. "We have to get back to work, critical work. What's your pleasure, sir?"

"I'll have a Murphy's, ma'am."

Before Erica followed Will to the bar, she looked at Kate and winked.

"I'm amazed to see you here tonight."

"Why is that, Detective?"

Kate looked disinterestedly at Madley and then scanned the room. While she planned a graceful exit, he asked, "Hey in your experience, is it normal for a cod's insides to be green?"

She sensed some suspicion. What was he getting at?

"Not really. After a few days when it spoils, it goes from gray to black."

Now she was especially anxious to get back to her sample and run some tests.

"Did you examine the fish when you opened his jacket?"

She was convinced this was not a social visit.

"I was in shock, Detective. You can imagine. Right?"

"Rich. My name is Rich. By the way, what were you all laughing at when I came into the bar?"

"Probably not your humor, just some local gossip."

"An outsider wouldn't get it, eh?"

"Exactly, Detective Rich."

"You know what's funny though?"

Kate was lured in. "What's funny?"

"I'm a local."

"I've never run into you. You look about my age?"

"St. John's. I took the bus out of the city." They both laughed at his reference to Boston's notorious busing crisis.

"Catholic school boy. Sounds like I could be of service. Do you think I could get a look at this curious codfish?"

"The evidence is stored securely and will be released only through the proper channels."

"I'm not proper?"

"Anyone around when you were with the body?"

"Seagulls."

"Here's some peanuts for your table." Erica delivered two more Murphy's and disappeared.

Kate lined up her beer with Madley's. "Cheers, Detective Rich!

Got to bolt."

Will caught Kate at the door, hugged her and whispered, "Rich? You got to Rich in a short time."

"Bye, Will. He's still a dick. Don't tell him anything. Bye to Erica."

She glanced back at Madley, smiling down on his beer.

Kate tiptoed past her parents' downstairs bedroom and walked softly up the steps to her own bedroom, but the wooden stairs whined with age and her phone buzzed. She fumbled quickly to answer it, but not before her mother yelled, "Kate. Kate. Is that you?"

"It's fine," Kate called out. "Go back to sleep. Pierre, what's up?"

"I heard what happened to you today. Unbelievable, a murder right at your workplace. Are you okay?" Pierre asked.

"Tough day." She told him all that had happened.

"That is tough. Why don't you come down a little early this year for the lobster bake? You can stay with us. We have plenty of room."

They invited her to stay with them every year, but she chose to stay at the Knotty Sea Inn overlooking Woods Hole.

"Thanks for calling, Pierre. I'll think about it."

"Of course. Love ya, kid!"

She hung up without responding. There was a time when she would have clung to the thought that maybe Pierre did love her.

She put on pajamas and slid into bed. Her thoughts drifted back to how she had found Sammy. Pop was quick to believe the heart attack story. But what the hell was a fish doing inside his jacket and why were its guts green?

Chapter Four

The drive down to Falmouth usually relaxed Kate. She'd track her progress with each passing town; if she got to Pierre and Haley's house in less than two hours, she was satisfied. Today she was too preoccupied to notice the time, never mind what towns she'd passed. On the passenger seat were three double packs of Sno Balls, slightly thawed. Tasty at any temperature, she especially loved them slightly frozen, like an ice cream treat.

She sank her teeth into the marshmallow coconut topping, knowing there was another behind it and more behind that one, so much better than the soft single at her mother's house the day Sammy died.

Almost two weeks had passed since she'd found Sammy dead on the docks and the autopsy was still not completed. Since then she'd met with Detective Madley twice for more questioning about the morning of the murder and to explain her daily FDA testing and tracking procedures. The Globe and Herald both reported that

Sammy's death was considered suspicious. Madley didn't tip his hand on anything except that there was an ongoing investigation.

The annual lobster bake at the Gosselins' place was Saturday, so Kate had decided to drive down early on Friday to visit Nobska Fisheries and use their labs to test her chunk of Sammy's fish. On the Monday after she found Sammy, she had returned to work and while running the daily catch, she discretely performed tests on his fish. No unusual results, so she packed the remains of the codfish with other camouflage samples for the trip to the Cape.

Today would be awkward, just like each time she greeted the Gosselins. Pierre never seemed uncomfortable, but of course he had never known how deep her feelings had been for him, and she had never shared her feelings about Pierre with Haley. It wasn't really Haley's fault, even if it felt that way sometimes. Anyway, who could blame him for falling for Haley, any man would. She beamed with energy, had dark silky brown hair, blue eyes and stood tall and lean. Her smile would captivate even a hardened criminal. On a weekend trip down to Falmouth, Kate had introduced them and asked them to keep each other company while she finished up some research in the lab. They found each other very good company and continued to keep company at Pierre's apartment on a permanent basis.

It had only been five years since Kate had introduced them, and four that they were married, and three since they bought their dream home in the Woods Hole section of Falmouth. This devastated Kate. She loved Pierre but never had the strength to tell him. They were colleagues. That's all. Sometimes Kate admitted to herself that Haley and Pierre had been a solid match, but it still tested her to see them together. Now she kept in touch, mostly with Pierre, and visited the happy couple every early May for their annual lobster bake.

Kate approached the Gosselins' driveway, framed by beach rose bushes. Their brilliant pink flowers bloomed fully in July; until then the rose buds were still sealed tight. The house was invisible from the main road, and broken quahog shells covered the sandy driveway. The shells crunched under the tires of her red Honda Accord. Branches brushed against her car as it turned the last curve to the gray shingled house regally staged on a slight incline overlooking the harbor. A Boston Whaler was tied up at their dock. Haley stood looking out from the open top half of the kitchen's Dutch door.

"You made it early. I thought you were coming Saturday morning." She walked toward Kate's car, smiling warmly at her.

"Um. I told Pierre I'd be here today."

"Let me help you with your bags."

"Oh, no, I'm staying at the Knotty Sea, thanks." They stood uncomfortably for a few seconds before they headed into the house.

"Pierre is at your favorite, Coffee Haute, he should be back shortly."

Coffee Haute in Woods Hole, where townies, scientists and tourists hung out, opened early and closed late. They served humungous popovers and the best coffee in Falmouth. Pierre and Kate used to study outside at the picnic tables and watch what they called the beat of the Hole.

"I'm so sorry about your father's friend. I remember meeting him at your parents' house. He seemed like a great guy."

"The best," Kate replied, an edge in her voice as they made their way to the kitchen.

Another uncomfortable silence. Kate began to ruminate. Even though they were the perfect couple, Haley should have checked with her before diving into a relationship with Pierre. After all, they were the closest of friends all four years at UMass Boston, where they had met the first day in chemistry class. They were the smartest girls in the room. But she checked herself for becoming irrational. All in the past. Love observes no rules.

"Hey, Katie! How are you?" Pierre burst into the kitchen, kissed Kate on her head, and placed the coffees on the granite counter. Everyone else had stopped using her childhood nickname when she entered high school. She didn't mind how he said it.

"Fair and maudlin." Kate smiled.

"Coffee Haute's café au lait will cure your ills."

"How French. We just say coffee where I come from."

He handed Kate a coffee. "Two creams, one sugar."

"Good memory. And you take yours black."

"Pierre's transitioned to adding cream," Haley said, standing behind him with her hands around his waist. "We'll get a little sugar into him eventually."

Kate laughed politely.

"You said you were bringing some work down." Pierre opened the creamer and poured it into his coffee, spilling half of it on the kitchen counter. "Damn it."

Haley wiped up his mess with paper towels. "How come you told me Kate was coming tomorrow?" She kept her head down while she cleaned.

Pierre shot his wife a dirty look. "You don't listen, do you? I said quite clearly, she was coming on Friday."

Haley's posture shrunk.

Kate wanted to comfort her. When did Pierre become so harsh? Now she wanted to leave to get away from the tension in the room. Where had the lovebirds gone?

"So I have samples to run. Special projects for work. I just wanted to touch base before I checked in at the Knotty Sea. Shall I meet you at Nobska?"

"Sounds good." He sipped his coffee. "I have a couple of phone calls to make here."

"Oh, yeah," Haley said. "Ed McGann called while you were out. Said you knew how to get in touch with him."

Pierre's posture stiffened.

"Funny." Kate took a giant gulp of her coffee. "That name sounds so familiar."

Pierre laughed. "Okay, I'll see you later." He retreated into the study adjacent to the kitchen to make the call.

At the Knotty Sea, Kate chose a room with a king-size bed overlooking Woods Hole. Watching the ferries coming and going raised Kate's energy. Loud horns signaling the embarkation and debarkation reminded her of her days here. She freshened up in the basic all-white bathroom, and headed back to her car for the short drive up to Nobska Fisheries, which was located behind the Nobska Point Lighthouse and overlooked Vineyard Sound. Doctor Zachary Zion had recently taken a role as a principal scientist. Kate had been under his tutelage at WHOI when he'd taken an interest in her studies. Dr. Zion had said on many occasions that she was a rare jewel, both the brightest and most down-to-earth student he had ever had the pleasure to work with. His constant encouragement shaped her into a confident scientist.

Along the drive up the hill past the regal lighthouse, she looked down at the soft blue water rolling in gentle waves onto a cove beach. Around the bend from the lighthouse on the left was the loose-pebbled road where the laboratory buildings were hidden behind heavy foliage. The shushing of the smooth pebbles under her car's tires had a soothing tone unlike the harsh crunch of quahog driveways.

Kate parked in a visitor's parking space. It seemed odd, considering she had spent long hours here for many years. She walked around the building to the front entrance, entered the double doors into the waiting area, and took a seat.

"Excuse me, I don't think you belong here."

"Dr. Zion! I was hoping you would be here."

Gently he offered his hand. They shook for a long time.

"You look wonderful, Kate. How are you?"

"I'm pretty well, thank you. And you?"

"Life is good. I continue to do what I love. I'm a grandfather again for the fourth time. What could be better?"

"Still the perpetual optimist, I see," she said.

"Only way to live. What brings you to Falmouth?"

"My annual visit to the Gosselins' party combined with some work." She shifted her weight from side to side and looked nervously at the keypad door.

"Are you okay?"

"Not entirely. There was a tragedy in Boston. My father's best friend died, and I found him on his boat. I'm still a bit shaky. A bit of PTSD."

"I heard it on the scanner down here. We get the Boston maritime news. They found a large bloody fish inside his jacket."

"Something like that." Kate couldn't believe Sammy's cod was reported as bloody. The reports said nothing about the green tint. She hadn't seen much blood anywhere except a bit where the cheeks had been filleted. But she had been pretty traumatized so she couldn't swear to anything with certainty.

"Tragic. Did you bring us lunch?" Zion lifted the cooler she'd left on her chair.

"I'm meeting Pierre to look at some samples."

"Come on in. I'll take a look. Don't worry about Pierre. He'll find you."

He led her down the maze of the aqua-painted corridors to a large laboratory with multiple testing stations ergonomically arranged for ease of movement. She opened her cooler and took out four individually packed fish samples labeled by number. Sammy's fish was Sample #3.

Dr. Zion held each sample up for visual examination. "What's going on with this little fellow? He's practically a Martian." He guided Kate and Sample #3 over to the spectrometer.

"Detecting nothing unusual here… for an old dead fish… except for its rare color. Let's check his levels. We will use the new ion chromater. When I say state of the art, it's only because there are no other words to describe the ability of this piece of equipment. Oceanware Technologies just released it to only three facilities in the world and we were chosen as one, with some persuasion from their favorite scientist. I never said research wasn't political."

They both laughed.

"You did harp on the politics of research. 'Rally for your projects like a presidential candidate.' Wasn't that your mantra?"

Dr. Zion prepared the sample for the chromater. "Okay, let's see what our specimen is working up for us. If we can extract some of the foreign substances out of this little guy, then we will compare him to the other little fellows and see why he shot to Mars."

Dr. Zion spoke in a colloquial way when he worked. His style put the researchers at ease. However, there was nothing easy about his lectures and exams. He'd earned the reputation as the toughest and most well-respected scientist on staff.

"Holy Toledo, look at the levels of ammonium perchlorate pouring out of this guy!" Zion exclaimed. "No surprise, I guess. This stuff is used for rocket fuel. He could have blown up with these levels. I wouldn't be surprised if his arteries ruptured. It could have caused some discoloration but it usually needs a catalyst to do real damage."

"What kind of catalyst?" Kate asked.

"I don't know. The green is quite odd. I haven't seen this before, ever. There must be something else mixed in to cause this green presentation."

"His chloroform levels were harmless, like what they use at grocery stores to preserve produce, she said.

"I'm just the technician here," he said. "But what's going on with this sample?"

"I'm not sure yet. It has to do with my father's friend."

He put his hand up. "What?"

"This is a sample from the fish they found on Sammy's body."

"Are you authorized to have this?" he asked.

"Self-authorized."

"I don't want to know any more. Pack it up, Kate. Let the law handle this."

"They won't handle it well. I need to know what turned the fish green. I believe it's a key."

"What makes you think that?"

"Intuition. Please, I had to tell you. You're the only one who'll ever know. For science?"

"How is possessing illegal evidence helping science?" He removed the fish particles from the test equipment and started to clean up.

"Sammy must have been into something." Kate felt like a betrayer.

"What do you think he was involved in?" he asked.

"I don't really know. Green stuff on his face and the fish ... so abnormal."

Dr. Zion squinted. "The shade looks like the color of one of those green apple martinis my daughter and her husband drink."

"Greentini." She mimed a drink. "Drink at your own risk. But it may kill you." Her voice faltered. "You know, his minimal fallout was suspicious. All the guys were calling him the Codfather. I should have looked closer. I could have caught something and Sammy would still be alive."

"You did your job. What else could you have done?" His firm tone soothed her. "Although."

"What? Just say it?"

"Why didn't you see the green on the fish samples you inspected and approved on the docks?"

Kate squirmed. "I've thought about that. Believe me. It keeps me up at night. I don't know. I never saw anything like this. Never came across any Greentini on any of the fish samples."

Pierre strutted into the lab. "There you are. I was looking around the campus for you."

"Hello, Dr. Gosselin," Zion teased Pierre.

"Doctor," Pierre bantered back in Curly Howard's voice from The Three Stooges. This was an old routine Dr. Zion performed during labs. At first Kate and her fellow students thought it was corny and dated, but soon enough mimicked it and found it stress-relieving.

"Dr. Zion was kind enough to run a couple of tests with me. We got some interesting results."

"What's interesting?" Pierre asked.

Zion raised a warning eyebrow to her. She looked at him skeptically. His usual relaxed demeanor was strained, his voice edgy. "Kate was checking out our new chromater," Zion said.

"You guys have better toys than I do," she said.

Pierre looked distracted as he scanned the room, then suddenly joked, "Watson's super gonkulator. Loads of fun."

Some of the tension he'd brought into the room dissipated and the three laughed at their pet name for all equipment.

"Are you all set here, then?" Pierre asked.

"For now. If you have work to do, I'll head back to the motel."

"I've got reams of data to analyze for a project. But Haley told me to let you know she'll be finished party prepping soon and to meet her at Ensign's Pub at six."

Kate hesitated. She tried to think of a good reason to decline but couldn't come up with one. "No. Yeah. That would be fun." She was committed to dinner plans when she just wanted to go back to the inn, rest, and get takeout.

The evening air brought a chill off the harbor. Kate wore her standard Ensign's cool-weather outfit: a cream-colored Irish knit sweater under a navy-blue windbreaker with tan khakis and comfortable brown leather heeled clogs. She walked down the hill from the Knotty Sea, breathing in the cool ocean air. Nothing filled her lungs or her soul so sweetly as Cape air. Maybe I belong down here, she thought. It was getting too difficult in Boston. With the restraints of the FDA's stifling organization and the lack of real professional relationships with her colleagues, she remained an outsider at the Fish Pier and was becoming a pariah among the fishermen. Maybe she was trying to live the dream of a little girl. Today's visit to Nobska reminded her that life was filled with options.

She walked onto the Eel Pond Bridge and paused, turning to face the boats. This was her favorite scene in Woods Hole. A menagerie of boats all shared one body of water. Some had flying bridges. Others were just dinghies. After a time, she crossed the bridge and turned into Ensign's.

"Over here, Kate." Haley waved from a barstool.

Kate approached the bar. "I almost forgot about these old stools. Same design as the legs of my mother's old Singer sewing machine."

"Unique and surprisingly comfortable." She sipped her white wine. "I got a booth overlooking the back pond. The gas fireplace is on—we'll be toasty warm."

She had forgotten how Haley took charge and how irritating it could be. Soon they were settled into their wooden booth behind the Ben Franklin stove.

"Are you up for some fish?" Haley asked.

Kate's stomach jumped at the thought of eating fish. "I could do that." Fish was the last food she wanted to eat.

"Steak sounds good for me. I have enough fish living down here. And finding uses for all the leftover lobster after the clambake makes me weary."

Kate's grip tightened on the menu as she stifled a humph. These were this woman's issues?

"I want steak, too." She refused to eat fish while Haley got off the hook.

Haley glanced over her menu. "Your prerogative."

"Thanks." Kate was triumphant. "You were saying, you're tired."

"If it wasn't for Pierre loving the bake, I think I'd stop holding the party. All left to me, now. Pierre used to do so much. Now he is so consumed with work, I hardly see him anymore." Haley's eyes filled up. She put her head down quickly to take a drink of wine.

A jab of empathy struck Kate. "I wish I had known. I would've come over after I left the lab and helped you out."

"Not a giant deal. I'm just overtired and feeling emotional. Selfish of me. Really." Haley forced a weak grin. "Did you get over to the lab today?"

"Yes. Dr. Zion was very helpful."

"Didn't Pierre help?"

"He came at the end. I was waiting for him in the lobby and Dr. Zion saw me. We did some analysis together."

"That's odd. Pierre left the house right after you. He said he didn't want you to have to wait."

"Maybe he was in his office," Kate offered, although she'd looked for his SUV in the parking lot and it wasn't there. Red Range Rovers generally stuck out.

Haley started to slug her wine.

"How's your teaching going?" Kate asked.

"Love my students. Most are hungry to transfer to four-year colleges. I often tout our alma mater."

"UMB was great for me," Kate said. "My family could barely afford the tuition and fees, never mind pay for room and board at some of those other schools."

"I admired your work ethic. I should have partied less." Haley motioned to the waiter. "Another glass, this time Pinot Noir, please." She smiled at Kate. "Steak works better with red wine and my whining about life."

"And you, miss?" he asked.

Kate raised her hand in refusal. "None for me."

"I shouldn't either but what the hell. Maybe I'll have two more," Haley said.

"You could always handle a lot more than me when we went out." Kate giggled. "Why don't you ever come into town anymore?"

"I do, Kate. Pierre has a lot of meetings in Boston. Sometimes I go with him and shop on Newbury Street. His colleague, Ed McGann, has a brownstone on Commonwealth Avenue. We go out to dinner as couples. They're originally from DC."

There was that name again, Ed McGann. And then she remembered he was one of Greely's guys, recently touted in the Boston Business Journal as one of the best research and development operations executives in Boston. She had read the article and wondered where the hell this guy had come from. He wasn't technical. His background was in communications. A real lightweight, she'd thought at the time. What was Pierre doing with McGann?

"What do they do for a living?" Kate asked.

"Wife shops, a lot. Pierre met him two years ago at a holiday party. Relationship building. That's what Pierre calls it."

"Chief Scientist Pierre Gosselin," Kate joked.

"That's what he aspires to. It's a double-edged sword, though. He works so much and he's changed. He's not the same guy I married. He's jumpy a lot and short-tempered, but don't get me wrong, we have a great life." She took her sweater off. "It's hot in here. I really shouldn't be talking. Way too much wine tonight."

Kate thought back to the afternoon and remembered how Pierre seemed kind of stiff. "I'm sure he's simply overtired. Just a phase."

Haley ordered a third glass of wine.

By mid-afternoon the next day, the lobster bake was hopping with old WHOI colleagues and new Nobska associates. After stuffing herself full of lobster, clams, and corn on the cob, Kate sat lounging on the Gosselins' boat, which was tied to the dock.

"Is that your boat, Miss?"

The sun's glare blocked her vision. All she could see were blue Dockers and boat shoes.

"No. Not mine."

"Want to take a spin into Buzzard's Bay?" His voice was clear, articulate. No Boston accent.

"I'll pass."

"Have we met?" He walked closer to her to block the sun. She could see crow's feet around his dark brown eyes. He stood about medium height, with white hair, and when he moved it was with authority.

"Seen you in town."

"How did I miss seeing you?"

"Irish luck."

The man she recognized as Ed McGann twirled his Rolex watch.

"Read about you and your work at Greely Labs," Kate added.

"Ah. The Boston Business snoops. We didn't give permission for that piece. At least there were no photo ops. Abhor that kind of exposure."

Kate was surprised to hear him dismiss the complimentary article. He seemed to guard his privacy.

"There you are. Did you have something to eat, Ed?" Pierre guided the man off the docks, ignoring Kate.

"Hey, why are you pushing me away from your friend?"

"So she remains my friend."

The men laughed.

McGann winked at her.

She sat in the captain's chair, turning the steering wheel. Who is this man? Why was he everywhere? One thing was for sure, McGann was definitely the man who used to visit Sammy at Fish Pier.

Haley was walking toward the boat when Kate's phone rang. She pulled it out of her jacket pocket. It was her parents' number.

"Pop got arrested."

"Michael, what are you talking about?"

"Just get home. I'm here with Mom."

"Wait. Why?"

"They accused him of killing Sammy, said he was the last person seen with him. Said they were seen fighting next door at Merrows' Marina. Some jerk of a dock detective, Madley, came with the arresting officers. Damn skeley. He snooped around in the house and then ransacked Pop's shed. Mom said they came out with two plastic gallon jugs that looked like antifreeze. It was hidden behind rags under his bench. Asshole spilled some on the driveway. I already hosed it off. Bastard." Michael never took a breath. "Pop's being arraigned on Monday. Come home."

"Wait!"

But he had hung up. She had trouble pulling the phone away from her ear. She tried to move off the dock toward her car but her legs were numb. The past two weeks were replaying in her mind like an old black-and-white movie, quick, jerky and unsettling. And now this. Unbelievable. Pop made a point of staying away from Merrows' Marina, the short pier next to Fish Pier. It was said to be haunted and Pop certainly held his Irish superstitions closely. Why would he abandon them now? Folklore dictated that if you fished off the pier, your skin would turn green, a curse handed out from the invisible merrows, or merfolk. The marina was usually empty except for the clergy who worked adjacent to it at the Salt House Mission. Why would Pop and Sammy go there?

"Hi-ho." Haley approached the boat with an unsteady gait. She took a long sip from a bottle of Perrier water. "Too much wine last night, even for me." She lowered the bottle. "Kate, Kate? What's wrong? You look sick."

"Greentini. Pop's shed."

"Okay. What did you have to drink?"

"I am sick. I have to go. Tell Pierre goodbye for me."

"I hope it wasn't the lobster. I can get Pierre to drive you back to the inn. He's just up in his study with Ed."

"Ed?"

"Yes, Ed McGann. You met him, right? I saw you talking to him down here. Handsome middle-aged guy."

"Uh, no, I mean yes. I'm sorry, I just have to go." Kate brushed by Haley and ran to her car.

She floored the car out of the driveway and got to the Knotty Sea in record time, packed her belongings, checked out and drove home. Once there, she tried to console her mother, tried to assure her that the arrest was just a formality, a giant error on the part of the skeleys. She ran through her meetings with the police and assured herself that she'd given them no reason to suspect her father. But Monday felt like it was light-years away and Kate's soul ached for her incarcerated father.

She needed to find out who the so-called witness was who had watched Pop and Sammy fight on Milady at Merrows' Marina.

Chapter Five

Monday morning, Kate, Michael, and their mother went to Suffolk Superior Court for the arraignment. Michael's friend, Kevin Byrne, two years out of law school and an associate at a criminal firm downtown—Ryan, Deluca, and Goldman LLP—had agreed to take the case. Over the weekend the one detail they were unanimous on was that Pop would choose someone he knew to represent him, even if he was a freshman attorney. Kevin had instructed them to meet just inside the front door of the courthouse. The three of them walked up the expansive stone courthouse stairway. By the time they got halfway up the steps to the beckoning halls of justice, they were panting in chorus because of the unseasonably hot and humid morning. A warm front had moved in from the west, mixed with ocean effects, leaving Boston with low lingering clouds and oppressive air, the kind of sticky, heavy air that is suffocating.

Kevin was waiting on a lobby bench alongside a tall white radiator. Dressed in a dark Brooks Brothers suit, he appeared fully engrossed in a brief. He stood when they approached him. He was short, handsome, and a fast talker.

Michael towered over his friend Kevin. "We really appreciate you coming on such short notice." Michael gave him a gentle hug and stepped back. They smiled at each other but Michael's eyes looked sunken and lifeless. Seamus often teased him about his brown eyes, saying that he was black Irish, probably due to some Spanish gene from Peggy's side.

"Mrs. Finn, I'm so sorry about your husband." Kevin wiped beads of sweat away from his forehead. "I want you to know, I'll do everything in my power to help him. I just read over the charges. I don't think we'll have too much trouble today."

"Thank you, Kevin. Thank you for helping us. A good soul you are, always were. Please call me Peggy. We're all grown-ups now."

They exchanged handshakes.

"I'll try. But twenty-something years of training will be hard to break. Let's run through this quickly. If things don't go as planned, you'll speak with the bondsman. What do you have for collateral?"

"We don't have much savings. Just our home and Seamus's boat. When we spoke over the weekend, you said the judge will let him out on personal recognizance."

"Exactly. He's not a flight risk. These are precautionary measures. This hearing will probably be a formality. No doubt Judge Poole will let him go into your custody. He's only tough on real heavies."

"He'll just go out of his mind if they attach our home or boat. It's all he's ever worked for."

Kate saw that her mother's hands were shaking as she moved her pocketbook from her right forearm to her left and then back. She had on her tan raincoat with the belt tied tightly. She stood a couple of inches taller than Kate. Her hair looked kinky, with shades of auburn, threads of gray, and in need of a good cut and color. It didn't matter because most people stared at her flawless peaches-and-cream complexion emphasized by neatly applied light foundation, pink blush, and mauve lipstick, to highlight her clear blue eyes. Kate eternally admired the erect and composed way her mother presented herself. Today was no different.

"Let's go in." Kevin placed his hand lightly on the center of Peggy's back and guided her into the courtroom. Kate and Michael followed behind.

The court was filled with what Pop called degenerates. Kate's stomach turned upside down. She'd never experienced a courtroom for any reason, let alone to see her father accused of killing his best friend. She bit the inside of her right cheek. The pain steadied her. Her mother stared straight ahead. Michael dug a pack of fruit-flavored Lifesavers from his black jeans pocket, placed one in his mouth and swaggered behind Kevin to a row of wooden chairs.

"I've never seen so many tattoos in one room," whispered Michael. He slipped his black leather jacket off and rolled up the sleeves of his striped pink oxford shirt to reveal a tattoo of a small mermaid on his right forearm.

"You mean body art." Kevin smirked. "At least your tattoo is tasteful. It's like these jokers pulled out a pen and marked themselves. Typos and all."

Kate was relieved to hear them joking. Black humor to relieve stress. Traditional Finn behavior. It was the Irish way.

"Where are these kids' parents?" Her mother chimed in. "They ought to scrape that ink off their skin." Everyone smirked now. She was not fond of tattoos and even less so of permissive parents. "Bunch of hoods."

The irony was too close for Kate because Pop was accused of murder.

"I'll be in the back room with Mr. Finn." Kevin left the seated Finns.

Kate turned. The faces in the rows behind them were filled with sadness. In the back of the courtroom in front of the grandiose doors, a middle-aged man dressed in a black cotton jacket and tan khaki pants talked to one of the court officers. His hands flailed animatedly. He had white hair but his head was turned so Kate could not see him clearly. He reminded her of Ed McGann, but she couldn't be sure because people kept milling around in front of him and the officer.

Three cases were called before Seamus's. A woman who looked like a homeless street person was convicted of possession of a Class A substance, with intent to distribute near a primary school, repeat offender. The judge ordered a five-year sentence, showing no mercy when the defendant cried that her children would be alone without their mother.

"What about the children you affect with this poison?" was his simple, dry retort. He motioned with his gavel to the court officer to move her along. "Next."

"Judge Poole, my client pleads not guilty."

"Your client what, Tony? You marched this guy out of here with an amended last time. I should have known better than to reduce his sentence. Now he breaks into a nursing home to steal televisions and gives a patient a coronary? Not this time, Mr. Wallace. Bail is set at five hundred thousand dollars."

Kate's stomach rumbled. Judge Poole was a no-nonsense man. Kevin had said he was hoping for Judge O'Hara, who was born and raised in Southie and was sensitive to the struggles of the locals, especially fishermen.

Kevin accompanied Pop while the court officer led him in front of the judge.

"Well, a murder case. How intriguing. Mr. Finn, you are accused of murdering Samuel Robbins. How do you plead?"

"My client pleads not guilty, sir."

"Of course. Of course. No one is ever guilty in my courtroom. Though, there are crimes committed, even people dead."

Poole rustled through some of the papers on his desk.

"This doesn't appear to be the first time you've been involved with some foul play on the docks, does it Mr. Finn?" Poole pointed his finger while leaning over the bench in an aggressive manner.

Seamus stared straight ahead, unflinching. His shoulders were erect but the skin under his eyes was baggy from what appeared to be not only a lack of sleep but of hope.

"Judge Poole, with all due respect, my client is a stand-up member of the fishing community in South Boston."

"And yet he has a previous, shall we say, situation with violence.

What do you have to say for yourself?"

"My client has nothing to say. It's beyond unwarranted to bring up his past."

"It was self-defense," Pop defended himself.

"Stop, Mr. Finn." Kevin placed his hand on his client's shoulder.

"This time or the first incident?" Poole asked.

Kevin interjected, "With all due respect, Judge Poole. I feel my client is being badgered."

"Well, with all due respect, counselor, your client left at-large could be a risk to society. No bail awarded. Mr. Finn, you'll be held at MCI Cedar Junction in Walpole until a trial date is set."

"Judge, please be reasonable."

"Watch yourself, counselor." Judge Poole raised his index finger to Kevin. "Next."

Mom, who made a point of never expressing emotion in public, wept openly. "It was an accident!" she yelled. "The man came at him with a knife. He was defending himself. Now they are going to reopen this wound for us? Seamus didn't mean for him to die."

Michael took his mother's hand and comforted her. Kate sat speechless, the insides of both her cheeks raw from biting them. She turned to the back of courtroom. The white-haired man was gone.

Chapter Six

They were silent on the drive home. At the house, Kate retreated to her room and sat on the floor at her window, gazing at the city street. The heavy haze was lifting slightly, but steam poured up through the storm drain grates from the temperature differential. Growing up she'd fantasized about a species of life living in the "sewers" as she called them. Not rodents, but angelfish with soft green wings and purple eyes floating in clouds of smoky sewer steam. If the angelfish wanted to head out to the ocean harbors or for a night in the city, they could freely and safely come and go. The fish were pacifists and worked together for each other's common good. Her window had framed the opening to this world. This evening, Kate noticed that the pure white woodwork had yellowed and the lavender walls bore a brown haze. How long ago had the walls turned from violet to mucky brown?

Nothing was clear anymore. Who had her father killed when he was young? She could understand why her parents had withheld that information. Still, she felt betrayed. Who are these people she lived with? Was it easier to kill a second time and cover it up? She didn't want to let her mind go there. Her father was innocent. The other incident was self-defense. Wasn't it? What was a man to do when someone came at him with a knife? But her parents constantly swept their lives under the rug. Especially her mother. She covered everything over. "He's tired, be patient; your father didn't mean that how he said it." Well then, what did he mean? Sometimes Kate and Michael discussed their father's coldness and their mother's lack of her own identity, but not enough to come to even a reasonable understanding of their parents' relationship. And now this. If he killed once, would it be easier for him to kill again? The question repeated itself over and over. No. Kate wouldn't allow her mind to continue to go there. There was something deeper. She thought about the chemicals on Sammy's fish. Inevitably she circled back to her father—her mind roamed back to that day on the docks so many years ago.

In autumn morning darkness, while the circling mist was still clearing, Seamus walked along the apron of Fish Pier with Kate and Michael in tow, holding each other's hands. Michael was six, and he didn't want to go to the fish auction that day or any, but Seamus had made him.

"It's loud and smelly." He held his nose and squinted. "And scary."

"It's okay, Michael." When her brother showed fear, Kate transformed into a protective big sister.

And whenever Seamus got busy with customers and Michael stood holding his crotch because he had to pee but wouldn't because he was afraid of rats inside the Porta-Potty, she accompanied him and turned her head while he went.

Michael was especially tense this autumn day, even with Kate's continual reassurances. She let go of his hand and messed up his hair, which usually led to him scrunching his hands at her and walking zombie-like, making them both laugh. But today it hadn't worked.

"Everyone is nice. They're just selling fish, like Pop catches." She pointed over at a display board.

FOR AUCTION:
COD
GREYSOLE
HADDOCK
OCEAN PERCH
POLLOCK large
WHITING mixed

Kate bent over and whispered, "Sammy might give us candy." She winked like Sammy did when he offered candy. Sammy was her father's best friend and Kate and Michael loved him.

Seamus led them past the fish stands where the sellers fumbled with money and credit cards from grocers, restaurateurs, and wholesalers. One fisherman shouted, "Hey Seamus, good-looking kids!" Pop acknowledged the compliment with a slight head waggle and turned around to check on his children. Michael lagged.

"C'mon, Michael," Seamus bellowed gruffly. "Let's go."

Tears filled Michael's eyes.

"Pop, he's only six," Kate said.

"You were barely walking when I brought you here. Couldn't get enough. Look at the state of him. Jeez. Who's the boy and who's the girl?"

Michael turned his lowered head away from his father and sister, attempting to dry his tears on his yellow slicker.

Kate looked sternly at her father like she'd seen Mom, Peggy Finn, do when he was too harsh with Michael. Her technique worked. Seamus pulled him tightly under his arm and with his huge hands wiped Michael's eyes and nose, shaking the excess onto the pavement. Then the three of them walked hand in hand with Michael in the middle.

They reached their selling station, sandwiched between Sammy's on one side and Louie's on the other.

Michael perked up when he saw Sammy, breaking the handhold with his father and sister, and ran over to him. "Do you have any candy?"

"Do I have any candy? Who told you I have candy?"

Sammy smiled at Michael.

"Kate."

"Well. As a matter of fact, I might. No telling what grows in these coolers. Step right up." Sammy unrolled a swab of paper towels and wiped off one of his dingy white fish coolers. "I have seats right here for you, my fine man, and your pretty auburn-haired sister, Kate." He reached into his cooler and pulled out a plastic bag with four large Hershey bars and handed Kate and Michael one each.

"Yummy." Michael ripped off the outer wrapper, unfolded the inner crinkly foil, and chowed down; chocolate covered his mouth, teeth, and cheeks. Kate thanked Sammy, broke half off and placed the other half in the pocket of her purple slicker for later.

By seven a.m. the fish had been sold. Seagulls screeched and circled overhead while the fishermen loaded their wares and equipment back into boats and trucks. Soon droves of gulls swooped to feast on dropped pieces of fish leaving their own excretions from on high. The smell was rancid but Kate didn't mind. Except for when he ate his candy bar, Michael had held his nose for most of the morning.

Sammy turned to Seamus. "A fisherman he's not."

Burly deckhand Rob Fitzpatrick scooped Michael up in his arms. "Michael's a smart boy. He'll be a businessman. I only work as a deckhand because I'm independently wealthy and these guys need me."

"No father wants his son in this business," Louie chimed in. "Better to stay off the docks, right, my man?" They fist-pumped as boxers do and Michael beamed.

Kate's stomach warmed with pleasure. These guys knew how to treat Michael. She wondered why Pop didn't.

Seamus lifted a leftover fish, turned it over and threw it back down. "Peggy's got them both over at the Dance Academy. He's got the bug more than her. Maybe he'll get into Riverdance like the Mahoney kid." He pulled his son out of Rob's hands, kissed him on the head, and set him down.

Kate grabbed Michael's hand and they both started a jig. Seamus and his friends whistled and clapped as the children flexed and pirouetted.

Meanwhile, three young white guys—baggy hooded sweatshirts, matching black Nike Cortez sneakers—strutted over to Louie's stand. "Hey, brah. What you got left today?"

"I'm not your brah," Louie said.

One of the three, who appeared to be the leader, pulled a wad of cash from his pocket. "This change your mind, brother?"

Seamus and Sammy both said "hooligans" at the same time.

Kate grinned at Michael as they mimicked the fishermen. "Hooligans." But Kate's lips trembled.

Seamus walked over to the three hooligans. "Is there a problem here?"

"Not your business." The leader spoke while the others stepped aside. "I'm talking to my man here." He adjusted his belt buckle and slid his thumb through a belt loop. Kate could see a leather knife case attached to the belt near his thumb.

"I'm not your man, your brother, or your brah." Louie pulled a large shiny knife out of his boot, picked one of his codfish off ice, and then jammed the knife straight through the middle of the fish.

"He's not your man." Seamus stood in solidarity. "Now get out of here. We don't need your kind around here."

Kate stared up at her father. She felt a mixture of fear and pride that he was sticking up for Louie because sometimes Pop said bad things about black people. He'd say stuff like "There's good, hard-working black people and then there's the welfare takers living off the dole." Her mother would nod her head in agreement and say, "Don't forget there's the white trash, too." Kate never knew what any of this meant—just that it sounded mean. Her teachers never talked like this and sometimes she feared they might find out and stop liking her because of her parents.

The thugs didn't leave. The main thug spread both his hands onto Louie's table and leaned in. "Are you going to sell to me, my brah, or not?"

Louie threw the fish back onto the ice and pointed his knife at the boy's chest. The early morning sun sparked shiny rays from parts of the knife that had not been inside the fish.

Rob and Sammy formed a wall next to Seamus and Louie. That's when Kate and Michael saw Seamus explode—face crimson, hands fisted. "Listen, you punk. This station is closed. Louie has a buyer for the rest so go shite in your hat."

Seamus pulled the table away and Kate saw the leader's hands fall off the table and that's when the hooligan lost his balance. His two friends grabbed his arms to steady him. He smoothed his sandy brown hair and tugged at the neckline of his sweatshirt. Rob and Sammy held their filet knives up in the air and ran their fingers down the blades.

"Let's go. I wouldn't eat *his* fish anyhow." The three of them sauntered off toward the parking lot.

Louie scowled at Seamus. "Thanks. But I had it." He put his knife away and packed the fish back onto ice.

"I know you did," said Seamus. "No disrespect." Seamus held

his giant hands up in an unguarded manner.

But Kate heard Louie mumble to Rob as he took up his station, "Crazy Mick, always looking for a fight. You think he would have learned his lesson."

"Hey, that wasn't his fault." Rob's voice was stern. "You know as well as I do what happened back then."

"Going to get us all killed," Louie was still mumbling. "Stupid Micks."

Through all the commotion, Kate didn't notice that Michael had run away. She panicked.

"Pop, where is Michael?"

"Where's Michael? He was with you. You were supposed to keep an eye on him."

"I'm sorry. He was here and then you were knife-fighting."

"Fighting! What are you talking about? Just getting rid of riff-raff." He grabbed her hand and ran up Fish Pier. Then he squeezed her hand too hard. "Don't tell your mother."

Kate could see Michael running down Northern Avenue. "Look, Pop. He's crossing the road. He's going to church."

Our Lady of Good Voyage's doors were wide open.

Inside the chapel, she smelled a stale, sweet smell. Michael was huddled sideways in a pew—feet up—staring at a stained-glass window with a huge fisherman at the helm. He was sobbing.

Seamus sat with him and consoled him. Kate sat quietly in the pew behind them.

"I don't want to go to the stupid auction. I hate it."

Seamus cuddled his son.

"I know, Michael. It's okay. You don't have to come anymore." He motioned to Kate to come sit with them and he put an arm around each child and pulled them in. She watched him stare up at Jesus on the cross, noticed when her father's face finally relaxed, and sighed in relief when he said, "Hey. Let's all light a candle."

Michael looked up at Seamus. "One for Mom, too," he commanded.

He rubbed his back. "Forever thinking of your Mom."

They approached the candle display in the back of the chapel where small and large lit candles glowed through red votive holders. Kate liked the smell of the burning candles and how air swept through the chapel, waving the flames back and forth, casting moving shadows on the ceiling and walls. Her father pulled the wooden lighting stick out of the metal container next to the offering slot. He gave them each a dollar to put into the slot. Kate folded and deposited hers. Michael followed, and Seamus added two more dollars. The three of them used the same stick, passing it around, to light their candles. After they were done, Seamus placed the stick in Kate's hand and pulled Michael's onto it while he covered both of their hands with his giant scratchy one. All together they lit a candle for Peggy Finn and Seamus recited, "Go raibh maith agat!" which Kate and Michael knew meant, "May you have goodness."

"One more for Sammy?" Kate pleaded with furrowed brow.

Michael nodded in agreement. "He's nice. He gives us candy."

So Seamus put another dollar in the slot and they repeated the lighting ritual, this time for Sammy, and then Seamus blew out the lit stick and stuck it with the other extinguished sticks in the small container of dirt next to the candles.

"Now let's get the hell out of here. It smells like a funeral."

"Deep thoughts?" Michael squeezed through her slightly ajar bedroom door.

He'd startled Kate out of her memory. "Yeah. Something like that." She tried to gather herself back to the present. "You've been sticking around a lot lately."

"I'm supporting you ladies."

"You're with someone. Who is it?"

"Well," he positioned his hands in an exaggerated manner, similar to a ballet dancer, the gesture he often used when he explained personal business, "about two months ago, I went to Champs to dance." He lowered his head and smiled that sweet grin Kate had seen since he was a little boy. "Bo Ming and I were attracted immediately. Love saying Bo Ming."

"Nice Irish lass."

"Pop's gold standard. Not mine."

"Details."

"Well, he's a Chinese immigrant," Michael drew a full circle in the air, "and he's gorgeous. He's trying to get into BU for, get this, marine biology. Same as you, Sis. His language skills are excellent, so no problem there. He's part of the family business so he's got the science by," Michael air-quoted, "osmosis."

"Science joke." Kate smiled. "Witty."

"But math's his Achilles' heel."

"Kind of the reverse of most Asians."

His eyebrows arched in the famous "you should be ashamed of yourself" look he gave her when she joked with him. "Kind of a stereotype. Anyhow, he works at Aga something in East Boston. His uncle runs it."

"AgaCulture? Poor guy. That place is supposed to be a pit, ripe with mistreated undocumented workers. They say they harbor them inside and work them twenty-four-seven."

"It can't be that bad. When Bo talks about the workers, he sounds so protective of them."

"Just telling you. The place has a reputation. I wouldn't set foot in it even if my life depended on it."

"Yeah. I get it, marine biology snob."

Kate blew her brother a raspberry.

"Hey! Wait a minute. You're helping him? How does that work when I used to do all your math homework?" She lightly punched his arm. "What are you guys really up to?"

"Smart ass."

"I hope he treats you good," Mom said.

Kate looked over at Mom standing in the doorway and drew a breath of relief that she didn't have to tiptoe around Michael's life anymore. Michael's sexual orientation had been clear to the Finns since junior high, but his parents never openly acknowledged it. Up until that moment, he'd only confided in one Finn, Kate.

Michael grinned at his mother. "Thank you, Mom." Then he turned to Kate. "By the way, don't forget who wrote the essay that got you into WHOI."

"I didn't have time for that literary drivel."

After dinner, when Kate had again retreated to her bedroom, Michael yelled up the stairs to tell her she had company. She stood up from her crouch by the window but charley horses thrust her back down. She arose again slowly, shaking her legs free of the cramps. She heard the crinkly sound of an empty Sno Ball packet and peeled it off the back of her leg, wondering if she had worn it to court, and then tossed it in the wastebasket. Navigating the narrow stairs with jiggly legs felt even more challenging than usual, seemingly harder than when she was in college and had attempted them hungover after a late night, trying to measure each step, often miscalculating and sliding down two or three before gaining her balance against the banister. The forest-green carpet was gone now, exposing bare oak. Mitzie was incontinent one too many times before being put down. Kate missed Mitzie. There was nothing more soothing than holding that big fluffy cat and feeling her thumping heartbeat.

"Pierre."

Pierre stood at the kitchen doorway where the Finns held all their drop-bys before inviting them in. He hugged Kate.

"I'm so sorry about your Pop. I was up on business and ran into some mutual acquaintances who told me what happened."

"Who? We were just in court this morning."

"My colleagues heard through the dock guys. Word travels fast, you know how it is. Anyhow, I have a friend who's a pretty good criminal attorney. He could help."

"We're all set. Got Kevin Byrne."

Michael came in to grab a beer from the fridge.

"My guy's the guy," said Pierre. "At least let your Pop speak with him. I can get him over to Walpole tomorrow."

"I guess it won't hurt for Pop to just talk to someone else. What's his name?"

"Anthony Monero."

Michael interrupted, "The guy who handled the Charlestown fiasco?"

"Yes. If anyone can strike a deal, Monero can."

"You're wasting your time, dude." He took a long swig of Bud Light. "Kate, tell him. Pop will never go for it."

"Why not?" asked Kate. "Pop deserves the best."

Pierre winked at her. "No pressure. We can talk. Hey, you probably need a break. Let's go over to that bar of yours. Who owns it? Bill and Erin?"

"Will and Erica. I think they're playing tonight. Michael come with?"

"Got plans."

"Bring him." Kate winked at her brother.

"Flute and Fiddle?" He seemed to reconsider. "They got the band back together?"

"All two of them," Kate chided.

"How can I say no to Flute and Fiddle?" He slipped into a fast jig. "We'll stop by for some beers."

Kate and Pierre followed the aroma of draft beer over to the bar. Will held up two fingers as he poured behind the bar. Kate nodded.

"I don't get a say here?" asked Pierre.

"You'll get Murphy's Irish Stout."

"Decisive. That's what they say about you, Katie."

"That's me. Decisive."

They moved to a square table for four.

Will came by and placed the drafts in front of his patrons.

Pierre stood up to shake hands. "You look great, Bill." He became dwarf-like in Will's shadow. Will ignored the handshake offer and patted Pierre on his shoulder. "It's Will. You're looking the same, Pierre. Kate, Erica should be coming down any minute. Enjoy your Murphy's."

"He doesn't care much for me." Pierre slugged his beer.

"You never remember his name."

"Bill, Will, Willie, Billie. What's the big deal? They're all nicknames for William!"

"Okay, Peter."

"Now that's just fresh."

"Ah, so it's only proper to address others improperly? I keep forgetting who I'm with. Is that how kids are brought up over the hill in Brookline?"

"Eh? Nah, I picked it up at my grandparents' in Nantucket when I was a kid. Those islanders are tough."

"I see, in the ghettos of Nantucket. Must have been rough for you at the yacht club."

They smirked comfortably at each other, downed their beer,

and ordered two more. Pierre fingered the condensation on his glass.

"Perhaps I'm totally out of line to say this considering your family circumstances, but you look amazing tonight. You have a certain appeal. You're fun to be with and decisive."

"Decisive. The word of the night. Are you for real? And yes, you are out of line."

"Haley used to be more decisive and fun. Now she works, cleans the house, and constantly asks me to scale back my schedule. These are the earning years, I tell her."

"Oh, God. Is this one of those 'I married the most beautiful girl and now we are bored and have nothing in common' conversations? I'm going to need another beer and maybe a shot of Baileys to listen to this." She raised two fingers and shot her left thumb up twice. "You know. Maybe we, I mean you, do work too much. Don't you want a family with Haley?"

"You're on her side?"

"Not about sides. She's so committed to you and you . . ."

"What? What me?"

"You're such a restless guy."

"If you want certain things, you have to work for them and not at some low-paying community college gig. She drinks too much, too."

"Harsh."

"Yeah, well I didn't really mean that. I'm just letting off some steam." With flexed arm, he made a sky fist. "Beer makes me brave."

Will approached their table. "Baileys will make you a regular warrior then, dude." From a shamrock-shaped tray, he served them two more stouts and two shots of Baileys. He sat down to drink his own glass of beer.

"Bud Light?" Kate asked.

"Yes, lassie, Bud Light, like true Irish men drink in Dublin. We can't drink those heavy beers all day and keep our fine physiques." Will rubbed his hand over his expansive belly.

"Oh, Will, you look great." She leaned over and rubbed his belly, too. "Burly, handsome man."

"And you are lovely tonight as usual." Will sipped. "She's the best, Pierre. Eh?"

Pierre nodded weakly.

Will drilled him. "What brings you over to my side?"

"Checking out your hood, buddy."

"Ha! Well, some of us consider where we live home not hood."

The tension was palpable. Kate's chest felt tight.

"You never want to get out, move on?" Pierre asked.

"Move on from what?"

"No offense meant," Pierre said.

Will stood up to down the rest of his Bud Light. "Ready for some Flute and Fiddle."

"Yes." Kate clapped. She was glad the tension was broken.

He hates me," Pierre said.

"Probably. He's protective of me."

Pierre leaned in closely and stroked her hand. "Why would you need protection?"

His grazing fingers excited Kate and she decided to allow herself the pleasure. Stuffing guilt into the back of her conscience, she opened her palms and Pierre slid his left hand on top of her right.

Flute and Fiddle began to play on stage. Will tapped his foot and waved to Kate to come up and step. She ferociously shook her head, at which point Michael walked in with someone Kate assumed was Bo, both of them dressed to the nines. Bo looked especially exquisite in his Tom Ford loafers, dark jeans, and a tan silk suit jacket that contrasted well with his dramatically dark layered hair. They made their way to the table but before they could all greet each other, Erica pulled Michael and Kate in front of the small stage.

Will broke out with "Peg O' My Heart" and Erica followed. Kate and Michael smiled at each other. It was the song Pop sang to Mom. Shoulders pulled back tight, they proceeded to reel. Then Michael took Kate's hand. She could barely keep up with him. He was on fire. His mocha Viberg boots only seemed to enhance his set. He moved into a hornpipe. She stepped back from her jig and cheered him on with the rest of the crowd. She looked over to Pierre, who was clapping and yelling with Bo as if they'd known each other for years.

Michael accelerated his dance. Perspiration poured from his forehead while sweat soaked his white oxford shirt. He finished the dance with a crossover to Kate and pulled her hand up for their final bow. They returned to their table.

"Hi, I'm Kate. Michael's older sister by thirteen months and ten days."

"Pleased to meet you." His handshake was firm.

"I didn't know I was dating such talent," Bo chided Michael.

"Michael danced in a troupe." Kate reached up and wiggled her brother's chin. "He didn't tell you?"

He tapped her hand off him. "Some things are private, Sister Kate. What happens in the Hub stays in the Hub." He nuzzled and kissed Bo. "Don't listen to anything she says. She's the family liar."

The men sat holding hands.

"Michael said you are applying to Boston University for marine biology," said Kate.

Bo's face dropped.

"I'm sorry. Did I say something wrong?"

"No. It's just that." He looked at Michael, who squeezed his shoulder in encouragement. "I don't want to be a marine biologist anymore."

"Why not?" Pierre abruptly chimed in.

"Because I am a poet."

Pierre started to laugh. "Buddy, you're kidding, right? Your uncle is one of the most powerful Chinese men in Boston and you want to ditz around as an English major? How does that go over?" He was on a roll. "Go for marine biology, dude. Make some coin."

Kate was dismayed by Pierre's rudeness, though she agreed wholeheartedly with his opinion about becoming an English major. In fact, at WHOI they often laughed about the budding writers sitting at Coffee Haute whiling away precious hours on writing that would never see the light of day, unlike their own scholarly research. A waste of precious time, they both said. At the same time, she thought it was odd that Pierre knew so much about Bo's uncle.

Bo continued, "Did you know it was Chinese who wrote poetry on the walls at Angel Island? During Chinese Exclusion Act. Your country didn't want us. Nothing much has changed in my opinion. Did you ever think about what it's like not to be able to live where you most want to? Chinese and Americans, unrequited love."

"That is poetic." Kate was moved by Bo's profundity. Like most Chinese she'd worked with over the years, he dropped articles like a, an, and the. She started to wonder if articles were just filler and Bo's version was more efficient.

"But you're here now with a good life." Apparently, Pierre wasn't as inspired.

"Seriously? I can be deported at any time. My uncle, he's trying to work things out but I might as well be one of his workers in between countries."

Michael choked out, "I'm sorry you feel this unsettled. Why haven't we talked about it?"

"There's a lot I don't say out loud. I used to keep journals of poems but my uncle discourages it."

Kate jumped in. "Our Pop is an immigrant. Ireland. His parents brought him over when he was two. He always said how hard it was seeing his parents struggle. They were simple people."

"My uncle is not simple."

Kate couldn't tell if Bo was arrogant or defensive.

"My father was a poet. He rebelled in verse disparaging the Republic and was sentenced to several months in prison where he performed self-criticism on his writings. About a year later my parents and sister were taken. No warning! I had stayed at a friend's house one night and came home to an empty house the next morning. In China, people get taken in the middle of the night and killed, children sold in the slave trade. No warning! Everyone knows it but the government lies."

"I don't know what to say." Michael stumbled over his words. "I'm so sorry."

Kate focused on how Bo said no warning. Twice. He had dramatic flair, for sure, but something more. An anger emanated from him. A kind of violence that made her squirm a bit. She supposed having family taken to the metaphorical gallows could cause such anger; however Pop was in a similar position. Out of the corner of her eye, Kate saw a distinguished man enter the bar.

"Shit. Uncle Li." Bo dropped Michael's hand and raced over to the newcomer. Bo motioned his uncle toward the side exit. They seemed to be arguing.

"What's up with that?" Kate asked Michael.

"He doesn't know about us. Wants Bo in an arranged marriage like him and his wife."

"That's still a thing?" Kate asked.

"Damn straight," Pierre said. "Not such a bad idea. Parents and uncles know a lot more than kids." Pierre continued to stare at Bo and Uncle Li. "Hey, looks like uncle and nephew are arguing." He coughed loudly and bowed to Mr. Ming, who abruptly bowed back to Pierre.

"What was that?" Kate asked.

"Just being friendly. And a gentle signal that we can hear them all the way from the entrance. Embarrassing!"

Kate noticed Bo pull his jacket back to reveal a gun. "Michael. Bo's carrying a gun."

"Everyone should pack in this neighborhood," Pierre said.

"Shut up, Pierre," Kate and Michael chorused.

"Sorry. Just saying."

"We hate guns," Kate continued.

"No. You hate guns."

"I don't even know you. Suddenly it's okay because your friend Bo has a gun."

"Bo. Friend," Pierre laughed. "Get it? Boyfriend."

Kate and Michael chorused again, "Shut up."

Pierre threw his arms in the air. "The Irish! If you can't score, fight."

"Stop sweating it, Sis."

"I worry. You know how many guns go off accidently. They cause a lot of damage, bro."

"I hate to break up this fam fight." Pierre pointed to the exit. "But Bo Bo's leaving."

Bo waved goodbye from the hallway.

Michael slumped back in his seat and finished the last of his Bud Light. "I'm out of here." He grabbed his jacket off the back of the chair and bailed.

"Bummer." Pierre leaned back on his chair.

"Poor Michael." Kate shook her head. "Bo is such an idealist, seems so sensitive except for the gun."

"Idealists. In the end, they are the deadliest."

"Will you give the guy a break?"

"He's well taken care of by uncle-dad."

"Insensitive. And how do you know so much about the Mings?"

"I get around, my dear." He swigged the last of his beer. "Speaking of which, why don't we go to your office and discuss some fish?"

Chapter Seven

It was one thing to accept a comforting hand. Was that what his stroking and hand-matching was? It was entirely another to be complicit in a compromising situation. He was married to the almighty Haley. Surely, Kate was just reading into things. Still, the way he looked at her with his piercing Pierre-ishness. Wow. Piercing Pierre-ishness. She had trouble wrapping her mind around that ungrammatical alliteration. She felt silly, light, and carefree. And it was good.

"Let's go see an office about some fish," she said.

They parked outside her office at Fish Pier. At the employee entrance, Kate fumbled with her purse and the bottle of wine they had picked up at a package store where Pierre got giddy over her reference to a packie.

"He runs a packie over in Back Bay." He mimicked an exaggerated Boston accent. "Why do we say package stores?" slurring the "s." "Shouldn't package stores be where one arranges or ships packages? And packies? Where is the logic there?"

She imitated his slurring and told him he couldn't handle his Baileys and beer.

"Here, let me hold the wine while you do your thing. In fact, let me hold your purse, but don't be telling anyone." He posed hand on hip and rocked with unsteady force back and forth. "It's a malebag. Get it? Mailbag. Never mind."

He supported his chin on her shoulder close to her neck while she entered her code. Again, she didn't retreat, not knowing why she felt so adventurous, reckless even. Perhaps it was because her father was sitting in prison. Still, her stomach already tugged with morning-after regrets. She assured herself this was a friend simply stopping by. Inside the office, Pierre moved her work paraphernalia to one side and sat on her desk, his legs splayed open exaggeratedly. She wondered why guys did the open-leg thing. Was it supposed to be virile? It seemed so juvenile, as if they were saying, come here baby, my parts are so big I must stretch this far. She pictured a little boy holding his hands at length to describe enormity.

"Glasses?" he asked.

Kate opened her desk drawer and pulled out some paper cups. "Voilà!"

"Ah, we are in style tonight, Mademoiselle."

"Only the finest for my office guest."

Using a corkscrew from his key chain, he opened the wine and poured it evenly into the cups. Kate accepted the wine and his dramatic hand motion to sit next to him. He closed his legs to make room for her. They sat for a minute looking out at the harbor lights. For the first time since she'd found Sammy dead, she felt at peace, even mysteriously content. She thought of Haley at home alone and wondered what she would think if she knew where her husband was. She shook off the thought. They were at work together, that's all. Pierre broke the silence.

"When are you going to get out of here, Katie?" He pulled her chin over with his thumb and forefinger, looking directly in her eyes. "You can't stay here forever. What happened to you? I thought you had higher hopes?"

Kate didn't want to admit to him that he had happened, and then Haley and he had happened, and she was shelved. Besides, she'd move on, just not yet.

"Hey. Want some food?" She retrieved a packet of Sno Balls from the freezer and broke the packet in half to share.

"You still eat these chemicals?"

"I revere them. Have some respect."

He took a disapproving bite of the snack and polished it off.

"Why are you avoiding the question?"

"I'm happy here," she said.

"I don't believe you."

"It's true," she lied.

"Here?"

He held her hand.

Doe-eyed, she looked up and he leaned down to kiss her on the lips.

Their breathing was labored.

She pulled away.

"I can't. It's not right. Haley."

He rumpled his hair and jumped off the desk. "Yes, Haley. Haley. Haley. Haley."

Chapter Eight

Light crept over Boston Harbor, notifying the city of morning. Kate lay still on the cot, feeling dizzy. She'd crashed first while Pierre had pulled a chair over to the window to stare over the twinkling harbor. Sometime during the night, she'd heard him snoring like a beast. This morning she opened her eyes to see him sitting at her desk moving papers around.

"Hey."

"Well, good morning. I was just looking for my phone. I think I dropped it somewhere, here." He peered underneath the desk.

She stretched her arms overhead and yawned. "Well, you won't find it in that data."

His phone rang. Smiling sheepishly, he pulled his phone out of the pocket of his pants. He looked at the phone and dismissed the call.

"Who was it?" she asked.

"Nothing, just a work call."

He looked down at his crumpled clothes and groaned. "I hope you have a change of clothes. At least one of us will be presentable."

The surprise wrinkles on her forehead lifted. "For what?"

"Well, I assumed you wanted to be at Walpole when Monero meets with your Pop."

"Why would you assume that?" It sounded weird to hear Pierre calling her father, Pop.

"You stated last night that you would be okay with him talking to your Pop." There it was again. She wasn't sure why it was weird. Too familiar, perhaps? Maybe it was actually sweet.

"Stated? I stated? What say you? Ms. Finn, would you please state for the court what you told Pierre in your boudoir on the fourteenth? I said it couldn't hurt. How do you even know Monero is available?"

"Boudoir? Is that what this place is?" Pierre came to the end of the cot and lightly grabbed her ankles. "Do you think I could take care of you for just a minute? A minute? That's all I'm asking. How can you even think straight with all that's gone on? I want to help and I have connections."

A cat padding to his prey, he pawed up the sheets until he reached her face. A flow of warm energy rushed into her belly. Pierre looked at her for an answer. She tried to keep a serious expression but a half-smile broke from the corner of her lips, then became a full smile with rolling eyes of exasperation.

"Okay. Of course I have fresh clothes here. I practically live here. I'm going to run down the hall and shower. There's a shower in the men's room, too. I have extra everything in the metal credenza: toothpaste, deodorant, shampoo, and shaving cream. They're all leftovers from hotel stays. Why not? The staff just throws them out anyhow."

"Handy. Thanks. I need to make a couple of calls, then I'll clean up."

"Your prerogative. You can stink up my office as long as you need to."

She shuffled down the corridor feeling the aftereffects of the beer, Baileys, and wine. Sno Balls were all that either of them had eaten all evening. Though she knew she couldn't drink as she had in her college days anymore, last night was such a release. But the more her head cleared, the more her conscience threatened to arise, like Venus rising from the sea. If only she could keep her mind quiescent like striped bass who didn't feed through the winter months. Schools of stripers sought out the warmest waters, the darkest holes, and stayed put until the water temperature began to rise in the spring. Maybe if she stayed in her office with Pierre into summer, Pop would be released and she could move freely again. But she knew he wouldn't stay with her, couldn't stay with her. He would pull away, forcing her back to her more solitary life.

Showers nourished her, cleansing body, mind, and even soul. This morning she needed some extra soul cleansing. Even though they hadn't had sex last night, they'd shared intimate space. She didn't want to hurt Haley and she'd never done anything like this before in her life. Why did I agree to come to my office? The alcohol wasn't totally to blame, although it certainly had helped. It was more, though. Anguish so raging that it seemed only misbehaving could soothe its current. Lately these emotions weren't prone to quelling.

After showering she stood eye to eye with the mirror to see if she had somehow changed. Freckles in place, eyes still green, same height. She brushed pieces of coconut from the night before out of her teeth and smiled to see that they were poker-straight. Michael's teeth took after her mother's—large, pearly white, and perfectly straight. Kate got the Finn picket fence teeth. Pop joked there was no need for braces and that Kate could "Elmer's Glue them together." One trip to the orthodontist assured them that this was not the case. Pop traded down on his fish radar to afford her braces. On nights when wires pressed on her gums, she moaned, grunted, and complained that she hated braces and wished she had her picket fence teeth back. These nights were the rare times she could remember her father's comfort. He came into her room and sat on her bed, placing his hands on her cheeks and telling her she'd love her beautiful new smile.

"You don't want to walk around like this, do you?" Pop had motioned to his own crooked teeth, clomping them down on his bottom lip for more effect. They wheezed in laughter, and she forgot about her pain for at least a moment that night. She wished pain was still as simple as cankers on her gums. Physical pain had a time line, a shelf life. She wondered what her father was thinking as he sat in prison. If he knew what she had done the night before, she knew he'd be ashamed of her. She hung her head under the hand dryer to dry her hair, as she did whenever she showered here, but today the dryer trickled cold air. She repeatedly hit the round stainless-steel button with the hope that the flow would become warm. Finally, she gave up and walked back to her office with an unruly auburn mane.

The door was slightly ajar. She peered at Pierre through the crack between the door and the doorjamb. He was speaking on the phone.

"I'm putting myself on the line here. Do you really think this is easy for me? Quite frankly, I'm finding it distasteful."

Silence.

The toothpaste slipped from Kate's hands and fell to the floor. She leaned down to recover it and heard the conversation trail off.

Pierre hung up as she rounded the doorway. They came face-to-face and she smiled a nervous smile. "I'm sorry, I didn't mean to interrupt your phone conversation. Clumsy me."

"Not to worry."

"Are you okay? I mean, is everything at work okay?"

He placed his hands on her forearms. "Just some government funding reviews. Sponsors are sensitive about where their money goes. You know the drill." Lowering his hands, he moved to the file cabinet that held the toiletries. "I'll be ready in a jiff and then we'll get going. Eh?"

"Right. A jiff. Okay."

"Okay, now you're mimicking me."

"No. Jiff is a perfectly acceptable word. I'm sure my father hears it all day at Walpole."

After his shower, they walked down the stairs to the parking lot.

He insisted on driving.

"Oh shit!" He grabbed the parking ticket off Kate's windshield.

"How much?" She leaned over the hood. "I never park in a service vehicle spot. What was I thinking?"

"Fifty bucks." He opened the driver's door and threw the ticket onto the dash and they both got into the car. "You can appeal it."

"On what grounds? I was upstairs messing around?"

"Harsh," he said.

A white Camry with the signature codfish skeleton on the driver's door pulled up next to them.

"Oh, Christ," Kate said. Detective Madley got out wearing his signature raincoat. He tapped the window with the back of his hand.

Pierre rolled down the window. "Can I help you?"

"Everything okay here?"

"Yes, sir." Pierre pointed to Kate. "She forgot something in her office. We're on our way, now."

Madley stuck his head into the car. "Helloooo, Doctor." He pulled the ticket off the dash. "Must have taken you all night to find it. Ticket was issued at three a.m. I trust the accommodations here are good?" He opened Pierre's door. "Step out of the car, please."

Pierre patted his curly hair and adjusted the top button of his polo shirt.

"License, please."

He handed Madley his license.

"What brings you to these parts, Pier from Falmouth?"

"It's Pierre. Work."

Madley walked away from him, turned back and said, "Your belt buckle is twisted, Pierre. You must have been in quite a hurry."

He opened the passenger door. Kate started to get out.

"No. No. Stay right there." Leaning into the car, he sorted through the glove compartment and took out the registration. "Should only take a few minutes to run this. Assuming there are no outstanding warrants." He winked at her.

She sat in the car while Madley took far too long and Pierre stood outside shivering. The static from the car's radio echoed across the pier. Madley walked back to them, paperwork in hand.

"Dr. Finn's car registration runs clean." He handed Kate's registration back to Pierre and held up his license. "But you, Pierre, have been bad. I see you had a BUI five years ago, still boating and drinking?"

"It was dismissed, Detective."

"Good lawyer?"

"Sometimes circumstances are not what they appear to be." Pierre smiled at Madley.

"Yeah. Yeah. Everyone is innocent." He shoved the license into Pierre's hand with an exaggerated almost-pat on his back. Kate heard Madley whisper, "You're all set" to Pierre before he bent down, waved to Kate, and walked back to his car.

Pierre put his license back in his wallet, fixed his belt.

"How are you all set?" she asked.

"Huh?"

"He said you were all set. Set with what?"

Pierre gripped the wheel. "Cops always say that. Hey, I'll take care of the ticket. I know a guy. Don't you worry about a thing."

At the moment, she wasn't sure who or what to worry about.

Walpole, former home to the Boston Strangler, killed in jail by a Winter Hill gangster, was not a place Kate had ever thought she'd visit her father. Walpole State Prison, had been officially changed to MCI-Cedar Junction at Walpole. But everyone stuck with the shorter version, "Walpole." And now Pop was stuck inside.

Pierre parked the car in the visitor's area and sat looking up at the brick and concrete fortress insulated by barbed wire.

He laid his right hand on her arm. "Are you ready for this, Kate?"

"Not really. I have no choice though."

She gathered up a stack of fishing journals she'd brought from her office. Pop was the fastest reader she'd ever seen. He whipped through text with a vengeance. He never read books, which she attributed to his preference for unwinding in front of the television.

The moment of reckoning. She shut her car door, looked up toward perdition, and lost her legs. Her body slid down the side of her car to the asphalt; she started to dry heave. Pierre ran around to her side of the car and lifted her up.

"No, no, no. We can't lose you now. Think about your father, Kate. You need to show him you're strong. Shake it off, Katie. You can handle this."

"Yes, of course. Kate can do this and Kate is strong enough to handle that. Why can't I be a weakling for a change?"

He stood over her.

"Great. Now you are feeling sorry for me."

His gaze darted away as she tried to probe further. "Don't flatter yourself."

"I hate pity." She rose.

"C'mon. We need to get over to the West Wing," he said.

Kate looked at her reflection in the side view mirror. "Ugh. Hopeless. I look like Medusa."

"You're beautiful. Let's go."

"That's convincing."

"We need to hurry. Monero is meeting us inside. Wait! Leave your purse in the car. Just bring your license." After security check, giant metal doors buzzed opened to reveal Monero standing outside a glass partition.

Through the glass, Kate could see Pop sitting at a table, head down to examine his fingernails. She choked back tears and extended her hand to meet Monero's handshake. He had the fleshy shake of a man who didn't use his hands for a living. The complete opposite of Pop's firm, sandpaper grip.

"Pleasure to meet you, Kate. Pierre has told me a bit about your father's situation."

"Nice to meet you. I just want to point out before we meet with my father that he's a proud man. Don't expect him to back down, or admit something that isn't true just to get off the hook."

"Well, aren't you the expert on your father? We'll have to see where he stands considering he's facing a murder charge. You'd be surprised how far some criminals will go to get, as you say, off the hook."

Face burning, hands stiff by her side, Kate said, "Don't call my father a criminal."

"Sorry. Force of habit."

Security let them behind the glass partition to Pop. Visitors were scattered around, meeting with their loved ones. Kate led the threesome over to her father's table; he didn't acknowledge them. Monero tried to shove his hand into Pop's sightline. He pulled away toward Kate.

"Who are these bozos you are with?"

"Hi, Pop. This is Pierre. You remember him from WHOI."

"Vaguely. What's wrong with your hair?"

Blushing, she patted down what looked like morning-after hair. "And this is Attorney Monero."

"Why is he here?"

"Yes, my name is Anthony Monero and I'm here as a favor to Pierre, who's a good friend of your daughter. She's very concerned about your case and feels you are being underrepresented by your lawyer."

"Is she? Are these her words or yours?"

"Mr. Finn, do you have any idea how serious the charges are against you and given your previous record . . ."

He slapped the table. "Get them out of here."

"Pop, please, just listen to what he has to say."

"I'm with Kevin. I have my attorney. Now get these guys out of here and don't bring them back."

"Pop, just listen."

"No. You listen and listen good." He leaned in, whispering, his finger raised. "Don't interfere here, Kate. You think you know what's going on down at the docks with your statistician job. You know nothing. You shouldn't be there. Why are you there? Sleeping in the office." He glared at Pierre. His hands were flat against the table as if he were holding them in check. "Get this silver spoon and his ginzo lawyer out of my face."

He motioned the guard to buzz him back to his cell.

"Pop. We don't talk like that."

It was all Kate could think of to say to her father. She was furious, hurt, and disgusted. He'd never been so cruel to her. She'd hated when he spieled bigotry at home, grateful that no one was witness there, but here at Walpole he was letting it all fly. Now she had witnessed firsthand the effects of prison on him, covered with cruelty to her.

Stern-faced and cold-eyed, Pop was led out of the area by a guard. Never turning back to look, he threw his right hand up and waved them off as the security doors closed behind him.

On the drive back to Boston Pierre stared straight ahead out the windshield while Kate drove. She didn't want to break the silence. For some reason, it seemed futile to try to explain her father's rage, her father's prejudice, her father's condition. Suddenly, the provincial lives of her parents and even Erica and Will irritated her. The circular swirl of her hometown. No wonder Michael was always staying out of town at friends' houses. But lately he was around a lot. He seemed very attached to this Bo Ming. She'd never seen him so in love.

She should have listened to Dr. Zion. When she was at WHOI, he was clear about scientists needing to cut familial ties if they got in the way of research. He believed that her gifts must manifest themselves to the entire world and not be left open to attack by unevolved individuals with their perpetual problems. Kate dismissed this manifesto because her mentor had a solid family and she wanted one, too. But today she realized that Dr. Zion had somehow foreshadowed this time in her life. She looked over at Pierre, who was still staring, expressionless. He turned and looked into her eyes with no compassion; in fact, his eyes looked as expressionless as Sammy's had the day she found him dead. Pierre wasn't at all the seductive man from the night before. She saw her lot with new clarity—daughter of a man up on murder charges.

She pulled up in front of her parents' house, Pierre's Range Rover parked in front of them on the street, beckoning him to head back to the Cape.

"I'll probably keep a bit of a low profile for a while," he said.

"Yeah. I kind of figured."

He pulled the silver door latch to exit Kate's car. She sat still.

"You know, it's kind of funny," she said, staring straight ahead.

"What's funny?"

"Just how interested you were in hooking my father up with a new attorney."

"I just wanted to help."

"You've never showed any interest in my family life. Maybe I've been through a lot this past month and I'm not seeing clearly. Certainly messed up last night."

"Kate, I, I have to go. Haley's going to be concerned."

"Yes. I get it." But she wasn't so sure she was getting anything except cast off. She was finally ready to tell Pierre how she had felt about him. And he wanted to go home.

He leaned over, kissed her on the cheek, turned, and leapt from her car. She listened as he sped away down O Street.

Chapter Nine

When Kate entered the house, Michael was sitting at the kitchen table with their mother, finishing up a bowl of beef stew.

"Hey. Where have you been?"

"Hi Mom. Here, there, and visiting Pop in prison."

Her mother lowered her head at the word "prison." She walked to the stove and stirred the stew. "How was he today?"

"Just great. First he refused counsel from Pierre's lawyer friend. Then he proceeded to insult and degrade me and my friends. Can't wait till next visit."

"Why are you so angry all the time? Why can't you just support your family?" Mom kept her back to Kate, stirring the stew.

"Whoa, you two," Michael said. "Kate, you know Pop isn't going to let some slickster handle his case. What were you thinking?"

"I don't know, Michael. What was I thinking? Maybe try a different approach. Maybe not stay inside the neighborhood mentality. Step out a little. Get a tried-and-true expert instead of Michael's friend."

"At least my friend Kevin is loyal."

"Loyal won't get Pop off. Do you realize what he's up against with a prior record? There are no other suspects! What the hell are you people thinking?"

"What are you thinking?" Michael pointed at Kate's hair and patted the back of his own.

"Just finish your stew and be on your way. Don't worry. I'll handle things here per standard. We'll stick with the freaking messed-up Kevin plan."

"Don't speak that language in my home." Mom glared at Kate, the spoon dripping stew onto the floor.

"Your home. Your wonderful house with all your secrets. Why didn't you tell us what happened to Pop? I bet everyone in Southie knows except for Michael and me."

Michael lunged out of his chair. "Kate! You've taken it too far."

Kate stormed upstairs to her bedroom.

She heard their voices below as she lay across her bed. Then a soft ascension of the stairs. A knock. A pause. Knock. Pause. Knock. The childhood code they had developed to enter each other's rooms.

"Come in, Michael."

"Hey, how did you know it was me?" He was calm.

"Don't you want to know the story?" Kate moved to the window, staring down at the storm drains. "Why shouldn't we know about our father's past?"

"Why does it matter so much to you? They said it was self-defense."

97

"Because. It matters."

"Sorry about the hair thing. Not used to seeing you the morning after. Don't tell me you were with the scientist."

"Yeah. Okay? I fell prey to his wiles. And I can't say that I regret it." She leaned her head back and rubbed the stiffness out of her neck with both her hands. "Kind of like it's out of the way. But I never had sex with him."

"No need to know the details."

They were quiet for a bit. Even as kids they'd been comfortable together in silence.

"When are you going to live your own life?" Michael asked.

"I thought I was."

"You cling here. Mom and Pop's life is not your future. Then you sleep with your friend's husband?"

"Sleep. In separate corners of my office. That's it, nothing more. Can we not talk about Pierre anymore?"

"Okay. Sorry. But it appears like more. Just saying."

The next morning, Kate did something unheard of. She went to Mass with her mother. She still felt nothing within the walls of the church. Ocean shores were her sanctuaries. On the way home, they drove around the neighborhood while Mom reminisced.

"I interrupt this story with a private broadcasting announcement," Kate joked. "This is a repeat. I repeat. This is a repeat."

"Very funny, my dear. The thing is when you get to my age, the stories have been lived. Your turn now. I know you kids didn't have all you dreamed of but it was our dream to see you through college and help you on your feet."

"You did great, Mom. I never wanted anything more."

"Except a smart mother. Someone you could have discussed your science with. I'm sorry for that."

"Don't be stupid. You are so good with kids and you understand people. You do everything well. You cook and sew and knit. Remember when you tried to teach me to knit?"

"Let's not go there." She jokingly chided Kate about her inability learn to knit. "The dent is still in the living room wall where you whipped them needles, young lady."

They drove past the playground across from Carson Beach. When Kate was a child, Mom had brought her here to play on the monkey bars. When Kate was in junior high, she and Erica had teamed up with Jason and Connor to experience their first kisses. Quid pro quo, first Connor, then Jason. Nobody was remotely interested in anybody so it was the perfect exercise to get rid of the awkwards, as they called their inexperienced kissing techniques. Then came Randall, first love. They did it on a Sunday while his parents were at a church fundraiser. It hurt. Not physically. It hurt when Randall said he'd love her to infinity as his parents watched them on the curb next to the U-Haul. They were heading to Wisconsin to manage a dairy farm. Even now it seemed odd to her that a guy from Southie had turned agrarian, but from Randall's letters she learned the farm was quite successful. Then the letters slowed and finally ceased.

Now everyone was telling her to move, move on, let go, don't cling. Everyone knows what's right for me except me, she thought. She didn't want to admit out loud that she feared the unknown, the unfamiliar. Still, she knew they were right—all of them, Michael, Dr. Zion, even Pierre. Oh, Pierre. What did I do? Haley will never forgive me. What am I becoming? They passed Randall's old house.

"He's back."

Kate pulled her hair into a ponytail, holding it in place with both hands. "Who's back?"

"Randall. Your first love."

She blushed and looked out the side window. "Seriously, Mom."

"His preschooler is at my bus stop. Randall's wife brings her most of the time. She seems like a nice young woman. Accent sounds like she's from Wisconsin, too. And, guess what the daughter's name is?"

"I don't care?"

"Funny." Mom smiled. "Her name is not 'I don't care.' It's Caitlin. Catie for short. And get this, she loves fish. She talks about how her daddy takes her to a lake for catch and release."

"Good to know that little Catie won't have to milk cows in Wisconsin. I'm eternally happy for Randall and his beautiful family. Now please release me from this conversation."

"Okay." Mom nodded. "Apparently still a sensitive topic." She paused. "You do have to admit the name thing is probably more than coincidence. Even if subconscious. You know, first love is lasting in many ways. We don't get to choose who we fall in love with."

"And I think that line of thinking is kind of creepy, Mom."

They both laughed as they turned up O Street. Kate could tell by the way her mother gripped the steering wheel that she was mulling something over and ready to pounce. When she was relaxed, she placed her left hand on her lap. When she was nervous, she grasped the wheel with both hands. Mom had both hands on the wheel. And then she came out with her news.

"Don't take offense, Kate, but after Pop gets off, you need to find your own place to live. Michael soon after."

"Well, that's rather abrupt. I thought we were helping you."

"You are, but it's time for you, especially, to find a nice guy and settle down. You're not getting any younger."

"I'm twenty-seven. Michael's twenty-six. You and Pop didn't get married until your thirties. Oh. Wait a minute. I get it. Meanwhile, Michael and I will put things on hold until you are settled."

"What? Why are you talking all angry again?"

"Do you hear yourself? What are we, temporary help until you and Pop are back under the same roof? I have a slot for you right here until."

"I'll never understand you."

"Don't worry, Mom. I'll be out of your hair by the time Pop gets out."

"I didn't say that. You completely misunderstood."

"I understand perfectly. You're right. And don't think I haven't had plenty of offers from men. Plenty." Maybe no real ones, but she wouldn't admit that today.

When they pulled into the driveway, she spotted Rich Madley at their door, writing a note on a piece of paper from his notepad.

She slouched in the passenger seat.

"Great. More good news."

"What now, Kate? Will you please get a hold of yourself?"

Kate eased out of her mother's car and slammed the door.

"Can I help you? Because there is no one left here to harass, issue tickets to, or arrest." Kate thrust her wrists out. "Unless you want to book me now, too?"

"Actually, I came to apologize to you and your mother. I felt terrible about the arrest."

"Then you shouldn't have arrested him," Kate said.

"Kate, invite the detective in." Her mother's voice was cold.

Instead, Kate walked back to the car, pretending to look for something inside on the floor. Mom had opened the door for the detective. Kate looked up and saw the door still open for her. "Shit." She walked into the kitchen where the two stood in a face-off.

"How is the investigation going, Detective?"

"Well to be blunt, Mrs. Finn, I can't discuss it with you."

"Oh. Then why are you here?"

Kate didn't want him in the house either, but she was surprised by her mother's open hostility toward him.

"Detective, my mother asked you why you are here." Kate's voice was harsher than she'd intended.

For a split second, she saw him clench his jaw in anger. "As I said, I want to apologize for your family's situation."

The words sounded right, well-placed, neutral even, but Kate felt a kind of force behind them that was aggressive. A tonal shift to what she thought was the same arrogance she felt from him on the docks. Was he too good to answer a question? Did he think he was better than them?

"Noble of you," Kate said.

"And, our experts have not been able to determine exactly why the fish turned green.

I thought you might tell me, off the record, of course, if you know why?"

"I spoke to my father's attorney and he said I should not discuss anything with the skeleys or anyone else regarding my father's case."

Madley squinted. "As a Massachusetts Dock Police detective, I just thought, given your expertise and the situation, it could help your father."

"I'm sure your concern is with my father. Don't you have people to look into why a cod turns green? God knows there is plenty of cod evidence left."

"What do you mean 'left'?" asked Madley.

"I remember it was pretty big." Kate realized she had stumbled. "I have no ideas about the color of fish."

"Thank you for coming by." Mom opened the back door to show Madley out.

But he turned back to Kate. "Say hi to your friend Pierre. Make sure you take care of that ticket."

"What ticket? What's he talking about?" asked her mother.

Kate shrugged. "Don't know, Mom. He seems kind of crazy." She would never be able to tell her mother about her soiree with

Pierre, or any other man for that matter.

Mom put on the teakettle as Kate slumped into her father's living room chair. Intense pressure pulsed behind her eyes and for once she let herself release all that had been stacked inside since the day she'd found Sammy. Giant tears dropped onto the brown leather recliner. The once-smooth leather was worn down to suede, so the tears stared back at her in messy shapes. She didn't care. She missed Pop, the one she thought she knew, the one she had grown up with. She missed his solid presence, even his gruffness. She hated watching her mother without her partner and wanted to alleviate the loss. Salt from her tears slid over her mouth, some reaching her tongue. Her head burrowed into the worn wet leather. She felt her mother's hand touch her back, then her head and suddenly she was a small child, body throbbing, choking out her grief in thumping bass, ending in soft distant whimpers.

"John Brennan was his name. He was a transient deckhand. Your father didn't like him from the start and never used him on Truelight. He came cheap, so some of the other guys used him. You know those guys. Sammy was the worst. Tight as they come. Eternally trying to save a buck." Her voice lowered, talking more to herself than her daughter now. Kate witnessed her mother transported back in time. "Seamus said, 'They'll pay one way or the other. There's no free lunches.'"

Kate straightened her posture. "He still says that."

"You kids weren't born yet. It was in the middle of November. No one was on the docks. Pop stayed later than the rest of the guys to wait for me to get out of work. I went to pick him up. We'd planned to go to dinner that night at Durgin-Park to celebrate our three-month wedding anniversary."

"Why didn't you go to Amrheins?" Kate shook her head in confused disgust. "Durgin-Park? Those waitresses used to be so awful."

"They were hell on wheels." She smiled. "Funny as heck, though. We had our favorite waitress, Ginny. She took care of us. Even tied the red-and-white checkered cloth napkins around our necks. The good old days." Her eyes looked dreamy. "Seamus proposed to me there over coffee Jell-O. Ginny was in on it. She put a candle in the Jell-O." Mom focused back on Kate. "You know your father. He doesn't go for anything swanky."

Mom sat down on the couch.

"Brennan had been caught stealing from the boats and selling to his own private customers. He'd raided the boats at night, too, and took some of Sammy's gear off Milady, and a couple of other boats. Seamus was the one who confronted him. He should have let them all fight their own battles. But you know your father, it's his way. Always fighting for the underdogs. But Brennan denied it."

"Slime," Kate said.

"Days later, your father was working on Truelight's engine. Brennan came up behind him with a knife." Her mother's voice drifted. The look in her eyes shifted as if she was staring out at the ocean's horizon. "Seamus was able to get out of his boat and take it up on the docks. He got the best of Brennan. Brennan fell over the side. He didn't make it."

"Did you see him do it?" Kate asked.

"I got there right after. Seamus ran to our car and yelled at me to drive us home. His chin was sliced, and his arms and legs were cut. His jacket and pants were saturated with blood. Brennan was an animal. We went home. He called the police right away."

"I always thought the cuts were from the fishing lines. I asked him once and he changed the subject. I thought he was mad at me. I knew never to ask again."

She let out a shallow sigh. "We try to put it behind us."

"Did they give him any credit for calling right away?" Kate asked.

"Said he left the scene of the crime. Those skeleys came to the house. You know your father, he resisted and they weren't having it. Beat your father in front of me, as if he wasn't banged up enough." She placed her right hand on her forehead and covered her eyes. "They dragged him onto the front lawn in front of the neighbors. Mrs. Burke started yelling at them to stop but all the others were terrified. Can't blame them."

Kate sat beside her mother and pulled her close. "I'm so sorry, Mom."

Her head was down, eyes still covered with her hand. "Everyone on the docks stood by him. Said Brennan was a thug on the run. Preyed on hard-working guys in the trade. We got a decent lawyer. He found another fisherman down in New Bedford who said he'd been threatened and attacked by Brennan with the same knife. The hospital records could prove it. The state cut a deal to avoid a trial. Your father served six months in the Charles Street jail for assaulting an officer and resisting arrest."

"What a nightmare." She thought about how Pop's body tensed

and his voice shifted whenever he saw a skeley.

"Your father served six months," she cleared her throat, "plus the rest of his life."

Tears jetted down both their faces.

"There is one good part to this story." Mom coughed.

Kate could see that her mother was breaking down. "What's the good part, Mom?"

"I was going to tell your father at Durgin-Park over coffee Jell-O that I was pregnant with you."

Kate pulled Mom's wet hand away from her eyes and held it for a long time.

They moved around the house quietly for the rest of the day. That night Kate dreamed she was pulling silk rope out of her stomach. It kept coming out and coming out and coming out until an old barnacle-covered anchor ripped her insides.

Chapter Ten

O n the Fourth of July Kate awoke to the sound of fireworks from the direction of Carson Beach. She sprang
out of bed and neatly rearranged the new white eyelet
comforter her mother had made, parted the matching curtains, and
pulled up the green shades. The sky was shadowy and promising.
The alarm clock read 7:49 and she had a good feeling about this
day. The nautical layer of mist would soon dissipate to reveal a
stark blue sky, though not too soon. She hoped for the sun to ar-
rive in a gradual unveiling, like all things that moved her—the fore-
play of events was as fulfilling as the actual acts of life. She had
never been one for jarring drama and therefore couldn't help re-
senting Sammy for pulling her family into his death.

In the shower, she let the lukewarm flow hit the middle of her
forehead—Hindus referred to this clairvoyant area as the third eye.
Kate was far from clairvoyant, but today she felt clarity, something
she hadn't experienced since that April morning when she had
walked out of her office to find Sammy dead on the docks. She did

feel bad when she thought about her father spending Independence Day in jail. Even though she knew she should go visit him, she wasn't ready. He wouldn't want to see her anyhow. She was sure of that much. He had his pride and she'd crossed a line by taking Pierre and his prized lawyer to see him that unsettling morning. She choked back tears when she thought of how they had looked at Pop. He was a sideshow act to them. It was enough to make her never want to speak to Pierre again. Had he ever really been a friend? She didn't know anymore. Or maybe she simply assuaged her guilt by avoiding the Gosselins.

She felt like riding her bike over to the beach and around Castle Island. She pulled on khaki shorts, a white tank with a built-in bra, and her favorite new Nike sneakers with peach and gray swooshes on the sides. She wiped the steamed mirror with a thick poppy-colored towel, one of the few domestic items she'd bought since she moved back from Woods Hole. Bold colors captivated her. On a seventh-grade field trip to the Museum of Fine Arts, Kate had spotted Henri Matisse's Vase of Flowers. It was gripping how he mixed colors and texture. Left to her own tastes, she would have selected a screaming orange comforter and green polka dot curtains for her bedroom. Instead she graciously accepted her mother's staid choices. Decorating made Kate nervous and never seemed quite complete. Science was never complete, either, yet it was infinitely expansive, unlike a room with artifacts. She breathed more easily when others arranged her space.

In the kitchen, she downed a glass of orange juice. Then she stopped off in the brown-walled pantry and secured three Oreos for the ride. A power breakfast.

The morning sun danced off the chrome on Kate's bike as she traveled the tight streets. Thoughts of her father stole in again. She wondered how he was dealing with jail. She wondered if he was afraid now. He had never been afraid. He was the strongest man she knew. He would kill anyone who got in his family's way. This awareness sent a chill through her body. It was clear that her father was capable of killing, had killed, even if it was self-defense.

A car blasted its horn behind her. She tried to pull over, but the car trailed behind her and kept beeping. She pulled up on the sidewalk and watched as the black Lincoln Town Car pulled by her. The driver waved through the open sunroof and beeped one last time. "What the hell? Can't even take a bike ride without assholes," she yelled at the car and then read the rear license plate: GSL. Abbreviation for Greely Seafood Labs. She remembered it from Fish Pier, the day Sammy was killed.

Carson Beach on Pleasant Bay was already hopping with twenty-somethings drinking out of red cups and eating Sully's hot dogs for breakfast. She remembered her own morning-after beach parties from college. Even in high school, she would claim to be sleeping at Erica's house and vice versa; neither of their parents ever checked on their girls because they trusted them. A twinge of guilt tweaked inside her stomach at the memory of her deceit. Sometimes they stayed up all night visiting friends and got lobster rolls for breakfast. She bent her head in reverence to Sully's and rode toward Fort Independence, locked her bike in a rack under a tree and walked the two-mile loop around the bay. The morning breezes rushed at her and she took shallow breaths of relief with each step that no rats had scurried over her feet. They had been overbreeding here. Some said that the demolition of older buildings for new construction drove them out into the open. Rats terrified her.

Stepping down onto the beach, she took off her sneakers and carried them along with her bike helmet. The seasonably warm water relaxed her as she stood looking across the bay. Fourth of July revelers blasted their music behind her. At twenty-seven, she suddenly wished she could recapture her early twenties. A girl in a blue and pink polka-dot bikini lit a joint and passed it to another girl. Their conversation strayed toward philosophy. Kate remembered these kinds of talks with Erica and their high school friend, Melissa Ford. Their lack of logic had exhausted her. Often Melissa shifted into ethereal topics citing nonsense like the sky is an extension of the sea. Perpetually pragmatic, Kate argued the science. Usually these conversations also took place over a joint, when Melissa was most vehement in her position on sea-sky connections until shifting into other examples like butterflies are God's love messengers.

Melissa was a gentle soul, stunning with curly blond hair, deep-blue eyes, and a figure that wowed all their guy friends. But Melissa's struggles with everyday life led her to find destructive forms of relief. When Erica and Kate had walked into Reagan's Funeral Parlor and seen Melissa's crack-ravaged face at her wake one month before she would have turned twenty, they dutifully paid their respects and assured the Fords they'd loved their daughter and had tried to get her away from the wrong crowd. Then they drove home and cleared out their own pot and paraphernalia for good. Today Kate was enveloped in layers of blue sky nodding into the bay. She felt Melissa's spirit encircle her and conceded: Who's to say sea and sky are not connected?

It was time to head home, but first she wanted to buy a bottle of water for the ride. She cut through the parking lot in front of Sully's. Parked there with the ignition running was Greely's car. "Jackoff," said Kate, louder than she intended.

Each year on the Fourth, Erica and Will closed Dingles early and the three of them set up camp with blankets and coolers at the Hatch Shell on the Esplanade. Today they sat on their blanket facing the Charles River. Kate felt festive in her red and white sundress and blue wrap. Late afternoon wound into evening and the hum of the crowd pitched to a dull roar. Families walked by, some pushing strollers with balloons tied higher than children could reach.

"Why do people do that to their kids? My parents used to tie my balloon low on my arm so I could enjoy it. What is the point of having a balloon if you can't play with it?"

"Okay, calm down." Erica patted Will's leg. "We'll get you your own later."

"That's not the point. My kids will touch their balloons."

"That's settled." Kate pulled two plastic pitchers out of her cooler. "You all up for sangrias? I made red and white."

"Nah. I'll stick to beer. Erica won't be drinking." Will leaned over and took Erica's hand.

"Huh? Did you finally get accepted into a twelve-step program?"

"Better." Erica touched her belly.

Kate looked back and forth from Erica to Will. "Wow. When? This is incredible. I'm sorry about the stupid comments."

"Don't worry about it. About four months, give or take. It didn't seem right telling you when everything was coming down on your family. I'm due in December. I think. My math is a bit off."

"Where have I been? You don't even show."

"Right. You're being gentle." Erica rubbed her stomach. "I hide it under the fat."

"I'm so happy for you both. This is what you've wanted forever." She squeezed both their hands tightly and pushed the surging tears down. She was happy for them, but scared that she would lose her best friends. Surely they would include her as much as possible, but Kate had seen this routine over and over, losing single friends to marriage and then married friends to children. Now she needed a drink for sure, possibly two or three.

"Look who's here, Kate," Will said.

Kate saw him walk through the river of blankets. "That's Madley. What the hell is he doing here?"

Will called over to him. "Hey, hey, Detective."

"Will, stop. Please. I don't want him to see us." Kate put her head down.

"Stop stressing, Kate." But it was too late. Madley looked directly at Kate.

"Oh, Christ." Kate had looked forward to a relaxing night with her friends, probably one of the last for many years since they had officially entered precious prenatal time. Now Madley threatened. She turned to walk over to a popcorn vendor but Madley got to them first.

"Hey, what's up? Spending the Fourth in the city, huh?"

"No, we are actually down the Cape," Kate said. "You're seeing holograms."

"Hi, Detective, you remember my friendly friend, Kate?" Erica asked. "We've missed you around Dingles, lately."

"Oh, I'll be by this week." He winked at Will and patted his pocket. "Hey, do you guys want to take a ride up river? I'm off duty and one of my buddies has a boat right there." He pointed to a shiny green and white Grady White.

Kate couldn't get her thoughts into words. Erica had already obliged. "Well, I for one am sweltering in this heat. At least, I think it's the heat."

She looked at Kate with pleading eyes. Must be the mommy hormones kicking in. She looked vulnerable.

Will leaned over and rubbed Erica's stomach. "We want you to have fun tonight. It won't be as hot on the water." He looked at Kate, winked, and nodded at Detective Madley.

"We'd be happy to join you."

Before Kate could protest, Erica had directed Will to gather the picnic basket and coolers and to leave the blanket to save their spot. Kate hugged her cooler while Madley's buddy, Bob, helped her into the boat. Seated on the spotless white vinyl cushion, she sighed and glared at Erica.

"What?" Erica asked.

Kate mumbled, "Not how I wanted to spend my Fourth. Under river surveillance."

Erica sat down and admired the scenery. "But everything is different from this angle. Fabulous."

Kate sulked. There she goes again, fabulous. Who says fabulous besides gay decorators, especially about river boats on the Fourth of July? Amazing, maybe. Festive even.

Erica pinched Kate's leg. "Give him a chance."

"The man arrested my father."

"Technicality. Time to release and re-catch."

"Fishing jargon now? What in god's name are you talking about? What happened to my sardonic friend Erica?"

"She's grown up."

"Want one?" Madley lurched over to Kate with a blue plastic cup filled with fluid resembling beer.

Kate accepted the drink and thanked him, happy to discover it was beer. The perks of being a skeley. She remembered the skeleys confiscating liquor and threatening parental reports, the ultimate threat. Some skeleys poured it out in front of them. Others grabbed it as their own. Kate used to imagine skeley basement bars with granite countertops, leather stools, and bottles hijacked from traumatized teenagers. Tonight Madley seemed different from those skeleys, but it was probably just the beer skewing her judgment.

He offered her some mixed nuts out of a can. "I did try to call your house last week to pick up on our last conversation."

"I'm not home." She funneled the nuts into her mouth.

"You have amazing deflection capabilities. A natural reflex?"

"No detective-talk tonight, Detective. If you want us to hang out with you, you can't interrogate."

She poured out the beer backwash and opened the cooler to retrieve the sangria.

"Now, the question is red or white sangria?"

Madley drained his cup. "Red, of course. White is for girls."

"Red it is, macho man," Kate said.

Maybe the sangria helped, maybe not, but their conversation flowed easily.

He lifted his polo shirt and pulled a joint out of the front pocket of his shorts.

"Want some?"

Kate and Erica shook their heads.

Will took a hit and passed it to Bob, who pulled out a prescription bottle and swallowed some white pills.

Kate rolled her eyes.

Bob told Madley to take the helm, rummaged through the back of the boat, and came up with a guitar. He thrust it at Madley. "Play."

Madley pushed it away. "These guys don't want to hear me."

Erica and Will chimed, "Yes, we do."

Madley was a force as he strummed Led Zeppelin's "When the Levee Breaks." All of them sang. Will stood up waving and yelling to the nearby boats to join in for the last three lines. The serenade faded and Will sat as the rest of the boats and their and crews riotously applauded for more.

Erica cuddled up to Will.

Kate threw her arms up and applauded over her head. "You got some stuff."

Madley broke into a slow country tune Kate didn't recognize.

"Seriously?" Kate griped.

Erica lightly slapped Kate's head. "Ye doth protest too much. Country is the wave, baby."

"Never. Death to country." Kate toasted her cup to the sky.

Now the nearby boats chanted, "Dirty Water, Dirty Water, Dirty Water."

Madley faced the fleet of boats and belted out the song, sweat pouring off his forehead.

Erica and Will hung over the sides of the boat singing the lyrics in harmony with the adjacent boats. When the concert was over, everyone turned to look at Kate. She was disengaged, fingering her sangria fruit.

Erica sat next to her. "Hey, what wrong?"

"Not a thing," Kate said. "Can we get going? Now?"

Madley interrupted. "You can stay onboard for the fireworks."

Will looked like he was about to accept for all of them, until Erica gave him a stern stare. "We need to get back to our blanket, honey. Tradition."

Bob turned the boat around and headed downriver.

When they reached their blanket, it had been mangled and stomped. After they ate some snacks, Kate turned to Erica and thanked her. Erica's eyes filled. "I don't know what was wrong. But

117

I knew I had to get you off that boat."

"My father loves fireworks."

The three of them lay on the blanket, looking up at the fireworks.

After the fireworks finished, they stayed fixated on the sky, watching the fog of smoke float away.

"Remember how Melissa loved watching until the sky was clear enough to see stars again?" Erica asked.

"Never forget it," Kate responded. "She made us stay until all traces of smoke were gone. It took forever."

"I still miss her," Erica said as tears soaked her cheeks. "I hope my baby never gets hooked on drugs."

"She won't." Kate placed her hand on Erica's stomach and repeated, "She won't."

Chapter Eleven

They met at the Pour Over House on Tremont.

"This is my favorite Boston spot." Madley straightened his silverware. "Do you think it's dull?"

She leaned over the table and whispered. "A fine blend of blue blood and gold flow through those polished mahogany walls."

"We can leave."

"Never. This place is swanky."

"Thanks for coming." He unfolded his napkin and placed it on his lap. "We got off on the wrong foot."

"You mean the part about you arresting my father? Or interrogating me and Pierre? Or kidnapping me and my friends on the Fourth?"

Madley's mood soured. "Hardly a kidnapping." He looked around for the waiter.

"I wasn't going to come. But what the heck. How does a woman pass up the chance to have dinner with her father's arresting officer? Are you going to order haddock?"

"Wise guy," he gently chided. "I swore off haddock after the food poisoning at Jimbo's. I'm going for the lobster bisque, though."

"JFK's favorite," she observed.

"There's a suite upstairs named after him."

Shrimp cocktail came first. They shared six prawns.

For dinner Kate ordered the traditional clambake and Madley ordered halibut. They agreed on a bottle of Sauvignon blanc and then another. For dessert, Boston cream pie.

Tonight, she felt an ease between them and didn't resist when the conversation turned.

"Have you heard of Frankenfish?" he asked.

"Duh! Just every day since I can remember. All the real workers in Boston are pissed off about GE."

"GE? You talking about General Electric who brings good things to life?"

"Funny, Detective. I'm talking about genetic engineering, genetic modification, Frankenfish."

"I get it. I'm heavily invested in a local business that's trying to break in."

"Greely's," she asked.

"Hell, no."

"That's quite an exuberant no."

"What about your father. Does he like GE?"

"Are you insane? My father says it's Armageddon."

"Doesn't he support his daughter's scientific inquiry?"

"Don't kid yourself, Joe Friday."

"It's a logical step in the food supply chain but there's so much resistance," he said.

"Agreed. Been going on since the 1950s, anyhow."

"I guess." He seemed interested but not surprised. "So why do so many object to GE fish?"

"GE in the fishing industry can be scary business. A complete shift in the species genes, creating disease and possibly wiping out our oceans could happen if the fish farms move too fast. If they keep it to simply accelerating maturation, then maybe it would be fine if they can eliminate the bacteria. I'm not sure I'm onboard with any of it, yet."

"Same thing could happen to America's agriculture. Global chemical companies own agriculture now, plant and fish farms. What's the difference? We'll be left behind other countries if we don't stay ahead of them."

"You've done your research." She high-fived him. "I tend to agree within reason. The oceans are polluted. I think if GE is handled with proper safeguards; if there are the strictest of regulations, it could be revolutionary. But you didn't hear it here. Not from Seamus Finn's daughter."

He shifted in his seat. "What does he approve of?"

She laughed. "Certainly, not you."

"Friends?" He wiped the sides of his mouth with his napkin.

"My old friends, sure. New ones, not so much. He'd approve of my WHOI advisor, Dr. Zion."

"Isn't he in Planet of the Apes?"

"Zion, not Zaius."

"Sorry, just a lame joke. Great movie though. The original." He spoke rapidly in rat-a-tat-tat fashion that made Kate a bit untethered.

"Can you focus on a subject, Detective?"

"Sorry. Who's Dr. Zion?"

"Doctor Zachary Zion now works with my friend Pierre, whom you met," she sneered.

"Why don't you call him by his first name?"

"He's the leading expert in his field, the master. When I first met him, it seemed to be proper and then it stuck. Now I can't call him anything else."

"Master, huh?" He poured more wine. "Lucky we aren't driving. I arranged for the JFK suite."

"Have some respect." She toasted, "His spirit is still there."

"Do you have better sleeping quarters?" he asked.

A male voice came from behind.

"Hello, Kate. Still trying to find suitable sleeping quarters?"

Then a female's voice. "Yes. Seems you can never settle on one."

She turned to meet Haley's eyes.

"Oh, hi." Kate wiped her mouth, placed her napkin on the table, and stood to greet her friends while Madley nodded from his seat.

"Where have you been, Kate?" Haley's tone was not as enthusiastic as usual but not so edgy that it sounded like she was talking to the woman who had spent a night with her husband. They hugged one at a time. It was all so stiff, like the Finn hug.

Kate responded to Haley's question with another. "What are you doing here?"

"We come here a lot for Pierre's business dinners. Who's your friend?" Haley asked.

Kate was sitting now, fidgeting with her wine glass. "Sorry. This is Rich Madley."

Madley stood and shook hands with Haley and Pierre. He lingered over the shake until Pierre pulled his hand away.

"What is it you do again?" He winked at Pierre. "Go fishing? Or boating under the influence? I can't remember"

"Hah, good one, Officer." Pierre laughed louder than Kate had ever heard him laugh.

"Detective." Madley sat down.

"Detective. Please forgive me, Detective. I'm a scientist, Detective." Pierre exaggerated "detective" for effect. Everyone was uncomfortable.

Haley broke the tension. "Look, Pierre, there's Ed and Melissa."

Kate turned to see Ed McGann and his wife. Tonight McGann wore a traditional Bostonian navy blue blazer, golf shirt, and tan Dockers. He resembled a polished legislator with his white hair and classic dress. Melissa was overdressed in sparkly high pumps, a low-cut silk blouse, and a black leather skirt. She looked more southern than Brahmin. Haley and Pierre were dressed in their customary, understated classic attire.

Madley waved to the McGanns.

"Do you know the McGanns?" Haley asked.

"I've seen them around." Madley nodded toward their table.

"Looks like you have more company."

A tall, good-looking man waved over to them. Colin Greely.

"Great, Colin decided to come after all." Pierre slipped his arm through Haley's to lead her away.

Madley stood up and nodded in deference. "Haley, enjoy your evening. Good to see you again, Peter."

"That's Pierre. Not Peter. Not Pier."

Madley winked at Pierre. Haley motioned with her eyes to Pierre to get going.

"What was that?" Kate asked.

"What was what?"

"Please. You practically strip-searched the guy in front of his wife."

"Well everyone else has. Didn't you?" he asked. "Remember? At Fish Pier. Looks like the wife might be on to the two of you. Age-old story, woman beds her friend's husband."

"Funny." She slipped her napkin off her lap and onto the table. "Somehow, I'm not thirsting for an aperitif, anymore."

"Well, you did sleep with him. Right?"

"None of your business."

"I think they're talking about you." Madley cocked his head.

"You're insane." But when she looked over, Greely raised his wine glass and mimed a "cheers."

They walked silently down Tremont Street.

"I'm sorry, for being snarky. Come over to my apartment. I live in the South End."

"It's late," she said.

"Come up to my apartment and we'll have a drink."

"I'm not coming up," she said. "I'm not sleeping with you. Coming here tonight was a mistake. I'm going home." She'd mistakenly let her guard down, or maybe the wine had done that.

"No one said anything about sleeping over."

She turned and walked away. He ran after her and grabbed her arm. "Please, just forget what I said. It was a joke."

"I can't." She shook his arm off hers. "How could I be so stupid? You're just playing me for information. I feel it. Skeley on duty." She began walking again.

"I get it," he yelled after her. "You only date married men."

She ran toward the T station, darted down the stairs, and waited for the subway alongside a family of four. The little boy rode on his father's shoulders and the daughter held his right hand, the mom his left. Kate was overcome. Her chest murmured. She'd stayed away long enough. She needed to see Pop.

The next day she jumped on the Southeast Expressway by cutting through Quincy. Even with the windows rolled up and the sound of the air conditioning fan combatting the sweltering heat of the July day, she could hear the trucks that vibrated her Accord as they flew past her. Oddly, the noise pollution soothed her. Highway cruising allowed Kate to get out of her head. But the Jersey barriers lining the expressway were not so soothing. Sometimes she envisioned slamming into one, bouncing across the pavement upside down, and crashing into the onslaught of traffic. Shaking off the image, she turned up the radio and sang with the Stones, "(I Can't Get No) Satisfaction." Today she decided not to take her father's harsh comments personally. He'd suffered a lot over the last four months.

She pulled the car into the lot where she and Pierre had parked. The towering brick buildings shadowed the lot and the barbed wire weighed heavily on her eyes. Such a horrible place, she thought as she neared the visitor's entrance behind a parade of other visitors. She didn't make eye contact with them. Didn't want to get to know them or their stories. She just wanted to pretend Pop was in a holding pattern until she could somehow get him out.

She entered through the metal detector. She watched the guards shuffle through her purple leather hobo bag. Since she forgot to leave her cell phone in the car, the guard confiscated it and told her she could pick it up on the way out.

"You came back." Pop looked skeletal.

"Hi, Pop." She tried to hug him. He patted her back. "I didn't think you wanted to see me. So I stayed away. Probably for too long."

She sat across from him at the long visitor's table. They avoided eye contact.

"Which way did you come?" he asked.

"Ninety-three to ninety-five."

"How's the traffic?"

These were the same questions Bostonians asked on a continual basis. She never understood why people cared so much about the route taken.

"Lots of trucks. And some of the Jersey barriers were out of alignment."

"Those g-d things. They cause more trouble than the old permanent guardrails. They were supposed to be temporary thirty years ago. The Commonwealth is too cheap to fix them properly."

She was happy to hear him rage against the tide. It indicated that he still had some fight in him. He tilted his head at her and she met his eyes. They looked stern.

"Your mother says Erica is expecting."

Kate nodded.

"Are you still going to Dingles to visit them?"

"Free Murphy's."

"Still drinking your Irish stout, are you? I miss the neighborhood."

She looked down at her sweaty palms in her lap, switched the top hand to the bottom, then repeated the sequence. He rocked back in his chair, head slightly upright.

"I'm okay, dear."

She forgot he called all women "dear." She used to think it was Victorian, now it felt comforting.

"How's work?" he asked.

"Not bad. We've been getting some shellfish from Mass Marine Fisheries, a bivalve depuration plant."

"Bivalves. Jumping teams, are you?" Their eyes met and squinted. "Sorry, jail humor."

"Red tide is running amuck, again."

"Goodness." He looked at her face like he was studying her features.

"Rob's taking good care of Truelight. He gives Mom half of what he makes."

"Good man."

She didn't avert her eyes this time. "I talked to Kevin. The autopsy came back." She hesitated. "And it doesn't look good."

"Why? What's the cause of death?"

"Cardiac tamponade."

"Speak English, Kate."

"Heart failure. Bleeding around his heart." She drew a long breath. "Kevin said they suspect overexposure to ammonium perchlorate, but they've never seen so much in a deceased person before." She squinted at Pop. "So it's not conclusive."

"That's good news then," he said.

"They said force was used. Sammy may have been forced to ingest some of the chemical. They found bruises on his neck, arms, and back. And if the chemical didn't kill him, the stress of the struggle did."

"Mother of God." Seamus banged the table with his fist. "How did he swallow chemicals?"

She shushed him and looked around nervously. Craning her neck, she confided in her father. "I didn't tell you this because everything happened so fast and Mom never wants me to upset you. Then you got arrested."

"Geez, I'm fine," he said. "What do you need to tell me?"

"The morning I found Sammy. I took something."

He pulled his chair closer to the table. "What are you saying?"

"His chest was bulging, so I opened his jacket. There was a codfish propped inside."

"Yeah. It was in the papers."

"I took a piece of cod. It was green inside." She sighed. "Without thinking, I just grabbed it and threw it in my coffee cup and hid it behind my bookshelves. There was a close call when Madley came up to look around. The cup was rattling. I told him it was the AC system."

"Jesus. You tampered with evidence, Kate."

"Not intentionally." She looked behind her to see if the guard could hear. "Well. Maybe it was intentional."

"What did you find in the cod?"

"Traces of chloroform. But then I took it to Nobska Fisheries for analysis. It reeked of ammonium perchlorate."

"Have you told anyone what you've done?"

"Just Dr. Zion at Nobska Fisheries."

"Mary, Mother of God."

"I can trust him."

"Let's hope so. You've been a busy girl."

"That's not the half of it." She swung her hair over her shoulder.

"What are your conclusions, Doctor?"

"From what I can tell so far, Sammy may have used chemicals

on his fish to pass inspection. Chemicals that don't come up in my testing or maybe in any. Possibly with the dual effect of masking bacteria levels."

"That crazy, desperate bugger." His face turned red and he clenched his fists.

"He'd drifted, sold his catch to Greely Labs and the Ming operation over there in East Boston. I knew he was up to no good."

She wouldn't mention she'd had been out with a skeley and run into Pierre, Greely, and his man, McGann. Or that his son had dated a Ming. He was too agitated to handle this kind of information. She placed her hand on his forearm. "Chill. It's not illicit to sell to those guys."

He let out a huge sigh. "It's a crime against the real fishing trade."

"I need to ask you," she said.

Seamus raised his right hand to stop her from asking and looked around for a guard to remove him.

"Please, Pop. I just need to hear it from you. I know what I believe in my heart, but what if I'm wrong? I didn't know you killed that guy when you were young."

"Self-defense." His face tensed, hardened like a man who'd battled life, an almost-criminal.

"I know. This time it's different. We need everything to win your freedom this time." She kept her eyes level with his.

He squirmed and shook his head from side to side. "I can't believe this."

She spoke softly. "Pop. Did you kill Sammy?"

"Time for you to leave." He shook the room with his roar.

The guard started to approach them. With his hands, Pop motioned a "sorry" to him and the guard whipped a cautionary stare at them, holding it for a long while before turning away.

He leaned forward and crouched to talk. "Sammy was my best friend, brother to me, uncle to you. He'd been having some financial problems. You know he liked to play the ponies. Off-track. We all like to gamble a little but Sammy had the bug, got behind on bills. The banks were going to put a lien on his boat. Then he switched up customers. They were hanging around, trying to infiltrate. The rest of us were standing firm but Sammy let them in and others followed."

"Who?"

"Doesn't matter. Point is, Greely is major now with the Chinese on his heels. I'll sell my boat before I sell to either. These guys never even break a sweat. Just buy all our hard-earned catch for nothing, resell and take more markup. God only knows what goes on inside that fortress named after Greely. Word is he's breeding Frankenfish, and the Chinese, too. They've taken over the Seaport and East Boston."

"What happened that day?" Kate's voice softened. "Were you fighting?"

He opened his hands in a sign of defenselessness. "Sammy asked me to meet him at Merrows' Marina."

He took a deep breath.

"He didn't want to meet next door at Fish Pier, 'too many eyes' he said. So I did. He told me he wanted to get away from the big guys, get back to his smaller customers. But, someone, he wouldn't say who, had their hooks in him. I pressed him for more information, but he got mad. Started swearing and told me I didn't understand. His best friend and I don't understand. Insulting!" Seamus snorted. "Then he started to cry. The man was literally crying. I walked away to give him his dignity."

"How come when you were arrested, Michael said the skeleys said you were fighting."

"Never saw any skeleys. Never saw any white Camrys. A few sailors and seafarers were milling around the area from one of the docked cruise ships. That was it."

He folded his hands around the back of his head and pushed it down and let out a grunt.

Her eyes filled. "I've doubted you." She wiped them with her sweater sleeve, catching her dripping nose, too.

"I have a feeling your Pierre is involved, too. When I saw that weasel in here, I wanted to brain him. He's not to be trusted. Where do you find these people?" he asked.

"Now you sound like Erica," she said.

"Nice girl. She's loyal. You need more Ericas as friends."

"No time for more friends. We need to get you off." She patted his right hand. "No matter what it takes, Pop."

"Let it be. You worry about you, little lady." His eyes were lifeless. "Maybe Sammy got what was coming his way."

"Pop!" She took his hand in hers. "You don't believe that any more than I do."

He wiped his eyes with his sleeve. "Allergies. Damn dry in here."

She said goodbye to her father and picked up her phone at the visitor's entrance. One missed call. She didn't recognize the number. There was a message.

"Hello, Kate. I've heard of your work through mutual colleagues. I have a job offer for you. Let's arrange to meet. Please call me back at 617-555-0000, extension 1894."

"Service call freaks." She threw the phone into her purse. Outside the jail doors, she jetted toward her car.

Work was slow on Monday. Kate took a walk outside and stood on the pier where she had found Sammy. She looked around at the Seaport and was thoroughly disenchanted with all the changes. Some of the earlier changes had been good, even necessary, but now the old charm was gone. Most of the new architecture included towering, reflective nondescript glass boxes. What had happened to their gritty waterfront with the time-honored restaurants like Jimmy's Harborside and Anthony's Pier 4? It had become Any City, USA.

The boats cruised on the harbor and pier workers milled around on the docks, some enjoying a smoking break. A boy on a BMX bike rode around her in circles. "Are you Kate?"

"Who's asking?"

"He is." He pointed over at a black Lincoln Town Car. License plate: GSL. Reflections on the car windows prevented Kate from seeing who was in the driver's seat.

"Is this a joke?"

"No, ma'am."

"Ma'am? How old do you think …? Never mind. Who is he?"

"I don't know. He just asked me to tell you to go see him." The boy sped around to the front of the Fish Exchange and popped a wheelie.

Kate sashayed over to discover the mysterious visitor. The driver's side door kicked open. No surprise. Greely.

"Welcome, Ms. Finn."

He got out and opened the rear door, motioning for her to sit in the back seat. She shook her head, holding her ground.

"Please." It wasn't so much a request as a directive.

After she slid in, he followed and closed the door before she had a chance to think.

"I like efficiency. Don't you, Kate?"

He was tall even sitting down and handsome in a finely tailored green suit. His hair looked like it had been jet black when he was younger. Now it was smooth and shiny, streaked with gray. His blue eyes were magnetic, his ivory skin had soft creases unlike the hard-weathered face of a fisherman like Pop. She felt surprisingly calm in his presence.

"How do you know my name?"

"You come highly recommended from good sources and not that squirrely detective you were on a date with." He shook his head. "Skeleys."

"Not a date." Was it odd that he called Madley squirrelly?

"Why didn't you return my call? I left you a message about a job offer."

"Oh. I delete all those calls."

"You must be in high demand. I'm sorry about what's happened to your family."

"Are you?"

"Tragic." He shook his head.

"You only need to be sorry if you had something to do with Sammy's murder, or my father getting blamed for it. Did you?"

"Oh, my." He shot a wry smirk at her. "I'm not the monster you think I am."

"Well, you have a reputation for being a badass," she said.

"You neighborhood types, wanting goodness and badness. Duality is for simpletons. You're smarter than that."

"Am I?" She looked out the back window as if it were an escape hatch.

"Your friend was probably in the middle of it. All of us make our own choices."

Her hair practically hit his face as she whipped her head back around to glare at him. "I doubt that Sammy Robbins made his."

"I didn't know your friend. But self-destruction is more common than you think."

"I really need to get going, sir. Mr. GSL. Master of Greely Seafood Labs."

"We just say Greely's around these parts," he smiled at her. "BTW, Vanity plates are good for business."

"I assumed they were for egos."

"Before you leave, let's talk about something more pleasant."

"Like what?" she asked.

"Self-preservation."

"Whose? Yours or mine."

"Hear me out, Kate." Again his voice was dominant. "Some might say I'm here to pirate you. But I contend that if my offer is more attractive than what you have, and I can assure you it is, then you'll come of your own free will, no pirating needed. I've got an operation that needs technical support. I'm not a man of science by training, just instinct, so I rely on my chief scientific advisor, and your good friend from Nobska Fisheries."

"I'm thinking he's no longer my friend." She shifted her body farther away from him.

"Hard times."

His cavalier attitude infuriated her. "Pierre Gosselin can go to hell with you and your other goons." She pulled the door handle to get out of the car.

"Oh. Oh, Pierre?" Greely stuttered. "Well, he speaks highly of you. Very highly. I imagine his wife isn't fully aware of how highly he's held you in his esteem."

She stopped trying to open the door. "What are you getting at?"

"I'm here to offer you a position at the Labs. I can compensate you much better than those FDA curmudgeons. The work is more interesting."

"Work for you?" She leaned in close, staring into his eyes. "You know I can start screaming and the parking guard will be out here in a shot."

"John? Great guy," he said.

"You even know the parking attendant? Who are you?"

"Feisty one. Did you know I used to know your mom? Peggy, is it? She wasn't like you. She was quite reserved."

"Leave it alone. You don't know her or anyone in my family."

"Kate." Greely sighed and looked out his side window. He turned back to her and adjusted his suit jacket.

"What do you want from me, Greely?"

"Colin. Call me Colin. I want you to come work for me. I can pay you well. It will help your family."

"How?"

"Your father is a stubborn and prideful man. Old Irish. He'll destroy himself, Bobby Sands-style, before he'll save himself. A trial lawyer can be expensive."

"My father is a good man. And we have a lawyer."

"Good guys are all the same—filled with principles. Principles won't get you ahead in life." He twirled the claddagh on his right ring finger. "My father was similar."

"How did he die?"

"Does it matter?" He ran his fingers through his hair. "In an accident."

"I'm sorry for your loss." She lowered her head in respect, looked at his ring and wondered if it had been his father's.

"Don't be." His voice became lower, less assured. "It was a long time ago."

She tried to allow enough time to seem respectful in a detached manner. "It's been interesting sharing family stories with you, Colin. But, alas, I have to go."

He pulled his business card out of the breast pocket of his

jacket. "Call me. I'll give you a tour of our facility. You'll be blown away. All legit. We have government funding for a super project. That's why I want you."

"Inspiring." She leapt out of the car and threw the business card on the ground. He got out and moved around to the driver's seat.

After Greely drove away she retrieved the card.

"Kate, what's up? Who was that?" Rob yelled over to her from the docks.

"Hi, Rob. No one. I'll look at the catch in a minute. Just give me a minute to go the bathroom."

He yelled back at her. "The guys are getting restless."

She ran up the back steps to her office and locked the door. After she ran the daily catch, she stayed in her office to finish up some work, but Greely's visit had broken her ability to concentrate. Maybe I should seriously weigh this job opportunity, she thought. The money could feel dirty, but it might help write her own ticket and get Pop out of Walpole. After all, everyone was corrupt in gradation. Pop's trial date was set for early October and money was an issue. Kevin was working for them pro bono, but fees for expenses were adding up. She knew she could handle anything Greely Labs threw at her. She was a better scientist than Pierre. Dr. Zion had repeatedly said so. Such a forthright man. Still he had warned her that perception was reality and told her she was too humble; Pierre would surpass her because he used everything he had, including his friends, to get what he wanted.

Before Sammy's death, she had focused on the purity of science. Now she understood what her father had been saying to her. She realized now that she had been a bit Pollyanna-ish in how she looked at the world, up until the day he was arrested. She thought about him being in jail. It was the opposite of how she'd thought he'd end up. Was it fair that he had to work so hard for so little? The work had taken its toll on his body; he had to pop ibuprofen daily for his aches and pains, which often upset his stomach. Meanwhile, others floated through life, people like Dr. Zion, an idealistic academic, not street-savvy at all. He'd never had to struggle. In the beginning, it was why Kate admired him so. He got to be a purist, but being a purist was a luxury, one that wouldn't save Pop.

The Finns had been cornered in survival mode and she was furious. She didn't owe anyone anything, including an explanation. Even soldiers in battle did the wrong things for the right reasons. They negotiated with terrorists, even bribed them to get them on the "right" side and discarded them after they served their purpose. She wasn't ashamed of what she needed to do for herself and her family. Hadn't Greely handed her a kind of olive branch? He needed her and right now she needed money to save her father.

Chapter Twelve

K ate approached the guard shack at Greely Seafood Labs off Northern Avenue where a once-falling-down abandoned brick factory building had been gutted and remodeled. Her heart raced. She wasn't sure if she was impressed by this huge modern building with reflective glass trimmed in white brick and had won many prestigious architectural awards for design and functionality, or if she was having a slight panic attack.

She told the guard her name and that Colin Greely was expecting her. He checked his computer, asked for her driver's license, and pointed her in the direction of visitor parking.

A slim, attractive, middle-aged woman with straight blond hair reaching the collar of her pink dress greeted Kate from the reception desk. Her name was prominently displayed on a wooden plaque as Executive Assistant: Norah Woodstone.

"May I help you?"

"Kate Finn. I'm here to see Colin Greely."

Norah Woodstone looked Kate up and down and shot her a

stiff smile. "Please take a seat."

The décor of the lobby was just as stunning as the outside. Brick walls and wooden beams complemented the nautical artwork and industrial copper pendant lights hanging from the rafters. Kate smoothed her black A-line skirt and checked to see if all the buttons were fastened on her white silk blouse. She felt good all dressed up for a change, though somehow the receptionist had made her feel dowdy. She started to slump a bit until she remembered how her mother called women like Norah "babes." Look at the babe over there all dolled up, as if they were a bit of a joke, transparent, and totally self-conscious. Her mother had taught her to never be intimidated by anyone, especially these kinds of women. Kate sat up straight and stopped fidgeting.

Colin Greely came through a door on the left side of the lobby. "Kate." He held his right hand out.

"Colin." She shook it.

He turned to the receptionist. "She'll need to fill out the nondisclosure form, Norah."

Norah opened a desk drawer, pulled out a form, attached it to a clipboard, and handed it to Kate. Her signature swore her to secrecy. Colin led her to a locked door that had a retinal reader. He blinked twice and entered a code on a keypad, the door buzzed and he motioned for Kate to enter. They stood in a small dressing area where white suits on hangers were encased in hermetically sealed plastic bags.

"Clean area?"

"Cleanest around. You'll need to suit up over your clothes."

Inside the giant, spotless white warehouse, she walked with Greely alongside seemingly endless multi-level tanks full of live seafood. There were no windows. Soothing simulated ocean music played over the ceiling speakers. Robotic cranes moved gracefully, filling separate tanks with fish from plastic tubs labeled WILD and FARM.

"Black ops," he said. "No one else in the industry is this advanced. Yet."

"Nice touch with the music," Kate teased.

She felt like she was starring in a James Bond movie. Quickly, she identified the fish in three nearby tanks. One was Arctic char, another cod, and another anglerfish (also known as monkfish). The monkfish's anatomy was a source of terror to Kate. It looked demonic and sometimes grew beyond five feet long and several hundred pounds in weight. Some people liked the taste, even comparing the sweetness to lobster, but she couldn't get past the beady eyes and wide-gaping mouth that threatened to drag her to hell. Turning away from the monkfish, she decided to think better thoughts, like those of her imaginary angelfish from childhood.

Three open floors resembling a giant billiards hall were filled with fish tanks instead of pool tables. Each tank had been labeled with black painted letters designating the fish it contained. The two upper levels were for shellfish. The labels read: Cherrystones; Quahogs; Oysters; Snails; Crab: Blue, Soft-shell and Alaskan; Shrimp: Jumbo, Medium, Mini; Lobster, Langostinos, Rock Lobster; Periwinkles; Crawfish; and Squid.

Kate felt like she needed to pinch herself. "What is this place?"

"The future, Kate. The future of fish."

"Madness," she said. She'd heard of these kinds of labs but had never seen one until now.

"People have an appetite for fish. Since the available levels are finite and the laws limit fishermen more and more, we intend to take the 'erman' out of 'fisherman' by mass breeding. Farming is our cash cow here. But we have to do it quicker. We also need to address next-generation methods to perfect other kinds of fish. Still we need to be aware that there are toxicity issues. And if we resort to antibiotic use, probably an uptake in consumer allergic reactions. There are many barriers, possibly years of clinical trials before full FDA approval of additional consumer lines, here at Greely's. That's part of your mission, Kate."

This area felt too cold for human comfort and Kate started to shiver. In front of her, two large tanks looked to be over twenty feet tall. One was labeled "Wild Caught," the other "Incubator." The smell overpowered her. She gagged then shrugged off the nausea, silently assuring herself she'd seen worse.

"We're going to get you started in the groundfish section. Your mission is to isolate reproduction and make every day mating season."

"Romantic." She rolled her eyes.

He pointed at one of the wild tanks. "This is filled with fresh healthy haddock and the incubator is the reproduction tank simulating their spawning beds. As you know, haddock thrive in deep cold waters. Your end goal will be to cross-breed haddock with some of its neighbors, such as cod, dogfish, and perch, etcetera. If that goes well, who knows? Lobster could be next. How does lobdock sound?"

Flustered, and at the same time curious, Kate walked around the tanks. She couldn't help her questioning nature; it came with the profession.

"Who is responsible for this place? How does it even exist?"

"In fact, the USDA has released grant funding. I mean I do well for myself, but a facility like this? And we have an association with Nobska Fisheries."

"Thus Pierre," she said.

He shook his head. "Yeah well, Pierre."

"Well, I know about fish farming, of course." She winced. "But let's face it, the stuff sucks."

"Not ours. Our farming method infuses sea salt and good bacteria into the fish cell targeting the nucleus for cell division. Our experimentation involves tricking the fish into reproducing like they do in the wild rather than suffocating them in large farming beds that become bacteria-laden. After a while they aren't cod or haddock, they are a derivative and break down. We'll only breed them two times and then start again with wild-caught. We need to get another life cycle out of them."

"You mentioned next generation meaning GE, Frankenfish?"

"We prefer to use the term," he circled his hands like a professor reprimanding a student, "genetically engineered. GEs. I guess it all depends on your definition of perfection. Purists like you probably wouldn't take the risks we do, but then again, what's the saying? No risk, no reward."

"But bacteria levels in most Frankenfish are toxic."

"We're working on that. We need someone like you to get in here and make it happen."

"But why me? I'm no expert in GE. In fact, I have some reservations."

"That's good. You think I want someone here who doesn't have reservations about changing sea life as we know it?"

"So you're confident that these fish will be wholly consumable?"

"I'm a businessman, not a scientist. But you said it yourself. They are vulnerable to disease. My scientific sources claim there's a genetic breakdown when they reproduce."

"Right. Not to mention regulating the production and distribution. It's a whole new species. Probably why none of the agencies want to touch it."

"To the contrary. There's quite a bit of interest." He looked at his watch. "We still have some time before lunch. I take all my job candidates to lunch. It gives me a chance to get to know you. We have a team spirit here."

"With the robots? Where are all the workers?" she asked.

"We are ninety-nine percent automated. No need for human resources except at the highest levels and shipping and receiving."

The tour continued.

"This is our automatic boning, portioning, and packaging area."

"All robotic?"

"Absolutely. It'll prevent virtually all industrial injuries. And a full bar-coding system includes a track back to the origination point, your current expertise. If there was a product recall, we can track back and notify the source immediately. But you know that drill, working for the FDA."

"Assuming you can actually get this operation fully functional. Seems like you might be getting a bit ahead of yourself."

"That's what visionaries do," Greely retorted. "Someone has to think big."

"When do you intend to get them to market?"

"ASAP. It's like the old US and Russian space race. The Asians have been messing with this stuff well before us. We're coming late to the party."

He led her to the exit.

"Any preference: Harborside or Oceanus?"

"I like Salacia's."

"Salacia's, huh? Okay. Goddess of the sea it will be."

They were seated outside on the deck. Colin insisted they drink white wine.

"Still the best view in Boston and the food is reliable. I've tried to sell to them for years. They insist on the fresh-caught stuff. No better than frozen. They'll be gone soon. Too old-school."

"Fresh is a better value. Frozen fish give a false weight, which is a rip-off for the consumer."

"Precisely. Consumers have to leave some money on the table

for places like my Labs to do business."

"That's your justification for tricking us?" Kate shook her head in disgust.

"Who are you, Ralph Nader?"

"Touché." She laughed and they raised their wine glasses.

Colin rambled on about his business prowess and how he had started Greely Seafood Labs on his own. How he lost his parents when he was young and how he'd brought up his younger sister. She ignored his bragging and focused on the harbor, wondering what Pop would think if he knew she was here. The wine tasted good and she swilled it.

"Slow down. This is a fine French blend, not to be gulped like those barflies do at places like Dingles."

Kate lifted her head at the reference to her friends' bar.

"My best friends own Dingles."

"Sorry." He lifted his glass in a toast. "Dingles is a nice neighborhood beer spot, but old world wine is so much more refined. Don't you think, Kate?"

Not a natural wine enthusiast, she nodded in oblivious agreement, because she was really enjoying this wine.

The waiter came over to tie on their bibs before presenting them with their lobster plates.

"Shall we?" Colin cracked his lobster. He pulled the meat out of the claw and took it whole into his mouth.

Kate stared, reviewing his process. "I start with the claws, too. Don't you dip your lobster in butter?"

"What for? The taste is pure sweetness on its own. No makeup required. Do you know that a female lobster can mate only after she sheds her shell? She's the one who approaches the male's den with her pheromones." He wiped his mouth.

"Yeah, I know the lobster story. What's your version?"

"After the female chooses her mate, who is of course the strongest in the neighborhood, she molts in front of him and he shows his appreciation by becoming aggressive. Subsequently, they spar with raised claws, then he protects her in his den until she hardens but they still bicker."

"Quite the love story. I didn't know you were such a romantic, Mr. Greely."

"There's a lot you don't know about me," he said without raising his head. "In fact, you know nothing about me, Kate Finn."

Kate was unsettled now. "Do you know what happens after she hardens in the den?"

He was on to the tail now, taking his last bite.

"They part ways." He chewed the lobster tail, juices dripping from his lips.

Kate pointed and he wiped his mouth.

"They reenter cold waters, leave their story behind. They start again." He placed his napkin on the table and picked up his wine glass, offering a toast: "To new starts."

She clinked her wine glass against his. "Thank you for lunch." She sipped her wine and finished eating.

While Colin paid the check with his credit card, she gazed over the harbor. She turned back to see the folded receipt positioned in the middle of the table in a courtesy tray with cellophane-wrapped peppermints.

"It's my offer," he said.

"Candy?" she teased.

"Don't look at it now." He picked it up and offered it.

She picked up the receipt and held it without looking.

On their walk back to Greely's he asked how old she was.

"Well, since I already have the offer letter, I will answer your inappropriate and illegal question. Twenty-seven. How about you?"

"I'm thirty-eight." He cleared his throat. "To be honest, thirty-eight and a half."

"Really? What else have you lied about?"

He gave her a crooked smile.

"How do you know my mother?" she asked.

"She was my crossing guard lady. I also walked my sister to your mother's corner in the morning. I took all my classes in the morning, so I could work at night. Your mom," he hesitated as if he had a lump in his throat. "She made sure Molly got across safely to the school yard."

"Where did you go to school?"

"Northeastern."

"What did you take?"

"I was on scholarship in the honors business program, but I ran out of money in my junior year."

"Sad. You made it that far."

"Made me hungrier. I could teach those classes now. Nothing like real-life experience." He glanced at her. "College kids today, their parents practically tuck them in every night."

"You're not short on confidence," she said.

"Neither are you."

They were quiet the rest of the walk until they arrived in front of the Labs.

"Seriously consider my offer, Kate. It will be great for you and it will certainly help us. I've checked around and you have the skills and determination we need to bring this concept to market."

"I'll think about it."

"Sleep on it. Call me tomorrow with your answer." In front of the Labs, he patted her on the shoulder and walked back inside.

She thought about the offer as she walked to her car and wondered how a guy his age got to be so successful. She looked at the receipt: $182,000.00 with potential for bonus. She wondered if she'd read him wrong. The offer was strong, and if the Labs were government-funded, then legitimacy wouldn't be a problem. It was her own resistance to change, the one that had grown directly from her father's, that made her hesitate, yet it was for her parents that she would take the job. She thought of Michael and how he'd been the outlier for so long. She should've moved away and avoided all of this. She thought of Melissa and her drug issues, just one of the hundreds of kids lost from the neighborhood. No one went untouched. Even Will's father had to grease certain palms to keep Dingles going for the next generation, and so would Will and Erica. They never talked about it, but everyone knew it was the cost of doing business in the neighborhood. As long as the benefits outweighed the costs, people kept their mouths shut and went through their days without kicking.

On the second Monday of August, Kate started work at Greely Seafood Labs. After she finished onboarding with the Human Resource Department, Colin greeted her and led her into his office. Pierre sat in the visitor's chair.

"Hi, Kate. I'm handling your orientation," he said.

She barely grunted a hello.

They walked out to the haddock station.

"These are the synthetic hormones for you to work with. Inject them into the wild females, then place them in the incubator to spawn. Simple procedure for someone with your background. When the babies are born, we inject the hormones and combat disease with a slight dose of antibiotics. The problem we've been having is that the babies are stunting. You need to find the proper balance to allow us to grow them just large enough to get to market."

"That's it?" she asked.

"For now. Can you handle it?"

"No problem, Mr. CSA."

"What the hell are you talking about?"

"Chief scientific advisor, on this project."

"Not quite. You haven't been fully briefed, have you?"

"I guess I misunderstood."

"Don't worry about it. There's plenty more to do here. I'm only here on Mondays and I'm in meetings all day, but you have my number if you have any issues." He held his hand up in an air call.

Kate approached the tank that held hundreds of haddock and pulled out her first fish with a net. She brought her to the workbench and placed her in a large tub-shaped stainless steel bowl.

"You're a nice girl. Soon forced to be a mommy vessel. Sorry about this. Not my idea."

She tried to remember everything she could about this close relative to the cod. They both shared three dorsal and two anal fins, but haddock also had one spot and dark side stripes. They rarely grew larger than four pounds or two feet, with the largest almost forty pounds and forty inches. They spawned in the deep. She wondered if the tanks provided proper deep ocean simulations.

She injected the female haddock, walked over to the spawning tank with the netted fish, apologized to her for messing with motherhood, and sent her into the tank with a splash. Next victims. While she remastered the fish, she reflected on her scientific intentions and decided they'd been pure. So far. To play around with the mating process of groundfish was one thing but Frankenfish messed with the laws of nature. Surely there'd be backlash. The general public had become more aware, often vigilant, about what they ate. Still, she had to admit that Greely's research facility seemed solid. He'd nailed a strong position though no real results yet, though she did admire the state-of-the-art facility and the preliminary processes he'd implemented. Maybe she'd tell him she couldn't do it. That it was immoral. She realized he'd probably fire her. But she had time. For now, he had his robots at work in the black ops area.

The next day she worked on cod and dubbed her area Georges

Bank. She'd been to the real Georges Bank when she was an undergrad at UMass. It was a rough trip, not as bad as the "Perfect Storm" that sank the Andrea Gail and drowned its entire crew, but the waves crashed over the ship and twenty students, including Kate and Haley, lost their lunch and more into plastic bait buckets until they pulled into Boston Harbor. She'd never experienced such fear on the ocean. That day she defined her career path and decided to focus on the testing end of marine biology so she could to stay ashore as much as possible.

These days her fear was different. Her adrenaline constantly pumped. Even Pop's claim of innocence gave her little relief. She had doubted him. Kevin said the evidence from the first killing showed that it was clearly self-defense, but, like her mother told her, he'd resisted arrest then and more recently with Sammy. Judges and prosecutors don't care for defendants who wrestle with cops. Assault and battery on a police officer and resisting arrest might be seen as worse than murdering Sammy. The prior did not help his case even though they couldn't legally use it in court—people talked. Perception was everything. Who the hell knew Pop had killed Brennan all those years ago? But a lot of people surely would. Some of their neighbors had been there for fifty years; undoubtedly, they knew about the killing and the night Pop was beaten down.

Kate took two haddock to her station. She'd decided to go full speed, whip through these fish to find a solution. If GE was the new wave, then Greely was smart to catch it early. She injected the females, dumped them into the spawning tank, and continued at this pace for the rest of the day, working up to three and four fish at a time. She wondered how often they replenished the tanks.

By the end of the second week, she'd finished with the ground-fish and moved over to the adjacent lobster room. Her new directive was to accelerate the molting process, when the lobster's soft shell left it vulnerable to attack by other species and its own for six or more weeks. Pierre had given her white papers on molting, but Kate was having trouble isolating the chemical behaviors of captive versus wild lobsters. In captivity, lobsters tended to delay molting as long as possible to avoid vulnerability. Kate wasn't sure how to expedite molting when the lobsters were stubbornly avoiding it. She'd read that the ocean's warming was naturally accelerating this process and that other researchers had been able to accelerate molting, cutting a lobster's juvenile life cycle from seven years to three or four years. Not only did captive lobsters not taste as good as wild, there was a higher risk for bacteria. She decided to jack up the temperature of the tanks anyway.

During her third week of work, Colin came to visit her.

"Hi, Colin. I thought you'd left town?"

"I've been in and out. Thought I'd give you some space. You seem to prefer to work alone."

"It seems you're right." She held up a female lobster and showed him the eggs.

"Nice. You're doing good work out there. So good in fact, Pierre's nose is a little out of joint." He laughed at his own comment.

"Where has Pierre been this last week?"

"Let's just say he's on sabbatical. That's what the academics call it, right?" He motioned for her to follow him. "Let's talk."

His office was lush with furnishings. They sat facing each other in two leather swivel chairs in front of a gas fireplace. Photos of Dublin, Athens, and Paris lined the walls. There was a framed photo of Colin, in his high school cap and gown, receiving a scholarship from Boston's chief of police.

"You got the BPD scholarship? Remarkable."

"I suspect you were no slouch either. Doesn't take a genius to see that. I'm offering you a promotion. You'll work with the chief scientific advisor. I think you'll work well together with his guidance."

"Pierre?"

"I dismissed Pierre. He was too distracted and constantly looking for more money. He doesn't have passion for his work. You do. I informed Nobska today that we no longer need his services."

Colin stood up and moved to his desk. "Don't be afraid. You'll be fine."

She gazed over to the graduation photos.

"Top in my class at Boston Latin. And Chief Kelly put in a good word. He took me under his wing after my father died. He lost his when he was young, so he knew what it was like."

He rose.

She turned her chair and followed his athletic profile. His hair was generously sprinkled with gray like most of the Irish men she knew. She liked his tall, well-built body. He motioned for her to come over to his desk. She approached, pushed her long hair out of her face and looked directly into his eyes. These blue, magnetic eyes looked gentle today.

"Okay, let's shift gears here, Kate. How's the progress on molting lobsters?"

She was glad to shift gears. She stood in front of his desk. "Frankly, I'm a little stumped. How can I help them accelerate their molting when they cling to their hard shells?"

He nodded in affirmation. "A true conundrum. Come over here." He leaned over his desktop computer. "Look at this data. What do you see in the numbers?"

"Trends."

"What are you saying?"

"I see rising trends, then a falloff, then a flattening. What do these numbers represent?"

"Life cycles of ocean life—simulated ocean life. Test results from each of the tanks in the facility. We take the babies once spawned and move them to another area. You haven't been in there yet. After spawning and some growth, poof, flat-liners. How do we get these up?"

"I can look at it. Do you have the actuals for each lot of them?"

He whisked through the files showing her each species. She was overwhelmed. She'd need printouts and time to isolate what was truly going on.

She felt his presence behind her while she studied the data.

When he asked to use the mouse to show her other files, his hand brushed hers and she pulled it away.

"I better go back to work. If you run those reports, I'll take them home and look at them tonight." She hurried out of his office, but his touch lingered.

Chapter Thirteen

By the end of her fourth week Kate was still struggling with artificial lobster mutation. Greely's head of research and operations, Ed McGann, informed her she needed more field experience and directed her to look for the infamous lobster-woman named Rhonda over at Cardinal Medeiros Dock.

"You'll have no trouble finding her since she's the only lady at the dock," McGann said. And then he added, index finger raised in warning, "Don't mention my name."

Cardinal Medeiros Dock, on the opposite side of the harbor from Greely Labs, close to South Boston beaches, had been dedicated to Cardinal Humberto Medeiros because of his dying wish to give the Boston lobstermen a permanent dock.

Most of the guys at the dock were friendly. All wore the thick skin of their trade.

There was one woman among them working on a boat named Catch Me. Kate waved to her and she waved back. Captain Rhonda

Conway, slim, tall, and healthy looking, had perfectly aligned white teeth and a sun-bronzed face. She was severely striking with her sun-streaked hair. Up close her hands didn't look worn like those of the men. Kate did notice she was missing her left pinky finger but the rest of her nails were perfectly manicured in vibrant red polish. She compared her own ungroomed nails, quickly concluding that she preferred both pinkies over a perfect manicure.

The lobsterwoman gazed up at Kate.

"Snapped it off bringing one of the traps up during a thunderstorm. It was my own fault. I was rushing to get in. Should have just left the traps until morning. God, the blood was the worst. It went everywhere. Everywhere."

"Sounds painful."

"Obviously." Her eyes were aqua glass. "So, what brings you over here to the dark side?"

"My employer wants me to run some numbers on your daily catch."

"FDA?"

"Something like that," Kate said.

"Well, feel free to come aboard. My sternman is off today. And every day. I work alone."

Kate hesitated, plagued by her mercurial relationship with the deep ocean.

"How far out do you go?"

"Sometimes pretty far. But today just in the harbor. I need to gather and repair the traps. C'mon. You'll enjoy it."

"Okay," Kate said. "But I have to be back soon to check in with some of the other boats."

Rhonda seemed like a good captain. She waved to the harbor-master as he patrolled alongside her boat.

"Where has the prettiest lobster boat captain been hiding? What are you, a hobbyist, now? Not going to pay the rent on those hours."

"No worries, Master. I came into some new opportunities."

"Hope it's legal!" he yelled.

"Ha." Kate saw Rhonda's knuckles go white from gripping the steering wheel. "You're looking fit. How did you survive the appendectomy?"

"Piece of cake." He grabbed his side, pretending to keel over from the pain, then sped off toward another lobster boat called Hysteria.

The horizon had a yellow tinge. As promised, they proceeded slowly, with Rhonda pulling up traps and repairing lines. Kate kept count of how many lobsters had been trapped in Rhonda's lobster pots, but mostly she tried to keep her head as straight as possible so she didn't vomit. It was easy at this clip, nearly fun. From her angle the Harbor Islands looked like separated puzzle pieces.

"Supposed to get some weather later." Rhonda sounded excited. "I love right before a storm. Everything is so calm and then it blows wide open."

"You do?"

"Ah, yeah. It's freakin' exciting."

"I prefer just calm, no storm," Kate said.

"Is that why you got involved in the paper side of this business?"

"Probably my father's warnings to stay clear of the daily grind and my mother's landlubber spirit. I get seasick easy."

"Not me. Never get it."

"Where are we going?" Kate asked.

"Channels. That's where my traps are."

"It gets rough there."

"Only when the cruise ships go in and out. None due until tonight. We'll be fine."

Kate felt queasy. "I hope I don't throw up. Last time I did was when I found my father's friend."

"Who?"

"Sammy Robbins. He was a friend of the family. I found him dead in April."

"I read about that. Some guy named Finn is in jail for the murder," Rhonda said.

"Yeah. Some guy." Kate looked over at Winthrop to the Deer Island Sewage Treatment Plant, which used to be the site of the Deer Island Prison. Now it looked like a futuristic national park with state-of-the-art pumps to cleanse Bostonians' shit. People were running and walking with their dogs along the promenade as if it was the Santa Cruz Beach Boardwalk. She imagined the hipsters' horror if the pump station suddenly exploded waste, and on the flip side supposed the pups would think it was Disney for dogs. "I heard lobsters eat the garbage around the wastewater plant."

"Not anymore. Fully encapsulated. Closed-loop system. Nothing to feed from anymore." She turned the boat. "I've got a few traps to check over near Thompson Island."

"Perfect." The boat challenged the currents head-on. Kate's stomach soured. She barely hung on.

"When did you start working for the FDA?" Rhonda asked.

"After I finished school. I was a contractor. Now I work over at the Labs where it's somewhat government-funded but strictly for profit."

"Greely Labs?"

"Do you sell to them?" Kate asked.

Rhonda shook her head. When they arrived at the traps the wind hit them sideways, bouncing and tossing them. She asked Kate to hold the wheel as she opened the glove compartment and took out large pliers. Kate was happy to have a mission to take her mind off her nausea. Rhonda turned serious, absorbed in her task, untangling line. She didn't speak for some time. Kate just watched. After Rhonda finished, she turned the boat and opened throttle. Somehow Kate held it together without throwing up and asked, "Why are we turning around?"

"I'm going to head in. I've got to get more supplies. You'll need to disembark. I'm going out farther."

It felt like an eternity before Catch Me reached the lobster dock. Rhonda tied up loosely and asked Kate to step out. Both boat and dock rocked furiously, but Kate made it across.

"Good luck with your work at Greely's." Rhonda stood at the helm.

"Did I do something to offend you?" Kate asked.

"Nope."

Rhonda pulled the boat up to Cardinal Medeiros Dock. "Good-bye, Kate."

On shore Kate felt unsteady. Her head was filled with the sound of the motor and confluent smells of oil and sea water. She had to remind herself she hadn't meant to upset Rhonda.

She composed herself and watched as a man pulled his boat alongside the pier, grabbed the piling to dock his boat, and threw down anchor. Skinny and middle-aged with sun-kissed brown hair, he moved about the boat hunched over like he suffered from musculoskeletal pain.

"Hi, Captain."

"Hiya. Your friend left in hurry. Catch me if you can indeed."

"How was your catch?"

"Not bad but it won't amount to much." His eyes squinted when he spoke. "We used to keep seventy percent of our take. Now we're lucky to get twenty-five."

"I get it. My Pop's a fisherman. Hey, how does Captain Rhonda there do?"

He slammed down another lobster. "Okay for a part-timer. Must have a sugar daddy. Never seen her work a full day. Got something going on the side, I guess."

She was surprised to hear this considering Rhonda's blood and guts attitude, but the harbormaster also said she was rarely at work. And that perfect manicure. Not so gritty after all?

Kate didn't have the heart to stick around. She wasn't making any friends here. She didn't take the cold shoulders personally; she'd grown up with them. Besides, her mission was different from that of the Greely Labs buyers who bought up as much as they could each day. She was just on a research mission. The buyers could handle the rest for Colin, who had told her he had single-source contracts with many of the Boston-area fish markets and restaurants to help the fishing industry. Times had changed. He reasoned that it was easier for businesses to work with one company than several fishing boats. As Colin saw it, everyone won. But the lobster boat captains knew Greely Labs could undercut the lobster boats by selling in bulk at lower prices to customers. They lost. Colin was a shrewd man.

Today Colin had arranged for his chief scientific advisor to come to the Labs to meet Kate at one o'clock after her Cardinal Medeiros site visit. She ran home to shower and change. When she sprinted into the building a half-hour late, Colin was talking to Norah at the reception desk.

"You're late, Kate." He was not pleased. "Our guest had to leave."

"They were doing construction on the Summer Street Bridge and I had to reroute near South Station. I called Norah to tell her I ran into traffic."

Norah looked at Colin. "Oh, yes. She did. I was on my way to lunch and it must have slipped my mind."

"You'll need to manage your time more appropriately." His voice was terse. "Tomorrow cocktails at my house, where I'll announce the re-org. Please be there no later than seven. Norah will follow up with directions." He left the two women alone.

Norah resumed work without looking at Kate. "He won't tolerate tardiness."

"Thanks for the unsolicited advice," Kate retorted.

She entered the closed area to gown up for work. Doug Middleton was also gowning up. It was a good thing because he was the kind of guy whose feet smelled through his shoes. The clean room clothes masked a lot of sins for scientists who had personal hygiene issues. Washing wasn't a top priority for them.

Kate yanked a suit off the garment rack. Under her breath, she mimicked Norah's words. "He won't tolerate tardiness."

"What was that?" Doug asked.

"Nothing. I missed a meeting with Colin. I did call. But Norah didn't forward the message."

"She's all right to me. But be careful. She doesn't treat the women scientists the same as men."

"Seriously, in this day and age?"

"Just beware. Colin relies on her for everything." He lifted one foot at a time onto the bench and put dust booties on his shoes. He leaned down to adjust them. His scalp was covered with dandruff.

"Good advice. I appreciate you telling me the ugly truth."

"I feel kind of bad for her," he said. "Her ex-husband is a researcher, left her for his lab assistant. She never really recovered."

Kate tripped into her overalls and had to steady herself against the bench.

"Don't make me feel for her." She regained her balance and pointed her finger at him. "I feel bad and try to be nice, she treats me like crap, and then we are back to where we started. It's too complicated."

He scratched his head and white flakes flew around. "Ew." Kate couldn't hold back.

"I know I have a dandruff issue – seborrheic dermatitis. Had it all my life. Kids teased me in school. Called me Buggy Dougie."

"What?" She feigned disbelief. "No. I was still thinking about Norah the Whora. You have a dandruff problem? Really?"

He smiled appreciatively and held the door open to the inside labs. "You missed Zion."

"Excuse me?" she asked.

"The new chief scientific advisor from Nobska Fisheries." He scratched his head and released another blizzard of dandruff, practically sending Kate into bronchial asthma.

She cleared her throat. "Dr. Zachary Zion is the new chief scientific advisor?"

"That's the one. Colin invited some of us to his office to meet him. Zion won't be here too often, though. He'll be working from Nobska Fisheries. A one-year joint contract. Colin said he was lucky to get him for a year. By the way, there's a party tomorrow night at Colin's."

Kate drove up the long driveway to Colin's home. She had to admit that she was impressed that he had stayed in Southie and bought an 1860s mansard on East Broadway, thoroughly impressive from the outside. At the same time, she felt a twinge of loyalty to the old-timers who called people like Colin "lace-curtain Irish." It was rarely a compliment.

Colin greeted her at the door. The kitchen had been modernized with state-of-the-art appliances and exquisite stonework on the floor, on the counters, on the backsplash. The ceilings had to be eleven feet high, with ornate crown molding and crystal chandeliers. She couldn't imagine a more beautiful house.

Colin handed her a glass of champagne from the kitchen counter. "Make yourself at home."

"I wish." She was feeling loose from just two sips of champagne.

"Yes." He pointed into the adjoining room. "Well, look around and then I'll come gather you to join us in the study in a bit."

There was certainly no slouching around this estate. She threw back her shoulders and joined the party. Acting casual, she strolled into the posh living room. It was pleasingly opulent with a blue and tan mosaic-tiled fireplace. The artwork alone was worth a pretty sum, including the statues and busts along the marble front foyer and hallways. The furniture looked imported and high-end, nothing like the comfortable J. C. Penney's furniture her parents purchased, however rarely.

Norah had arrived and was chatting with a circle of scientists who looked bored. Kate overheard her conversation.

"Well, if they're here illegally, then they don't belong. I have to work for a living. I'm not paying their damn tuition either. I say, dump all those illegals and their kids, too. Even if they're born here —it's a racket anyway. They come over the borders and give birth and claim to be Americans. They're trouble." She took a large swig from her champagne. "Nothin' ba trouble." Her speech was slurred.

Kate bristled. She moved over across the room to converse with Doug.

"On top of being a first-class bitch, the woman is intolerant. Sounds like my folks. But isn't she kind of young to be so prejudiced?"

"She'll never be accused of having empathy for undocumented immigrants." Doug raised his left eyebrow. "And since when is there an age limit for unkindness?"

They tapped champagne glasses.

"By the way, I love when you get all snarky. It brings out the beast in you."

"Shut up, Dougie."

She held her glass at the stem and sipped her champagne.

"I see McGann didn't make it tonight," Doug said.

"He probably had a better offer."

"No. Heard him talking to Colin. He's on his way to DC for a meeting."

"What's in DC?"

"President. Pentagon. FBI."

"Funny guy. On a roll tonight, aren't you?"

Colin sought her out as promised and led her into the den where Dr. Zion sat, legs crossed, in a plaid Queen Anne chair, holding a Manhattan on the rocks.

"Here she is. Hello, Kate." Dr. Zion stood and patted her on her shoulder. Gentle as always, his presence still comforted her.

"Dr. Zion." When she reached out to shake his hand she dropped her empty champagne glass on the Oriental rug. "I'm so sorry, Colin. Your beautiful rug." She quickly retrieved the unbroken glass. "Look, it's empty. No stains. I promise."

"Butterfingers?" Zion laughed.

"Relax. It's only a rug." Colin put her at ease. "Sit down. Let's talk."

Zion began, "I'm thrilled that you are working on this project, Kate. This science is cutting-edge."

"I guess I am, too." She'd never imagined that her mentor would be involved with GE. Then again, she was involved and somehow that was making sense.

By eight o'clock all the guests had arrived and enjoyed drinks and hors d'oeuvres. Colin was the consummate host, even when Norah, sloppy with drinks, slithered up and pawed his chest in a provocative manner. He gently excused himself to make a speech about the history of South Boston and its future in the twenty-first century. He said it would become the fish innovation mecca of the world. Then he introduced Dr. Zion, who swore his commitment to the race for edible genetically engineered fish.

Pop was right; Colin had covered all his bases in the industry, especially research and development. The new order had taken hold.

"Great party." Doug came up behind Kate inside Georges Bank. She looked at him in the cleanroom garb. It made his squat body look even more horizontal. His smoky green eyes peered at her as his right hand fought to rearrange the jet-black locks of hair falling across them. "Don't you think? You left before we had a chance to chat."

"There were so many people." Kate turned back to her microscope.

"Norah missed you," he said.

"Did she tell you that?"

"No. Just the way she was pacing, looking around like she had lost her best friend."

"You're a funny one, Mr. Middleton." She didn't look up from her microscope.

"Seriously, she could have used a girlfriend when she was having her way with the toilet."

She looked up at the ceiling and laughed out loud. "Disgusting."

"Apparently, she missed receptionist class 101: Never get drunk at the boss's house. But Colin covered her. Told everyone she had food poisoning from a bad ham sandwich at lunch."

"Excellent." She adjusted the setting on the microscope. "Now he's her boss and her enabler."

"Methinks she'd like him to be more than that. Hey, come over to bivalves so I can show you something."

"Bivalves? Sorry I'm a fishmonger and crustacean queen."

"Come on. It could be lucrative."

Kate followed him through a doorway to an annex where the large tanks looked like giant soapstone sinks anchored by pipes leading to twisted drain systems running underneath multiple tanks over to a receptacle station. "Ah, vertical stack systems. Smart move for your space challenge."

"It's what I do." Doug opened his arms in a comical show of hubris.

He was smart, and funny. "Stainless steel. I'm thoroughly amazed."

"Colin threw me a funding bone last year, so I devoured it." He walked around to check the temperature levels displayed digitally on the sides of the tanks. "Check this out." He loaded some cherrystones into a hopper that fed into a cleansing mechanism with a loud flushing sound. At the end of the cleaning run he had set up the adjacent counter with paper plates and Tabasco sauce. "Cherrystones on the half shell." He handed her a plate with three sauced cherrystones.

"Why thank you, sir." She swallowed them one by one. "Swanky raw bar you're running."

"Copycat clams are us. Why would you want any other kind?"

"My dad is a commercial fisherman."

"Ouch. What brought the daughter of a wild fisherman here?"

"The science."

He quickly raised and lowered his eyebrows like Groucho Marx.

"Money?" She tried again.

"You're not sleeping with Colin?"

"Not quite. What the hell is your problem?"

"I'm just saying. Norah thinks you are, except she didn't say sleeping."

"Okay, Bivalves. I'm going back to work. Thanks for the fake cherrystones."

"Okay. Just remember science is a cruel lover. If you get lonely, you know where to find me."

She waved him off. On her way out of the area she noticed an unusual piece of equipment. "Hey, what's this?" She walked back to him.

"I knew you'd be back. Couldn't stay away, could you?"

"Seriously, Doug. What's this for?"

"Prototype from Sea Agora for cytogenetic testing. Can even pick up nanobacteria."

"Are you shitting me? Not much can pick up nanobacterium. That's why we say they aren't really biological agents."

"Right." He looked at her smugly. "Tell the NASA astronauts' kidney stones that. They come home from missions keeling over from exposure to these self-replicating mini-beasts."

"Look at all these wires and test leads jutting out all over the place. Looks like an old woman's messy hair."

"Yeah. A hag for sure. Hag. I like that." He moved over to the machine and patted the equipment. "Today you've been given a name. No longer will you be known as DC5007. From this day forward you will be called Hag."

"How long will you have Hag?"

"Until I say I'm done testing, could be never." He stroked Hag. "Right, lover?"

"Are you done?" she asked.

"Finished up this morning." He scratched his face with one of the leads. "Pulled an all-nighter with my Hag."

"Good to know."

Back in Georges Bank she became engrossed in her research. Receiving had dropped off another batch of wild haddock. She scanned the bar code. They were from Fish Pier. She looked at the new batch. The telltale black devil's thumbprints on the shoulders of the fish were not as dark as usual.

An employee from the loading dock came back into the room. "I'm sorry, Kate. I left one of the crates here."

Kate watched as he dragged the crate across the floor onto his dolly without looking behind him. It left a liquid trail on the dark cement floor. Great, she thought, now I must clean up his mess. She grabbed some paper towels and mindlessly threw some over the liquid trail. When she kneeled to pick them up she saw that the towels were wet and tinted. She froze. Greentini.

She sidled back to her workstation and squeezed some drips onto a glass slide and looked at it under the microscope. Nothing to decipher. She ripped a piece of the saturated paper towel and placed it on another glass slide. Nothing was clear. She wasn't sure what she had expected to find but she ran back to the bivalve area.

"How do you use this thing?" She was practically yelling at Doug.

"Slow down. What do you have?"

"I need to use Hag. Can you set me up?"

"It's going to cost you." He prepared the equipment.

She inserted the paper towel into a mechanism that looked like a tiny Hubble telescope. The computer screen read the data. Ammonium perchlorate. No surprise. And anti-chromatin. Big surprise.

"What is this stuff?" Doug asked.

She didn't know if he could be trusted and decided to be vague. "It's acting like an anti-chromatin. Nothing would grow with this stuff on it." She looked at Doug without seeing him. "But I still can't get at why the color is green. Something else is at play here. Something undetectable. Greentini."

"Huh?" he asked.

"You know, like the shade of a green apple martini."

"Where did you find such libation?" he asked.

"I didn't," she said. "You can't tell anyone about this. Can you print it out and delete it?"

He printed photos and the file data, handed them to her and shut down the equipment. "Something tells me I don't want to know anything about this."

Colin was sitting on Norah's desk chatting about the party and complimenting her on her party planning skills. Kate casually adjusted her briefcase strap slung across her shoulder, aware of the Hag's data inside her bag.

Colin smiled and waved to her, "There she is. Good night, Kate."

Norah barely looked up. "Night."

That's how it went every day, but she wouldn't let Norah off the hook by ignoring her or not being polite, which seemed to irritate Norah more.

"Good night, Colin. Norah!" She smiled and waved to them. "Enjoy your evenings."

Norah didn't respond—just lifted her head and pointed her nose like a show dog.

Outside in the fall air she breathed a sigh of relief. Questions about the solution had gnawed at her all afternoon. Where did this chemical come from? Who was responsible for compounding it? It had to be the same chemical she'd found on Sammy. She questioned if fish were simply minimally coated, could they repel the chemical compound but still mask bacteria? Naturally, Kate allowed the fishermen to choose their own samples from the daily catches because she trusted them. Maybe Sammy treated his catch with Greentini before presenting samples to Kate. If she could find out where this stuff was coming from and who else was using it on the docks, she might be able to prove that Sammy was involved with something her father didn't know about. She had to go back to the docks and talk to some of the guys.

Chapter Fourteen

On Friday, she left work early to meet the incoming boats at Fish Pier. From a distance, she could see Rob Fitzpatrick's white hair, which contrasted with his red face and freckles. He reeled the last bit of rope into Truelight. He was strong. "Strongest man on the docks," Pop always proclaimed. Big, too. His beer gut hung over his belt.

Kate stepped onto the boat for the first time since Pop had been arrested.

"Good to see you, Kate." He gave her a hug. "We miss you around here. The new guy isn't as fast as you with the test results."

"How was your catch today?" she asked.

"Not bad, but the fallouts have been tough for most of us. Spence is doing good, though."

"Really?" She had her guy. John Spencer was never her father's favorite person. He once told Kate that Spence was the kind of guy who chased the shiny penny. Repeatedly the willing target of pyramid schemes, Spencer had been advised by Seamus to fish harder for his family instead of looking for the quick buck. Seamus liked Spencer's wife Doreen and said she was a lot like his Peggy. Kate remembered Doreen coming to the docks with their two boys and she didn't see what Pop was talking about. The Doreen Kate saw was gorgeous, not pretty in a motherly way like Mom. Skinny and tall with dark hazel eyes and jet-black hair, Doreen turned crewmen's' heads on the docks whenever she showed up. Maybe Pop was projecting what he wanted Mom to be. "Where is Spence?"

"Over at the lot having a beer. I'm heading there now. You want to come?"

"Love to, but I'm a little nervous."

"Why? We all know who you're working for. Word gets out. Frankly, I don't blame you. Smart girl like you. I'm only hanging in to help your Pop because he's loyal to me. When he gets out, bon voyage." Rob lifted his right and wiggled it like he was flying. "It's sunny Florida for me."

Hearing Rob say when your father gets out relaxed her, as if there were no questions about his innocence. "Sure. I'll take a cold beer on a cool day." She grabbed the last of the rope and helped Rob finish cleaning up the boat.

The lot bordered the right side of Yanks Lobster Company, where they still allowed the fishermen to park their cars for free and have a couple of beers in the lot, if they were discreet. Pop had sold his fish to Yanks for years. He called the owner "good people." Many of the locals used this colloquialism—He's good people. She's good people.—and it made Kate cringe with the same chills she got when an ink marker squealed on a whiteboard.

177

Rob was right. All the guys were happy to see Kate.

Spence was dressed in dark jeans and a leather coat. His blond hair and youthful skin stood out among the rest of the fishermen. He was handsome and fit.

"I hear you've been cleaning up, Spence?" She raised her Bud Light to him.

"Not really." Spence's beer hand shook a little. "Just doing a little better than most."

"Who're your customers?"

Spence shrugged. "So how are you doing over at Greely's?"

"Oh boy. I guess the word's out," she said.

"Just don't let Seamus find out. He'll disown you." Spence edged away from her to talk to the others.

She wondered if he was threatening her.

She joined them. One by one they finished their beers and left. Just Spence, Rob, and Kate were left. When Spence opened his trunk to get three more beers from his cooler, Rob grasped her hand and walked them over to Spence's white Dodge Ram.

Spence blocked them. "I'll get it, back off." He slowly opened the hard-top bed cover.

"Times are good. Nice ride, especially the cover."

"It's called undercover," Spence corrected him.

Rob let go of her hand and started rummaging through his friend's bed. "Look at all this shit." He held up socks, hats, and rain slickers.

Spence was angry now. "Leave my stuff alone."

But Rob had a playful beer buzz going and kept pulling stuff out of the trunk. "Why do you carry antifreeze?" He held up the jug.

Spence grabbed the plastic jug from him. "Give me that, you a-hole."

"Touchy," Rob teased.

Spence softened his tone. "Nothing, just some stuff from my garage. I use it on the boat sometimes to clean."

But Kate knew it had to be the indefinable Greentini. The same as the two jugs Madley had removed from the shed the morning he arrested Pop?

He offered them each a beer.

Kate refused the beer and grabbed Spence's forearm. "I think I know what's going on here, Spence. Who are you selling to?"

Spence shook her hand off of him.

"I've got to bolt." He jumped into his truck.

Kate followed him yelling. "My father is in jail and you can help him. I thought he was your friend!"

Spence rolled the window a crack. "Get out of the way. I don't want to hit you."

Kate slammed both of her hands against the window. Spence whipped the truck away from her and drove away.

"Who's he been selling to?" Kate stood still with her back to Rob.

"Wow. Take a breath." Rob approached her and patted her back. "Calm down, Little Seamus."

His quip broke the tension.

"McGann had been making the rounds with Pierre. Some of us

held back, but Spence was on board even before Sammy died."

She had a vague recollection of Spence's takes rising before she left Fish Pier. Today he was physically shaky, like Pop had said Sammy was the morning of his death.

"McGann and Pierre?" she clarified.

"I never see McGann anymore. Just Pierre now; sometimes he's with an Asian kid."

That night in bed Kate stared at the ceiling and wondered how to get Spence to talk to her. He was scared. She had to find out who was compounding the chemicals and the full recipe. Was Pierre now the main force supplying the fishermen with Greentini?

In her research, she'd read about experimentation with nano-bacteria and antibiotics to alleviate heart disease. On the other hand, an anti-chromatin could mask all kinds of bacteria on a human being and even hide the side effects of ammonium perchlorate. The heart would rupture, just like Sammy's. Thinking factually kept her from facing her fear that Spence was deeply involved. Could he have killed Sammy? Was Spence the kind of man who would let Pop rot in jail for a crime he didn't commit? And, who was this Asian kid on the docks with Pierre?

The next day McGann was waiting for Kate at her workspace.

"Sea Agora called to get their equipment back. I did a once-over and found some data on some fish, Kate. You've been playing with DC5007."

He held a tiny disk in his hand.

She blurted out, "Hag."

"Doug doesn't work with groundfish, so of course I thought of you."

"What's your point, McGann?"

"My point is this data is quite interesting. Thank you." He headed toward Doug's area.

"I did a once-over." She mimicked him. "Dope. You can barely find the power button to your computer."

"I couldn't quite hear that." He put his hand to his ear. "Are you prone to mumbling?"

"I said, sorry to see it go."

He smoothed his white hair, and his body language softened. In what sounded to her like a fatherly, even kindly manner, he said, "Just be careful what you get your hands into."

That afternoon Hag went back to Sea Agora.

"I'm sorry we lost our super equipment." Doug paced.

She didn't respond.

"You're not even going to look at me?"

"I have work to do." She checked the temperature levels of the tanks with a hand thermometer.

"State-of-the-art tanks with temp gauges and you use a manual?" he asked.

"Yeah. All right. Some things need to be triple-checked."

"What was I going to say? He was snooping around. It was like he already knew."

"You were supposed to delete the files," she said.

"I thought I did. There was a backup drive. IT came down to

clear it, copied all the files onto a disk and gave it to McGann."

She almost felt sorry for him. He had an edge of desperation in his voice. "Okay. I'm just preoccupied here. We'll talk later."

"Just think how Hag feels. She'd found a better life here. Now it's back to being objectified as DC5007. Make no mistake!" He threw his finger toward the ceiling. "She'll be sold on the open market." He kneeled on one knee, arms reached up to the ceiling. "Who knows what kinds of perverts will get their hands on her?" He stood, shook his head, and walked away

Kate stifled the urge to smile until he was out of sight.

She worked in the lobster area for the rest of the day. She had been slowly ratcheting up the water temperature to increase their potential to shed. The lobsters were starting to molt but they were clinging to the sides of the tank and she wasn't sure why. She had an idea. She hurried down to inventory stores.

"Hey, Kate." Al's interpersonal skills were superior to most of the staff at the Labs.

"Hiya, Al. I need some dive heaters."

"You a diver?"

She shuddered at the thought of being fully immersed in the ocean, dressed in a wet suit, laboring for breath. "God, no. It's for an experiment."

He grabbed some catalogues off the bookshelf. "Look through these and I'll check the Dive Live online catalogue. They're the best."

McGann walked by with Norah. He was bragging about his son's prowess as a Blue Devils point guard while Norah interjected praises about how his parenting must have resulted in his son's success. "Duke basketball, nothing to scoff at!" Norah flashed a friendly smile at Al, then swept by Kate with her eyes fixed on McGann.

Kate grunted a sardonic hello and rolled her eyes.

"She's tough," Al said. "Don't mess with her."

"She doesn't know what tough is. Stone-Age bitch."

"Wow. The scientist swears." Al covered his ears in apparent shock.

"We invented swearing."

She found the heaters she thought would work and he put in the order.

"I can overnight them and you'll get them tomorrow afternoon after they clear receiving."

"Do it." They slapped a high five and she returned to her area. As she stared into the tanks another thought occurred to her. She'd go back to Cardinal Medeiros Dock, ready to go deep.

Two days later, Kate walked down the gangplank of the docks at 5:30 a.m., pulling a large rolling suitcase with the heaters inside. Just as she had hoped, Rhonda was gearing up for the day. Maybe she never did put in a full day's work, but she was at work nice and early this day.

"Remember me?"

"Yeah. Greely's girl." Rhonda started the engine.

Kate wasn't deterred. "I have a proposition."

Rhonda put on a headset. "Sorry, I can't hear you." She threw her hands up, pointing index fingers to her ears.

Kate jumped onto the back of the boat, stood on her toes to try and reach Rhonda's height and pulled the headset blaring Aerosmith away from her left ear. "Hi." She let the earpiece snap back.

Rhonda ignored her and sang as she moved around the boat prepping for the day. Finally, she shut off her music. "You're not leaving, are you?"

"I have an idea that could help you," Kate said.

"I'm listening."

"I've been working with lobsters at the Labs, cranking up the temperature of the tanks to see if they would molt faster as they do in the wild. They do seem less stressed but the process has not sped up."

Kate could tell that Rhonda was only half-listening while she prepared the boat for its morning run. She pulled up anchor.

Kate continued, "I thought if I could add some dive heaters to a few of your tanks we could see if they molt faster in the wild, even though they're in traps. We'd leave them in place. Think about it. We can change history. The ocean is warming as it is. We're not freakishly modifying nature, just enhancing things a bit. Whenever lobsters lose their claws, rather than waiting three to four molting periods for regrowth, they'll bounce back sooner. More money in your pocket."

"I'm telling ya, you're relentless."

"Thank you, Captain."

"There is only one problem with your hypothesis. We have a glut."

"Northern waters have the glut. You guys are maintaining but global warming has hit these shores. Supply will significantly dip sooner rather than later." Kate turned to the horizon. The sky was starting to show signs of awakening. "We're looking toward the future. You've said it yourself. It's a hard life."

"Get your stuff."

"Thanks." Kate lifted her suitcase onto the boat and pulled out the heaters to show Rhonda.

"Do those work for you?" Rhonda asked, staring at Kate's arms.

Kate wore seasick bracelets on both wrists. "We'll see . . . won't we?"

"You look like a kid going to camp."

"I also took Dramamine. I feel confident today."

Rhonda took a bucket from the back of the boat and placed it at Kate's feet. "Make sure you don't splash on my boat."

"I'm a good shot."

They both smiled.

Rhonda's smile faded first. "Why me?"

"If not you, then who?"

"Charming." Rhonda cocked her head and started the engines. Kate sat across from her on the glossy white bench running along the side of the boat.

"We can fit these inside the parlor." Kate pointed at her heaters. "The bugs will stay warm."

"What makes you think they'll molt faster in traps rather than your simulated lobster tanks?" Rhonda studied the heaters.

"They need to experience something I'm not capturing in the

lab. Maybe they need vibrations or tidal shifts from the sea floor that aren't being properly replicated in captivity."

Rhonda turned on her GPS then pointed to a chart of the bay area covered in plastic and taped beside the steering wheel. "See how my traps are laid out?"

"Looks like a cartographer drew this map." Kate kneeled to get a better look.

"A hobby of mine." Rhonda twirled the wheel, making a ninety-degree turn.

Kate swayed and scrambled back to the bench.

Rhonda reduced speed to handle the wake of a larger boat and Catch Me bobbed over the giant ripples. "Did you know Colin and I had a thing after high school? I was the one who talked him into going to Northeastern. I knew he was smart. I pushed him even though I'm only one year older. Forty next year," she shivered. "He dumped me for a Northeastern girl. They were co-opping together at Gillette. I guess she was the best a man can get. Suddenly I was the chick who worked at the doughnut shop. The good part? She eventually dumped him. What goes around comes around, I always say."

"A true love story. Did you go to high school together?"

"No. I was working the Dunkin's near his mother's shop down-town."

"Isn't his mother dead?"

"What are you talking about? His mother is the Seamstress."

"The Seamstress?"

"Colleen Couture on Washington Street, on the edge of Chinatown."

"I've seen that shop. My mother used to drag me to the fabric stores in Chinatown."

"Colleen made costumes for the exotic dancers in the Combat Zone. She still does some local theater work, mostly easy stuff. Seams, hems, buttons." Rhonda continued, "I take my nets to her. She sews an extra cross stitch across the holes so the bug claws don't fall through and rip as much, and she seals the loose edges with epoxy and wax. It drives Colin crazy that she stays in touch with me. Aidan Greely fried on his lobster boat in a lightning storm. Colleen and Colin saw the whole thing from Fish Pier. Molly was in her mother's arms, so I guess you could say Colleen died that day."

"Molly. Right. Colin mentioned her once." Kate hung on the new information.

They were quiet for a time. Kate took in her surroundings. The sky was an amalgamation of pink and blue. Soon the GPS signaled and Rhonda hauled her first trap. Kate prepared the heaters for insertion.

Washington Street buzzed with the lunch crowd. The Seamstress sat inside her shop sewing. Kate passed by three times before she got the courage to enter the store. A chime rang when Kate entered the shop.

"I was wondering when you'd finish pacing outside and come through that door." Colleen did not look up from her sewing machine for some time. "So. How can I help you, miss?"

"These jeans need to be hemmed." Kate held up a plastic bag containing her jeans.

"I don't think I've ever seen you in here. Are you new in town?"

"No. I grew up in South Boston. I heard about you from Rhonda Conway."

"Rhonda! My dear Rhonda keeps me connected. What's your name?"

"Kate."

Shifting the dress she was working on to an adjacent white marble side table, the woman stood and offered her hand. "I'm Colleen." Her green eyes were muddy and her skin sallow. Kate grasped her hand. It felt thick and dry, old, a working hand. Still there was a definitive elegance in her manner, a lightness in her grip. She wore a silk orange top with bell sleeves that practically covered her hands over a pair of slim tan pants. But then why wouldn't she be stylish? She was a seamstress—a costume designer—after all.

Colleen opened her palms and flexed her fingers like a baby grabbing for a bottle. "Let me see what you have."

Kate pulled three pairs of jeans out of the bag and held them up to her. They were all different lengths, all too long for Kate's small frame.

"Typical. Offshore sweatshops. Sizes all over the place. They think Americans are giants." She held the legs up to Kate. "Go in the back and put them on and I'll get the proper length for you."

Kate stood on a round carpeted platform while Colleen knelt and pinned the hems of the pants. Colleen's silver hair shimmered in the mirror. She looked up and Kate noticed that her skin bore faded freckles. Miniature lines were carved into her face and forehead.

"Where do you work, Miss Kate? Ouch." She pricked her finger. "Dammit. That's a good one!" She sucked the blood from her left index finger, but it kept bleeding. Kate was glad because it gave her more time to formulate an answer. The blood dripped on Colleen's sleeve and she pulled it up, exposing larger pinholes on her wrist and arm. She quickly pulled her sleeve back down and went into the back of the store. Kate was relieved when Colleen came back and said she better concentrate instead of making idle chatter. The whole process took less than twenty minutes, including Kate's back and forth to change jeans.

"Give me until Wednesday. It's a small job but I have some work in front of you for some of the performers." Colleen moved over to her counter to fill out an invoice. "Your last name, Kate? And a number where I can reach you."

Kate recited her name and number.

"Finn. Finn as in Peggy's daughter?"

"Yes. You know my mother?"

"Of course. We grew up near each other. We weren't close growing up. I'm older, but she used to help my little son and daughter at the crosswalk for me. After my husband died. I was, ah, working two jobs."

Kate was permanently baffled by her parents' lives. They had so

189

many connections she knew nothing about. It was a mystery to her that she could come from these people, live with them, and be in the dark about their connections to others.

"That's wonderful. I'll tell my mother. Where is your daughter now?"

"My Molly passed."

"I'm so sorry." Why hadn't Rhonda told her?

"It's been several years." Colleen's voice was low. She brushed her hair off her forehead where beads of sweat had formed.

"Still," Kate tried to empathize. She didn't know why she did, but she pressed it. "And you said you had a son?"

Her face contorted and she let out a cackle. She stared through Kate in an otherworldly way as if her body was still intact but she'd left it many years ago to live someplace hellish.

"Well I'm here. And he's where he is, does what he does." Her focus shifted back to the invoice. She ripped it off the pad and handed it to Kate. "I'll see you Wednesday."

"Yeah." Kate's hands trembled receiving the bill.

She walked down Tremont Street watching the Emerson College students – a rainbow of fluorescent hair colors – and listened to their chorus of like ums, every statement ending in a question. She overheard a skinny blond guy tell his black-haired, punked-out girlfriend to meet him in like um an hour at the café and maybe get him um a chai tea? She dodged many more ums on her way back to her car.

Colin lounged in the lobby with his legs crossed in a manly half-yoga position, right over left. He was reading Boston Magazine. Kate breezed by him.

"What's your hurry?" He did not look up. She could see Colleen's mannerisms in him—cool, seemingly disinterested but attuned to every movement and rhythm in a room.

She stopped in her tracks. "No hurry."

"Come here and sit for a bit."

Why did his so-called invitations deliver as commands, directives? This time she would not kowtow.

"I'm not kidding. I have to get back to the lab to verify some temperature shifts in the bug room."

"The lobsters can wait. I need to discuss something with you."

She walked over and sat on a chair perpendicular to him.

He put down the magazine, leaned over the arm of his chair, and spoke in a low voice. "You visited my mother today."

"What?"

"Exactly my response."

"Are you spying on me?" she asked.

"I wondered the same thing."

"I needed some jeans hemmed and I heard she was a great seamstress."

"The city of Boston has many seamstresses."

She couldn't think of anything to say so she blurted out that Rhonda had referred her.

People were walking in and out from lunch. Colin looked up and waved, threw friendly greetings to them. Kate felt trapped in this open lobby. Her instinct had been not to tell Colleen that she worked for Colin because she had detected a disconnect, a deep wound. She had read once that death could break a family apart. She assumed they were that kind of family. But she must have been wrong.

He continued, "Rhonda referred you? She's a dragon lady, that one. My mother likes her, so I don't interfere." He re-crossed his legs. "However, I want you stay out of her shop. I don't even set foot in it. Not in ten years until today. She stays out of my work, etcetera, etcetera."

"Etcetera, etcetera?"

"Just don't make me have to go over there again." He stood up. "Your jeans are in a bag under my chair. Take them when I leave." He held out his hand for her to shake and said, "Good talk."

Norah looked over from her desk, one eyebrow up. Kate casually dipped her head in disrespectful affirmation.

He sat back down and adjusted his suit jacket so that he was not sitting on it. Leaning close to her, he explained in a low voice, "My mother's not a bad lady. She struggled after my father died and I took care of my little sister. Mother thought Molly would thrive in a Catholic high school but she got in with the wrong crowd. Started dealing and other raunchy stuff I don't want to think about. Familiar story?" He wrung his hands but his voice stayed even. "Couldn't stop her habit so one day she threw herself off the back of a tenement, landed inside the trash dumpster below. Mother blamed herself."

Kate was silent.

"End of story. Mother has her shop and does her thing, but we talk every day. Every day!" he reiterated with emphasis. "Last thing she needs is the past getting dug up around her. Now, are we done here?"

"I guess so." But she pushed harder, "How did you know I went there?"

"My mother called to tell me a good-looking neighborhood girl just left her shop and I'd be lucky to meet her."

Kate blushed. "She said that?"

Colin walked away, shaking his head.

Kate turned to Norah, who was obviously straining to hear. "Did you catch all that?"

Norah shifted her attention back to her computer screen.

That evening Mom offered more insight about the Greelys while Kate helped her mother prepare a corned beef dinner. Mom described Colleen as the "it" girl in the neighborhood. All the younger girls looked up to her, her wardrobe and how her hair was perfectly coiffed. She married young, at nineteen, and had Colin right away. Colin's father Aidan was a tough one. Colleen's mother and father never approved of him and wouldn't help their daughter out after he died at sea.

Mom threw the cabbage into a stainless-steel colander for a quick rinse. "I remember Colin walking Molly to school. Colleen had really hit the skids and was dancing in the Zone." She sprayed the cabbage on all sides. "That Molly was a precious child. Gorgeous, too. Such a waste."

"What?" The water spilled onto the worn counter. Kate wiped it down. "Colleen was a stripper in the old Combat Zone?"

"Yes. She worked at the Teddy Bare Lounge at night and ran her costume design shop during the day. From what I heard she made all the dancers' costumes. Not that I ever went down to that godforsaken den of iniquity."

She salted the corned beef and threw it into the Dutch oven on the stove. "Nothing but trouble down there. Started out clean, almost cabaret-style like old Scollay Square. Then it all turned. Drugs. Prostitution. Gambling. Weapons. Usual cast of criminals. I was glad when they finally cleaned it up." She licked her salty fingers. "Though it's still not the purest place."

"What made them shut it down?"

"Harvard football player got knifed down there. Wouldn't have mattered if it was a kid from Dorchester. Well, you get this. I don't have to tell you the ways of the world."

Kate tore a piece of cabbage out of the pot and burnt her tongue. "Ouch."

"What do you expect? It's hot."

Kate ran over to the freezer for some ice and held an ice cube on her extended tongue. "Is he embarrassed about his mother?" she asked with a burnt lisp.

"Probably. She was arrested for possession a few times."

"Of what?"

"Heroin. Junkie."

"And I'm an idiot." She told her mother how she'd thought the pin marks on Colleen's wrist and arm were from accidental pokes from common pins.

"She went through a lot but no excuse. Her kids needed her. That Colin was an intense one. He used to give me the same instructions every day in case Molly needed him. 'Call the business office at Northeastern and leave a message for me. I'll check in after each class.' She was with me for all of fifteen minutes in the morning. Of course there were no cell phones back then."

"She was really nice today." Kate sprinkled more salt into the pot. "She's had a tough life."

"Don't be such a bleeding heart. She left her son with her responsibilities. It's unnatural."

"Wow. Shall I tell Pop you are now defending Colin Greely?"

"Shall I also mention that you work for him?"

"No, Mom! Are you trying to give him a stroke?"

"Don't you think it's time you told your father what you've been up to?"

"Absolutely not. I need more time."

Michael burst through the back door with his work backpack. "Good timing. My favorite dish." He stuck his nose up in the air and moved it as if he were a golden retriever following a powerful and pleasant scent.

Kate was on tiptoes, reaching to get dinner plates out of the cupboard. Michael reached over her head, pulled out the plates, and handed them to her.

"I'm going to visit Pop tomorrow. Do either of you want to come with?"

"I think I can rearrange my schedule," Kate said.

"Kevin called today. The trial's been pushed out to early February. Courts are overloaded."

"Mom! Why didn't you tell me?" Kate threw her arms over her head.

"Because we didn't get there yet." She sounded defeated.

It had been a long time since they had all sat down to a meal together. Briny corned beef and cabbage fortified Kate.

Pop looked especially gaunt in his orange jumpsuit when the guard brought him into the family visiting room.

"I'm never going to get out of this dump alive." His head was down.

"Don't talk that way, Pop. It's good the trial is delayed." Kate leaned in and held his forearm. "It gives us more time to prepare evidence."

"Who's us?" He tightened his arm. "You aren't still dabbling around with the green fish? You don't know what those degenerates might do to you."

"No need to worry," Kate assured him.

But he wouldn't let up. "Are you still working? I heard you switched jobs."

Flabbergasted, Kate began to mumble a story about how she'd taken a family leave, when Michael jumped in to save the day.

"Pop. Mom made corned beef last night. Your favorite."

They all laughed. But Kate was still shocked that Pop was still privy to information about her life.

"Can't say I'm sorry I missed it," he said. "I hate that crap."

"My husband, the only Irish man I know who hates a boiled dinner."

"Boiling is for cleaning, not dinner, my dearest wife."

They flew home on the Expressway. A sense of heaviness pervaded the car.

"He's fading." Mom spoke with finality. "He won't make it in there much longer."

That afternoon Kate stopped off at Cardinal Medeiros Dock to check traps with Rhonda. It was a hazy afternoon and she felt untethered as she dragged herself down the ramp.

"Ready to check our traps?" Rhonda asked.

Kate whispered an affirmation.

"Hey G-girl, why the long face?"

"My Pop is dying in jail. My last name is Finn, not Greely's girl."

They cruised in silence. Rhonda lifted traps onto the boat and Kate took notes and photographs. The heating packs had taken a beating, but the lobsters were coming along on schedule. Kate should have been pleased with the results but the bay waters were rough and she wanted to be on shore.

"Colleen said you came to see her."

"Word travels. I took my jeans to her to be hemmed and Colin forbade me to see her. He doesn't want me near her."

"Think about it. It's part of his power act." She shook her head.

"You think he wants to keep her hidden? You know, with her heroin addiction?"

Rhonda sped up the boat. "She is what she is. He can't change that."

"You're right. He's controlling." Kate felt lighter. "I can't imagine telling my mother what to do."

"Hey. Why is this experiment so important to you? There's no shortage of lobster."

"We talked about this. Sure there's a lobster glut right now, but you know better than me that the supply goes up and down like a sine wave. Colin will probably eventually develop this as a green program. Totally self-contained facility. And less wear and tear on fishermen and their families. They won't have to struggle every single day at sea."

"You mean less jobs for fishermen! You're talking about their livelihood. I doubt Colin's worried about going green. Think about it. His father died in front of him," Rhonda snorted. "The real deal is that he's at war with the wild. Wants to put the ocean in a cocoon of his own making."

"At our first meeting, he did say his father was old Irish and so is my dad. Said my dad would die sticking to outdated principles, Bobby Sands style."

"Why? Is your father on a hunger strike?" Rhonda asked.

Kate looked at Rhonda skeptically. "Just his stubbornness is Sands-like. Don't be so literal."

"Don't be so smug, scientist girl." Her tone was venomous. She jerked the throttle and drove Catch Me around in a circle.

Kate was uncomfortable with the intensity of Rhonda's vehement response, as she had been that first day when she was abruptly dropped on the dock.

And then Rhonda seemed to reconsider her actions because she slowed down and yelled over her shoulder to Kate.

"Your boss is on to something big. Asians have the giant lobster farms, but only for those spiny creatures. Rock lobster ain't real lobster."

Chapter Fifteen

Morning rays burst through Kate's bedroom window. She always associated these rays with Pop. "The holy trilogy has arrived," Pop would say on early mornings in their kitchen when the rays poured through. As a child, Kate mimicked him but when she attended catechism classes, the religious instructors corrected her, insisting she say, "Holy Trinity." Kate liked trilogy better and stuck with it until the whole concept of three beings in one seemed ridiculous. She wasn't even sure what each member of the trilogy was responsible for. Weren't they redundant? Mom and Pop took these things on faith, never looking too deeply or questioning the raggedness of the argument of religion. What a gift, she had thought many times, to have that kind of unquestioning nature. She knew she'd question virtually everything, including God's existence, for the rest of her life. Coming up with inquiries and hypotheses to solve questions large and small was not just her job, it was her nature. Maybe her parents, playing by ear, were the more intelligent ones. She thought of the Native Americans whose many rituals relied on the vibrations of earth and signs from beyond. This made more sense to her than a multi-person deity.

This morning the sun's rays were mesmerizing and she stared into them against the advice of those who said she'd go blind; instead she absorbed their energies. Her imagination turned to her childhood sewer fish resting from their night out on Newbury Street. She felt in harmony with her invented friends, the angelfish with soft green wings and purple eyes floating in clouds of smoky sewer steam, because she toiled in the fancy sewers of Greely Labs and at night became whomever she pleased, at least in her own mind.

She took inventory of her current life. Pop was fading. Mom's hope had waned. Michael had been his elusive self since Bo Ming seemingly dumped him. And she couldn't even crack the DNA codes at work to artificially trigger fish to reproduce. Maybe because doing that would be the ultimate slap in Pop's face. The alarm jarred her and she reached over to her night table and pushed down the fifteen-minute snooze button.

Fog had settled over Nantucket Sound. The three of them jumped out of the Toyota Corolla and ran onto the beach underneath the Nobska Lighthouse. Kate clung to shore. "It's rough today. You'll never come in," Pierre and Haley yelled to Kate, who sat on the beach as they bounced in the currents of Nantucket Sound and hugged each other. The hypnagogic memory jarred her fully awake.

She strutted out of the house into an unseasonably warm November morning, glanced at her car, and decided to walk to work. On L Street, her phone vibrated.

"Haley, how are you?"

"Not so good," Haley said.

"What happened?"

"It's not what happened, it's what is happening. Pierre left. He's going to live in Boston. Said he never really loved me. Just an infatuation." Her voice broke. "And now it's dis-infatuation. That's what he said."

"Where are you?"

"At home. I can't afford to stay here. He said just sell it ASAP and we'll split the profit. Like he's giving me some kind of gift. It's the law."

"Slow down." Kate's breath was heavy. Commuters in passing cars cruised mercilessly by without regard for anyone but themselves. "Has he lost his mind?"

"That's what I said to him. And he just stared at me with a crazy look in his eyes. I was scared. He's been agitated all the time lately. There's a part of me that's glad he's gone."

"Bastard!" Kate said a little louder than she had intended. A bag lady passing by yelled at her to watch her "g-d mouth."

Smells from Tasty Burger wafted across the street.

"Is there someone else?" Kate felt dishonest asking.

"There've been many."

Kate held her breath.

"Do you want me to come down?"

"I didn't know who else to call." Haley's voice weakened. "Yes. I want you to come."

Kate sighed with relief that Haley had not specifically identified her as one of the many. Still, she really didn't want to face Haley.

"I can't tell my parents yet. You know how they are. They'll probably blame me."

She remembered the pressure Haley's WASP-y Southern Connecticut parents put on her. She hadn't lived up to the family legacy of law school and medical school like their other two daughters. But Haley was the nicest one, struggling to be herself. When she graduated from UMass Boston, she wanted to delay graduate school and travel to Haiti to work with underprivileged children, but her parents told her it was filthy there and if she risked her health in that way, they would not pay for a graduate program or her apartment in Boston. Instead she went to BU for her master's degree and landed the teaching job on the Cape. It was a respectable job, especially with the lack of higher ed options on the Cape, but not in her parents' eyes. Her mother told her she'd better raise her career stakes or she'd lose Pierre. When Kate stepped back and reviewed Haley's life, she could see that Haley wasn't the spoiled princess after all. Perhaps Kate had been the spoiled one, secretly thinking that Haley owed her restitution.

The sun set over the marsh as the evening breeze whistled across the tall yellow seagrass spreading the smell of low tide. Haley sat in a blue Adirondack chair on the dock, wearing a sweatshirt and a Falmouth Commodores baseball cap. Kate approached her gently. Haley gracefully stood up and greeted her with a smile and asked about her luggage. Kate hugged her tight. She felt her old friend's lack of energy. There was a hue of darkness, a sort of shadow around her. Kate guided her off the dock by her elbow and up to the house.

They sat at the white cottage kitchen table drinking hot tea. Haley filled her in on Pierre.

"He quit Nobska. Says he's going to work for some East Boston outfit."

Kate thought back to the night at Dingles when Pierre bowed toward Li Ming. She was somewhat foggy on that night but she remembered him saying he wanted to keep his options open with Ming in case he ever needed a job.

"AgaCulture Traders? Those fish farmers were written up by the FDA last year for mislabeling." She tried to lay it on thick in the hope of soothing Haley's pain. "They sold farm fish as ocean-caught and escolar as tuna to the sushi restaurants. Escolar is Ex-Lax. I wouldn't go near that place or the places they supply to. That said, Michael's old love works for his uncle there."

"Michael probably dodged a bullet. Pierre said it's a shithole with a shaky staff but that they offered him a honey of a deal and he took it. You know he was up for the promotion as liaison to Greely Labs and McGann screwed him, went behind his back and got Zion. McGann made him do all the dirty work and now he's out."

"What dirty work?" Kate asked.

"He wouldn't tell me. Just got angry. I kept trying to pry an answer out of him and he told me to stay out of his business."

Kate had never seen Pierre angry. She wasn't sure why, but she never saw him as having a proclivity for anger, never mind violence. But in high school psychology class, she'd studied sociopaths. There were disturbing examples of so-called nice men and women who murdered for insurance money. No one believed it at first because everyone assumed they were happily married couples. The more she thought about it, she realized nothing ever rattled Pierre. Could he be a sociopath who was capable of murder? Could Pierre have murdered Sammy? It didn't ring true in her gut. She had trouble believing. But if Pierre had killed for McGann, it was logical that McGann would want some distance.

"What's McGann's relationship with Dr. Zion?" Kate asked.

"Nothing. Greely wanted Zion. Read about him in Science magazine and said he was the guy."

"This is twisted. I work there too, you know. Not proud of it. Mostly monkey work—operational stuff for research and development."

"Ugh!" Haley scrunched up her face.

"The money is excellent." Did Haley really think her teaching job was superior?

The next morning, they drove to Woods Hole, got coffee at Coffee Haute, and walked around the village.

"I have to tell you something." Kate's hands were shaking as they waited for the Eel Pond drawbridge to be lowered so they could cross.

"You're going to do this now?" The horn from the Vineyard boat pumped. "I know you two were together in Boston this spring after the murder."

"Hal …" she couldn't get the words out.

"Really, Kate? You think I couldn't feel it? I called him over and over that night and he wouldn't answer. When he came home, he was totally vague and then you completely disappeared."

With no defense, Kate was glad it was out in the open. "I'm sorry. I was drunk and careless. But we didn't have sex."

"Who are you, Bill Clinton? I did not have sex with my friend's husband. If you were together all night, it's almost the same thing."

"I get it," Kate conceded. "But I passed out on my cot and he slept on a chair on the other side of the room."

Haley didn't respond. It was like she was in a dream state. "Well, you weren't the first. Just the only one who really mattered."

"Philanderer? I never would've guessed."

"Comforting." Haley's mouth contorted in pain.

"Sorry. I know, you can retaliate; hurt me like you were hurt."

Haley's sadness clouded her usually sparkling eyes. "Doesn't work that way, friend."

They crossed the drawbridge and walked over to the Woods Hole Science Aquarium to see the seals swim in the outside pool. Three seals swam playfully, and then one disappeared into the tunnel to the pool inside the aquarium. A second, white-spotted seal swam behind. The third squirmed up onto the side of the pool to bark and clap for a laughing audience.

"I was so pissed off at you at the time. Then I realized that Pierre …" Haley paused. "He gets what he wants. He took advantage of you for something."

There it was. That Haley arrogance. Pierre could never have been attracted to her; he only wanted something. "Thanks. I guess." But she knew Haley was right and it hurt.

The spotted seal swam back to the outside pool to join in the fun.

"Now he's with some gorgeous tall woman."

"Who is she?"

"I saw a picture on his phone. Checked it when he wasn't looking. She was holding up two lobsters, one in each hand. She didn't even look afraid of them snapping."

"There's a renowned lobster lady named Rhonda I know from Cardinal Medeiros Dock."

"This ain't no lobster lady." Haley shook her head and described the woman in the photo, "Gorgeous, bewitching, even with her missing pinkie finger."

Little did Haley know the woman she'd described was Rhonda, but why was Pierre with her? Was Rhonda selling to AgaCulture?

Kate tried to change the subject but Haley obsessed over her marriage. Finally, it was quiet for a bit as they watched the seals. Then Haley broke the silence.

"I did go through his pockets and found a parking ticket—for your car." Haley glared at her. "I ripped it into a gazillion tiny pieces and burned it. You have an outstanding ticket."

Kate protested without thinking. "Shit. He said he knew a guy who'd take care of it."

Chapter Sixteen

H is name is Reverend Jan Aaker and the prosecution says he will testify that he was on Merrows' Marina the morning of Sammy's death."

The district attorney, Suzanne Regan, had showed Kevin their witness list and he had stopped by the Finn's house with some news. They knew it couldn't be good.

"What in the hell is a minister doing at Merrows' at that time of the morning? Blessing of the Fleet?" asked Michael. "No one even docks there. Why did Pop have to meet Sammy there?"

"The minister was getting ready for the workers on the cruise ships and carriers. He runs that mission there. You know, the Salt House. They supply the seafarers with all kinds of humanitarian aid and services, even legal services. These folks are a long way from home and this organization gives them comfort."

"We're done." Kate paced between the kitchen and living room. "We are freaking screwed."

"What do you think?" Her mother did not flinch. "Will his testimony seal Seamus's fate?" She rose and snapped on the gas burner under the teakettle.

Kevin was gentle. "Hard to say. Maybe he was too far away to be completely definitive."

"But?" Mom prodded.

"But. Given no other suspects and the evidence of the chemicals found in the shed, things are stacking up. It doesn't look good, Mrs. Finn. I'm sorry."

They were all quiet for a few minutes. Then Kevin ventured, "Yesterday, the DA approached me. She may be willing to work out a deal."

"Your father said no deals," said Mom, shaking the kettle off the burner to stop the whistling.

Michael grabbed four teacups with matching saucers from the cupboard and slapped them on the counter. "Mom, just listen to him. Would you rather Pop stay in jail longer than he should? Swallow your pride."

"Our pride is ours and I'll thank you not to tell me what to do with it."

Kate was surprised at how sternly Mom had corrected Michael. She was usually protective of her son, even on the rare occasion when he said outrageous things.

She looked at Kate and said, "And you watch your mouth in this house, young lady. Just because your Pop isn't here doesn't mean you can drop the f-bomb."

There it is, thought Kate. She never has any trouble correcting me. "Freaking isn't a swear, Mom."

"It is in my house. So isn't the 's' word you used with it." Mom poured milk into her Belleek creamer and paired it with a matching sugar bowl, a wedding gift. Pop called his tea lucky tea after he poured from the creamer and spooned sugar from the shamrock-decorated porcelain. "I know my husband." She offered milk and sugar.

Kevin swept his light brown hair out of his eyes with his left hand, kept the heel of his right hand on the table and raised his five fingers in refusal. The Finns liberally added sugar and milk.

"How can you drink your tea black?" Kate asked.

"It's the only way to fly." Kevin took a swig and shook his head in pleasure. "A deal may be our only move. Suzanne said she could get the charges dropped to involuntary manslaughter. And drop the charge of leaving the scene of a murder. Generally, a three- to ten-year sentence. With time served, he could be out on parole," he hesitated, "in maybe two years."

"Two years?" Kate saw that Mom was clearly rattled. "Mother of God."

"I spoke to Seamus immediately after Suzanne approached me. You're right. He said, 'No deal.' That's why I came to you. You need to convince him it's a good move for all of you."

Mom stood up and walked over to the sink and looked out the window. After a moment, she turned to look at Kevin.

Kate held her breath. Mom, just say yes.

"No."

At some point during the negotiation, the air in the room had stopped circulating. Kate held her teacup and stared at one of the shamrocks painted on the sugar bowl. They were wearing away from use and age.

"Seamus won't go for it. He's determined to have his day in court."

"Well, it's my job to take the DA's deal to my client. I wanted to run it by you, too, so you'd have a chance to help Seamus make a good decision."

"Good decision?" Mom threw the rest of her tea into the sink. "You're starting to sound like you're working for the other side. Suzanne, is it? You knew when you took this case Seamus wouldn't budge." She held a preaching finger up in the air.

"That's enough, Mom. Kevin is just doing his job." Michael nodded to him. "And you probably need to get going."

"That I do. Indeed."

"Thank you so much for coming over to tell us face-to-face." Michael shook Kevin's hand at the door.

"No problem."

From her position at the table, Kate saw Kevin lean in and whisper something to Michael, and then the storm door closed with a clack.

"You've got him boxed into a corner, Mom," Michael said.

"I am your father's support. Are you? Why do you kids turn from him? Just respect his wishes. If Kevin can't handle this, I'll find someone who can." She stormed out of the kitchen, creating tremors as she pounded up the stairs.

"Wow. She's mad at you," Kate said. "That's new."

"They're making a mistake. Kevin said the minister is squeaky clean."

"Damn. Why couldn't he be a priest?" As she uttered the words, Kate felt bad about disparaging priests. Father Murphy had been so kind to Mom and Pop, even driving Mom to visit Pop in jail.

"Disparaging the Catholic Church now, are ya? I'll tell ya, you better watch yourself in this house, Katie. Wouldn't hurt you to have a little faith."

"Or Tony Monero on the case," she said.

He held both hands around his teacup. "That slimy wop? I'd sooner drown in the swill of Boston Harbor."

"Listen to you, Seamus Junior. You even have the voice down."

"Damn those Protestants." Michael hunched down toward his tea. "If only it was Father Mallory on the docks that mornin'."

"My son, Michael," Kate mimicked Seamus. "A fine altar boy, you were. Was it that, son, that made you a homo?"

"You are twisted, sister." He shook his head. "Should we go talk to Pop alone? Try to convince him he's hurting Mom with his stubbornness?"

"Maybe. Let me do a little recon on this Salt House minister. Maybe he isn't as squeaky clean as they think."

"They never are." He winked at her.

"Hey. How's Bo?"

"MIA. Doesn't return my calls. Just texts short notes. Says he's got to work around the clock."

"At least he's ambitious." She squeezed his right arm.

"His uncle has arranged for him to marry a Chinese-American." She could see him choke back tears. "Said it's the best way for him.

Says she's from a good family."

"Sorry, bro. But it's his loss."

"Yeah. Sure." His eyes filled. He turned from her as he had done since they were children.

"Hey, chin up. It's not like you have to go to the fish auction or something."

"What?" His tone shifted to false bravado. "No problem with the auction."

"You were afraid at the auction." She used her sing-song voice.

"I was not."

"Michael!" she yelled. "You were terrified. You made me go into the outhouse with you."

"It smelled and I thought there were rats in there." He rocked back on his chair.

"You look just like Pop when you do that," she said.

"You are Pop. You like all the same stuff he likes. You're the son he doesn't have."

"You're a great son. Pop is lucky to have you." She stood over him and mussed his hair like she used to do when they were little.

But Michael looked troubled.

"Remember when Pop lost it at the auction and I ran to the chapel?"

She nodded. She'd tried to shake off that day many times, but seeing her father threaten the teenage thugs almost to the point of provocation still disturbed her nineteen years later. What would have happened if the thugs hadn't backed down? She remembered hearing Louie say Pop was a crazy Mick who'd get them all killed.

Louie even moved to the Cape shortly after. Pop said he had family there. She wondered if Louie feared what could happen if he stuck around too long with the Fish Pier crew. She remembered what he said to Rob after, too. You think he would have learned his lesson. She knew Rob stuck up for Pop and was relieved that day, but now she knew what Louie had meant. Everyone on the docks knew Pop had killed before.

"Sometimes I think he did it."

Stunned by her brother's sudden admission, Kate tried to reassure him.

"Never."

It was an old habit to shield her brother.

"Pop would never kill Sammy." Her head shook with ferocity. "Never kill his best friend."

But she still held her own doubt.

Chapter Seventeen

I t was optional late arrival Friday at work and Kate decided to go in late. The road was blocked by skeley cruisers for the latest cruise ship in port, so Kate swung around Northern Avenue to the back side. She found parking and walked to the Salt House. She felt comfortable in her black jeans, hung low on her hips, with a long pink blouse covering the waistband. The early morning sun glistened off Juliette of the Eastern Seas cruise line. Seafarers swarmed the pier. One of the workers lay against the side of the brick mission building. Others were in a rage, pounding on the mission's doors, their teak faces matching the sea-salt-beaten door.

Kate approached a skinny man leaning against the front of the brick building, his right leg bent. "What's going on?"

He pulled out his wallet to show her he had no money.

"Yo necesito dinero," he sighed. "Dios me ayude!"

Another woman with bent shoulders and a permanent squint came face-to-face with Kate and put her hand to her ear in a mime air call. Then she pulled the air phone back, looked at it and shook her head.

"No teléfono." She threw her back against the building near the skinny man, her legs separated, not touching the brick.

A man in a tan overcoat and a minister's collar ran up the dock, waving his arms for people to get out of the doorway.

"Hang on. Hang on. Patience." He pulled a large jangling key chain out of his pocket. The seafarers pushed inside the ministry, chatting in Caribbean versions of Spanish, French and Portuguese. Kate could pick up some of the Spanish from her past studies of Spanish, a language choice that her father had not supported. She remembered him saying, "What the hell do you want to sound like a third-world national for? We got enough Puerto Ricans blathering that stuff. What's happened to studying Latin, where our language is rooted?"

She approached the rattled minister. "Excuse me. I speak a little Spanish. Is there anything I can do to help?"

"Yes. There certainly is."

His coat was wrinkled, collar disheveled, and his laptop fell on the floor when he pulled it out of his briefcase. He struggled to pull himself together.

"Get them in line and ask them to have their IDs ready. My wife will be here shortly. With any luck."

Every few seconds he swept his golden hair off his wide fore-head. He was a serious-looking man with a thick body. He set up his laptop in a deliberate manner on the countertop and typed the requests with his clumsy, thick fingers.

Most of the workers wanted hats and sweaters from the clothing donation box. Many wanted to buy discounted phone cards to call home. Some had not been paid wages in several weeks. Others wanted to know how to get to the Old Salt Manor in the North End where they could stay in plusher quarters for short money. As soon as Kate and the minister helped one wave of seafarers another line formed, which prompted Kate to call in late to work. After they serviced all the seafarers, she stood in front of him, hand out in a belated greeting. "Reverend? I'm Kate Finn."

"Well. Nice to meet another one of God's grace notes, Miss Finn." He clasped her hand. "I couldn't have done this without you today."

His grip was warm and steady.

"De nada, Reverend."

She felt a spiritual strength from him that she rarely sensed from other clergy, or people in general. It gave her the courage to tell him why she had come.

"My father's in jail for the murder of Sammy Robbins. I've been told that you saw the two of them fighting down here the morning Sammy was killed."

He retreated behind his computer, giving her a gentle but firm look.

"I've been called as a witness. This is inappropriate of you, Miss Finn."

"Kate. Just Kate. I understand. I'm not trying to sway you in any way. I just need to know what you saw. I must know. There might be other people's lives at stake here."

"That's quite dramatic." Frozen blue eyes challenged her. "You'll have to speak to the police about that. My part is to sit on the stand and tell what I saw."

"Which is?"

"Stop. You're coercing a witness."

"Reverend. I'm not a lawyer. Just a daughter. God's child if you wish. What did you say, a grace note?"

He smiled gently at her. "You are God's child. An unrelenting one." He snapped the laptop shut. "Have you asked your father what happened on his boat that morning?

"He said they didn't argue. They were just talking and Sammy was crying."

"Well then." He sifted through the donation box. "Here is an unused Irish knit sweater. Take it for all your help today?"

"God, no. I mean, I'm sorry. Thank you, but my parents brought us up never to accept any kind of secondhand clothing." She was afraid she had offended him. "Besides, my mother knits. I have more of those sweaters than anyone should."

He turned back to his sifting. "We share here."

"My family is a proud lot," she said. "That's why I need to help them."

He was not going to budge.

"What happened to your wife? I thought she was coming."

"Yeah." His voice hollowed along with his eyes. "She must have gotten hung up."

After the futile conversation with Reverend Aaker, Kate wasn't ready to walk into Greely Labs. She kept walking past the Labs to

Fish Pier. A foggy low-pressure system had come up the coast. Along the apron of the pier, vessels were coming in from their early morning runs. She turned to walk backward against the blurred view of Logan Airport. With eyes closed, she listened to the sound of planes bellowing in the thick air.

She chose the spot above where she had found Sammy dead. Careful not to crush the half-packet of Sno Balls inside, she laid her purse under her head, and rested on the cold dock enveloped by the milky air. Water splashed on the pier poles, swish, swish, swish. Tiny needles seemed to ping inside her belly, coconut from the Sno Ball she'd had with her coffee for breakfast. She really needed a better diet, but that would wait until after the trial.

Somehow, she had drifted into the fog and the docks felt dead, deader than she imagined the Dead Sea to be. She felt disconnected from her old world. How had everyone forgotten her so fast? She'd worked here since she left Woods Hole. What was the point of pouring heart and soul into a job? Stop wallowing, she thought. The Irish surpassed any other people in wallowing. Dwell, dwell, dwell. Even as recipients of the Nobel Peace Prize they could cast a pall of divisiveness by finding some conflict, some lack of fairness. Her heritage was a burden at times. She wished she was one of those light, expressively emotional French types. They experienced crises in full emotive release, then off they went, embracing life. Smiling, laughing, giggling.

A light tap on her shoulder startled her.

"What brings you back to the neighborhood?" Rob hovered over her with a black PENN rod in his hand. It looked like a pencil against his large frame.

"Hey. Did you hit me with that thing?" She didn't get up.

"Tapped you awake. For sure."

"Neptune called me over." She pointed at the stone sculpture of Neptune's head staring down to her from the conference center where she used to post her daily findings. "Somehow my family pissed him off and I'm trying to make peace. What's up with the PENN? Broken?"

"Nah. Just lending it to a friend. How is the trial prep coming?"

"Not great. The plot thickens. A guy named Reverend Aaker is the prosecution's key witness."

"Oh boy."

"Yeah. Enough said. How was your catch?"

"Hake, mostly. Dogfish. Stuff we wouldn't touch in the day. Good the restaurants are pushing it. Cod is untouchable. Damn environmentalists! Sorry, they just aggravate me."

Kate sympathized. "I hear you. They've gone too far."

On her feet again, she took a last deep whiff of the salty air. "I do miss this place."

"Come back." Rob's voice was weak.

"Not yet. I've got to work out some stuff."

"Hurry. The bottom-feeders are slipping in quicker than you think."

Back at the Labs, when Kate walked past Norah's desk, she jammed her hand straight out with a pink action note, never looking up. The directive was printed in all capital letters:

PLEASE SEE COLIN AS SOON AS YOU GET IN.

Even Norah's notes seemed hostile to Kate. What was her problem, anyhow? Jealousy? Disgust? Kate could never figure out Norah's game.

She walked to Colin's office and stood at the doorway. "You wanted to see me?"

"Come on in." Colin pulled a large file folder from the credenza behind his desk. It was one of Kate's technical files. "I want to review the cod findings with you. The market trends show a steady increase in demand for cod and I want to be ready to launch our findings to the FDA."

She briefed him on the latest activities.

"Fine work, Kate. Good stuff. I'll need you next Tuesday at the scientific advisory meetings to explain your findings."

"Next week is tough. We're briefing for my father's trial. Where are the meetings?"

"Here in the conference room. Norah's handling everything. They'll want a tour of the facility. Then we'll wine and dine these guys. They'll pretend they can't accept it, but I've never seen one of them turn down a free meal."

She fidgeted, shifting her weight from one leg to the other. "I never accepted anything when I contracted to the FDA."

He shook his head. "Quite rare, you are. Quite rare."

"It's illegal," she said.

"But customary, even expected in business. Quid pro quo, if you will. Anyhow, my executive and scientific staff must be there. Mandatory. After me, you have the most experience with the FDA." His blue eyes softened. "How are you coming along with my old friend Rhonda?"

"What? Did I give you the details of our experiment?"

"No. I just assumed you were working together given that she's not the type of friend you'd normally make."

"You think you have everyone figured out?"

"I think I have you nailed."

She did not shrink from his comment. His interest flattered her. "I have to get back over there on Monday and check the traps with her."

"Good. You've become a star staffer here." He pointed at his sitting area and they sat side by side. "I'm going to reward you."

"How?"

"How is your father's case coming along? Any new information?"

She thought about bolting from her seat and shouting at him to mind his business, but what was the use? He made it his business to know everything. He could probably tell her more than Kevin could about the case. She took the bait. "There's an eyewitness. A minister. I spoke to him this morning. He runs the Salt House Mission."

"Aaker?" he asked.

"You know him?"

"No. Just his wife."

"What? So now you run with the holy rollers?"

"Long time ago. Maddie, the good rev's wife, was a barmaid in the Combat Zone when I was little. My mother used to take me and Molly around. Maddie would put us up on the barstools and serve us Shirley Temples. Ah! The golden years. Now DSS would step in."

"How'd she hook up with the Reverend? He seems so pious."

"Humble guy. She cleaned up good. Stole his heart, I guess. Those guys are just as vulnerable as venerable. Last I heard she's back hanging on the other side of pious. Scandalous." He looked at her, long and hard. "Catch my drift?"

"Not sure. Where are you drifting?"

"Nowhere." He winked at her. "Except, he might not be happy to see photos of his wife showing up in compromising establishments."

Kate was ashamed that she was intrigued. She pushed forward, "Are you saying the Reverend can be influenced?"

"Did I say any such thing?"

Her body trembled. "Kind of."

"Then you didn't hear me. I'm saying a minister's wife who hangs with hipsters in Boston's nightlife scene dressed provocatively in ripe middle age could be an embarrassment."

"Now I see the difference." She shook her head and started to rise out her chair. "Chauvinism and ageism."

Colin placed his right hand on her left hand and tenderly squeezed it to stop her from leaving. His hand was warm and firm. "Not so fast. Think about it. This guy is willing to sink your father with a story that's subjective at best. Why does he get that power?"

"Pop is a sitting duck."

"If your Pop did pop Sammy, no pun intended, no doubt it was for a good reason."

"You're unbelievable." She could hear her heartbeat pounding through her eardrum. "My father didn't kill him. He loved Sammy like a brother."

"Remember what Oscar Wilde wrote, 'Each man kills the thing he loves.' Sammy probably broke code. It's honor with those guys. Brutus and Caesar. Cheech and Chong. Captain and Tennille. The list goes on and on."

"I don't know who Captain and Tennille are. Cheech and Chong? Hardly killers. How would the scene go? No more pot for you, Chong. Et tu, Cheech?"

"Point being, your Pop has his code. We all do." He slapped his thighs. "Do you want some help with this?"

Kate paced around the room, stopping by the window. It was foggy outside. No visibility.

"Yes. But don't take the minister down. My head is all twisted around on that. What else you got?"

"I know a guy."

"What are you saying?" she asked.

"Right now, Aaker is our best option."

"Please don't do anything without checking with me." She sank back into her chair.

"That's a chance you'll have to take. Do you want your Pop to live out his life with your mother, or in jail?"

"You know the answer." Exasperated, she looped her hands over her head.

"You gotta do yoga or something," he said. "You need to learn how to relax."

"Yoga is stupid and meditating makes me tense."

"Okay, science gal." He handed her some folders. "Let's get briefed for next week's meeting."

By eight o'clock, they were beat. He collected their work and placed it on his desk. "Excellent. Norah will put together the slides for the presentation. She does a fine job with that."

Kate mouthed his words.

"What was that snarky lip sync? Don't you like our star admin?"

"Lovely woman. Yes, indeed." She bowed her head. "Hey, I'm hungry. I'll be going."

"Let's grab a bite together," he said.

"I have some Sno Balls on reserve. Come down to Georges Bank. It's all set up."

The labs were deserted and the tank filters echoed throughout the walk to her area. She pulled a box of the pastries out of the cabinet above the sink. "Check this out." She retrieved her cryotherapy sprayer and doused two pink Sno Balls. They froze immediately. She handed him one and devoured the other.

"Shrinkage." He held it at bay. "Liquid nitrogen pastry. I don't think so. Is this what you eat?"

She grabbed it out of his hand and held it up to his mouth.

"Try a bite," she said. "You'll see. Most delicious dessert, ever."

"FDA approved?" He gingerly took one bite. "Mmm. Okay, let's go across the street and get some real food."

"Fine." She scarfed down his pastry. "Yummy."

They entered the double doors of the MilPort Hotel, stepping into a glistening lobby with white leather and chrome furniture and crystal chandeliers. A glass table held a tall vase with orange and purple dragon lilies. To their right was a swanky white backlit bar where the after-work crowd swarmed. She headed toward the dining room behind the bar.

"No. No. We have a suite on reserve for special clients. Follow me."

Kate wondered who we was. "A reserved suite? Is that a thing?"

"Sometimes I need to crash, close by."

"You live in the neighborhood," she said.

"I'm fond of room service."

"Okay. boss." Her body followed in Pavlovian fashion.

The steps to the suite were carpeted with oriental print stair runners. The banister was made of dark mahogany coordinated with white balusters. On the third rise, Colin opened a door numbered fifty-four.

"Wow. Who's your decorator?"

"Well, you know. Me."

Sheer curtains masked the lights from the commercial Seaport area. Heavy drapes were drawn halfway.

"It's amazing. Look at the couch and matching chairs." Kate plunked down on the brown leather couch. "I still live at home." She rearranged the throw pillows. "Not in the basement. Upstairs. In my old room."

Colin came closer. "It's not really great furniture. Impressive to the untrained eye, though." He sat next to her. "What else do you find impressive in this place?"

"Maybe a bathroom. Where is it?"

He sat, shoulders erect, and pointed at the left corner of the room.

In the bathroom where glass walls overlooked Logan, she was convinced that the planes could see in. Between the tub and glass shower stall another door opened to a bedroom with a king-size bed. The bathroom smelled like a luxury spa. The miniature soap bars emitting citrus smells of orange and lemon enlivened her senses. She primped, using the small treasures provided on the vanity—cotton balls, Q-tips, and orange blossom body lotion. She cleaned her ears, creamed her hands, face, neck, chest, and stomach, then refreshed her privates with makeup cleansing wipes. She nuzzled her face into the two plush white robes on the back of the door. Matching white slippers were enclosed in plastic and placed inside the front pockets of the bathrobes.

Colin sat at a room service table with two silver-domed covered dishes and a bottle of red wine. She sat across from him as he poured the wine. With a theatrical magician's move he unveiled the dinners.

"Hamburgers and beans."

"No good?" he asked.

"Fantastic. I love hamburgers. Not cheeseburgers, though."

"Course not. That's for people who live in flyover states. We salty dogs eat our burgers plain and burnt."

Over supper they discussed the upcoming meeting with the FDA.

"How did you become friends with Pierre?"

"What? Where did this come from?"

"He's a bit of a prick."

"We met at WHOI. He was different, then."

"So, you introduced him to your girlfriend. Emotions too complicated for you?"

"Dinner and psychoanalysis? What kind of racket are you running here?"

"I used to take the easy way out, too."

"I guess I might do that." She shrugged her shoulders.

"Though, not with your work. You give it your all. I'm impressed," he said. "By the way, what do you think of your work, knowing all fishermen are scared GE will replace them?"

She moved some beans onto her fork with her fingers.

"I get it. I'm fascinated by genetic modification of any kind, but manipulating genetic codes is still scary. It changes a species forever. You and I grew up here so we understand that fishermen know their stuff. They've seen it all, including virus outbreaks where no one gets paid. A lot of the scientists can't feel nature. Fishermen have a sixth sense."

"They'll come around if they find something in it for them. Certainly, scientists are in it for the money. I know. I deal with them every day. More corruption lies behind ivy walls than in the rackets."

"It's not the money," she said.

"It's always the money."

"It's about power. Star power. Glory. The chance to shine in research."

"How about your old friend, Pierre Gosselin?"

"You probably know more about Pierre than I do."

"Not really. He came with the package. We got funding from the government to work in a joint venture and used them for an offset partner. I wanted Zion, but he was working on an NSA project. Pierre looked good on paper. What about his wife? Wealthy?"

"Her family has some money."

"And Pierre's research? Besides chasing women." He cut his burger with his knife and fork and took a bite.

"Never saw it. Dr. Zion wasn't overly enthusiastic about him, though. He mentioned once that Pierre was short on integrity."

"Clearly Pierre has fidelity issues." He winked at her. "But Zion's been such a boost to Greely Labs. I'm glad I brought him on."

She hesitated for a moment and then decided to go for it. "He used test equipment, state-of-the-art chromate, to test the fish sample I got off Sammy's body."

"Whoa. Whoa. Whoa." He put his utensils down and wiped his mouth with his napkin. "The sample you got off Sammy's body? How did you manage that?"

"In a slightly unorthodox move. I had to research why there was green all over his mouth and on the fish."

"Ah, the green-eyed monster. The green fish."

"Yes. Greentini."

He didn't flinch at the nickname. "And I thought you were Saint Katherine." He reached across the table and squeezed her hands in his. "These lovely hands committed a crime."

"Anyhow, we found ammonium perchlorate pouring out of the fish. Dr. Zion said the fish could have blown up, literally blown up, with those kinds of levels, but he couldn't identify the properties of its catalyst versus activator, within the Greentini compound."

Colin leaned toward her and twirled a lock of her hair through his fingers. "What if we could prove your father didn't kill Sammy Robbins?"

Kate moved over to him.

"Do you have evidence? What's going on?"

"Nothing I can put my finger on yet. I just have a hunch that something else is in the pipeline. Come here."

She leaned in and he touched Kate's lips with his fingers. He rubbed her legs and then her backside. She did not stop him. She rambled on about her belief in her father's innocence while he nodded his head from time to time. Eventually he stood up.

"Let's go in the bedroom," he said.

He sat on the bed first and reached for her to sit next to him. Then he leaned her head back and kissed her. He lifted her hair and kissed the back of her neck and then her chest. He put both hands on her shoulders and rubbed them. His hands were the warmth she felt inside herself on a summer day at the Cape; she didn't want him to remove them. This felt right to her. She unbuttoned her blouse and he caressed her breasts, delicately circling the nipples with his tongue. She sighed. He reached for her jeans and lifted her hand onto his crotch and she started to rub him there. Soon they were naked.

They stood in front of the closet mirror admiring each other.

"You're beautiful," he said.

Now she replied fully, inhaling his breath passing into the abyss of tongues and hollow spaces. Slowly, rewinding each move, eyes glazed, he sat back gazing at her and she wondered why she had never been with someone like this before.

She opened the bedding for them and they slipped into bed. The duvet cover and sheets felt like a thread count of a thousand plus, and she appreciated the luxuries. Colin was on top of her, moving inside her. He was gentle and fierce and even though that made no sense, the sense was made in her. Their lovemaking went on and on and afterward she felt a contented fullness.

"Did you sleep well?"

Kate rubbed her eyes. Looking down she noticed that her right breast was sticking out. She covered it. Colin turned back the covers to expose her body and they made love again. They stayed in bed all that Saturday and into Sunday.

On Sunday evening, she left the suite.

Chapter Eighteen

On Monday morning, Kate and Rhonda pulled out of Cardinal Medeiros Dock to observe the lobster traps. They tooled past the longshoremen and harbor workers.

"Got your seasick jewelry on, I see." Rhonda pointed at Kate's wrists.

"Don't leave home without them. Even wear them for motion sickness when I walk to work."

"Funny. You look refreshed," Rhonda said. "Good weekend?"

"Average." Kate leaned back on the seat and crossed her feet. "Worked, mostly."

She watched the longshoremen operate the cranes. Pop told her that he tried to get a job with them but the local union made it virtually impossible. It was legacy for dock workers. Wharfies took pride in handing down their jobs through generations. He said when a baby boy was born into a longshoreman's family, plans were made for his future on the docks. Highest-paid labor in the city, her father had railed with envy.

"What did you do over the weekend?" Kate asked.

"Dinner with a friend."

"What kind of friend?"

"The kind you keep to yourself. MYOB."

Kate pushed it. "Do you know a guy named Pierre?"

Rhonda, at the helm, didn't flinch. "Can't say that I do."

They approached the first trap.

Rhonda stopped the engine.

The trap buoy had been cut in half. It was a clean cut.

"Help me out here." Rhonda pushed Kate over to the steering wheel. "Let's pull it up. Keep the boat steady." The choppy current bounced the boat around. Rhonda yelled at her, "I said keep it steady."

Kate thrust her upper body into the steering wheel, holding it with all her power while Rhonda pulled the trap onto the boat.

"Mothers!" Screaming into the sky, Rhonda threw her up arms.

The lobsters were gone, along with the heaters.

They checked the rest of Rhonda's traps. All of them had been pirated.

"This has never happened to me," Rhonda said.

"Never?" Kate asked.

"It's a warning."

"From whom?"

"From whom? What are you, from Harvard?"

"Who did it?" Kate asked again.

"Only happens when the guys have a bone to pick with one of

their own." Rhonda threw the last trap into the water and took the wheel. "I shouldn't have gotten involved with you. I knew it."

"I'm sorry," Kate said.

Rhonda did not respond.

"I'll make it up to you," Kate pleaded.

"You're going to make my peace with these guys? Don't be ridiculous. I know how to fix this. Stop coming around here."

When they docked, Kate was dismissed.

"I'm telling you right now. You're in over your head, Kate Finn."

Outside the conference room a banquet table was laid with smoked salmon, bagels, fruit, pastry and coffee for the meeting with the FDA. Norah stood next to the table and received the three FDA agents, one woman and two men. She handed them badges and navy blue folders containing marketing brochures and agendas for the meeting. Inside was the history of Greely Labs, including a timeline and short biographies of the principal staff: Colin Greely, Ed McGann, Dr. Zion. Norah had credited herself: prepared by Norah Woodstone, Executive Assistant. Kate signed in and took a badge and folder.

The conference room was warm but her body still felt stiff from the rawness of the air outside. She shrugged off the chill, sat across the round table from Colin, and fiddled nervously with the rose centerpiece. The water was halfway up the vase and it tipped over. She recovered it without soaking the tablecloth but feared that someone might have seen her clumsiness. She feared every-thing today. When she looked up at Colin, he was laughing.

"Come sit over here." He motioned for her to sit next to him, loosely paraphrasing Thomas Paine. "Unity in numbers."

Her stomach churned loudly. Colin looked at her. "Hungry?"

"Anything but."

"You've had your share of Sno Balls today?" He leaned over and patted her hand and she was at ease for a moment. "What happened with Rhonda yesterday?"

"The experiment was sabotaged."

"Dammit. I'd hoped to dangle a carrot to these guys." He turned away from her. "Don't bring it up."

Each with a coffee and a pastry in hand, the three FDA agents filed in, followed by Dr. Zion, Doug, McGann, and Norah. Mc-Gann raised an eyebrow at Kate, pointed at Colin, and nodded in a way that Kate understood to be tribal. Or, her mind creating tension in her entire body, was it thumbs-up for seducing one of his workers? No. McGann was just toying with her. Colin would never talk about their intimate weekend. Would he?

Nausea rose. She wanted the meeting to be over. She wanted to go to Dingles and have a Murphy's. She wished she was anywhere but here.

Colin stood and greeted the agents, directing his staff to intro-duce themselves. Then he got down to business. He pitched the genetically engineered processes underway at Greely Labs. Dr. Zion briefed them on the latest experiments. Kate and Doug described their progress with cod, haddock, and bivalves.

Colin conducted the tour. He had given the staff strict instructions to parade behind him and refer questions to him whenever possible. If questions could not be referred to him they were to answer briefly, preferably yes or no. These were the rules for FDA visits. Give the inspectors the minimum. Colin insisted that the FDA agents accompany him and his staff to dinner at Legal Seafoods and the agents graciously accepted. And they graciously and illegally allowed Colin to pay the check. When the dinner party broke up, Colin asked Kate to stay for debriefing.

"That went well," he said. "We're building a tighter relationship with the agency. They know what we're doing and respect the work. When the time comes, it'll be easier to get the approvals we need."

"I think they're here for the free dinner." She threw her hair over her shoulder. "Scumbags."

"You are so beautiful when you get all fired up," he said.

"Right. Fired up is my strong suit. I'm the redheaded cliché."

The restaurant started to empty. He gave the room a global scan. "I spoke to my contact in the Justice Department." He looked out the window at the harbor. Lights twinkled from every direction. "He'll work with us."

"Us?" She shook her head.

"The authorities want this to go away as much as you do. There's no room for violence here. We finally got rid of the likes of Whitey Bulger and his crowd. Now the waterfront is clean, upscale. Ed is always saying how we are making a positive difference."

She shook her head. "Your boy Ed McGann is quite elusive."

"He's on the right side. Above reproach. We need him. Look."

He pointed at her. "I've never pretended to be anyone but who I am. I have interests here. I don't want to hear you spieling about McGann. He's a loyal soldier."

"Loyal? Didn't he just cut Pierre off when you hired Dr. Zion? I thought they were friends."

"Pierre's a sore loser. Let's get back to your father. My guy says there may be enough evidence to slant the crime back to the victim."

"Suicide?" Kate asked. "Sammy would never. What about the bruises? He was attacked."

"How do you know? Were you there?"

"I'm listening."

"We already have reasonable doubt."

"But the minister."

"We can get to him," he said. "Okay?"

"He's starting to get under my skin."

"After meeting him once? You're tough."

"Yeah, He's got that save-the-world complex. Holier than thou attitude while his wife is on tour with other guys in the same city. To think I worked at the mission for nothing."

"Mercenary eh?" he asked.

"Yeah. Time is money."

"I can get my guy on it and try to get a compromise."

"Your guy? We've been down the deal road already. Tony Monero?" she asked.

"That jackleg?" he roared. "You watch too much TV."

"Pierre thought Tony could help, so we all went to visit Pop."

"You took Tony Monero to Walpole to see your father? The guy whose ads say: 'Have you been accused of a crime you didn't commit? We can get you off.' "

She leaned on the table, dropped her head into her right hand and covered her eyes. "I know. I know."

"Oh, that's rich." Gingerly he moved her hand away from her eyes.

She smiled at him.

"Let's go across the street for a change of scenery."

He rose and took her hand as if they were headed to the dance floor.

The next morning she woke in the MilPort suite to the sound of Colin's voice.

"Got the cameras on him at the right time," he said, sipping his coffee.

She wrapped the sheet around her, jumped out of bed, and walked out into the living room. He was pacing in front of the window fully dressed and wearing a headset. She could tell that he had not heard her come out of the bedroom.

He adjusted his mouthpiece. "Right. His voice was cracking the other night on Channel Seven when they drilled him about his floozy wife. It's been all over social media. The DA will take him off their witness list for sure. He's toast."

Kate felt a surge of energy. Though she had respected Aaker and didn't want him to suffer, even asked Colin to spare him, she couldn't feel bad for him. He was weak for a pathetic wife. At least her parents stood together, worked together, and did not risk their marriage for their own appetites. Why should the Finn family suffer so much when the rest of the world acted immorally and covered it over with ministries? With this revelation came another feeling. A kind of excitement she had never felt. A liberation from guilt. Maybe, she thought, guilt must be battled with action. Why had it taken her all this time to understand that long-suffering humility was utterly overrated?

"I can get back to you later." Colin clicked off his phone.

"Are we going to hell?" she asked.

He did an exaggerated about-face. "I didn't know you were there."

In full sheet regalia, she folded into his arms. He held her tight.

"We'll burn together," he said.

"Who were you talking to?"

"Colleague." His chin was on her head. "We work to keep the waterfront clean."

"What else you cleaning?"

"Got to get rid of sinkholes like AgaCulture, too. They'll undercut to get the market. Leave nothing on the table."

"Uh-huh. The good Bostonian-Irishman would never undercut anyone."

"It's different. Greely Labs leaves a bit on the table for the boys." This was the first time she had seen him visibly rattled. "I could tell you stories about how workers are treated in sweatshops like AgaCulture."

Kate spoke with passion. "Shameful. Sadly, it's the only survival the workers know."

His voice softened. "Forget it. New subject."

"Thank you." She kissed him. "Admittedly, I like the part about squelching Aaker. Does that make me a bad person?"

He kissed her back. "Maybe. But it weakens the prosecution. The beauty is, even if your father is guilty, no one will ever know."

"Pop is innocent."

He let out a deep sigh. "Correction: What if we could prove that your father didn't kill Sammy Robbins?"

She backed away from him. "I'm getting dressed."

"I'm sorry. You said yourself, there are the bruises. And we know they fought that morning." He followed her, tapped her behind with his hand. "We'll get him off, Kate."

For the rest of the week Kate concentrated only on her work at the Labs. She bargained with herself that if she spent time with Colin, their latest plan to help free her father would fall apart. He called her into his office once to tell her the wheels were in motion. Then Kevin called with news that Aaker's story, when fully evaluated by the DA, wasn't conclusive. Suddenly, the DA was willing to work with Kevin. She wanted a charge, some charge, but given an unreliable eyewitness, Suzanne Regan knew she could lose in court. The Finns were afraid to get too excited, yet. Kate still tried to believe in her father's innocence, but didn't care anymore how he was released from prison. For her, this end could justify the means.

On Thursday night when she arrived home she found a note from her mother on the kitchen counter. Erica had a girl. She is at Mass General Room 25.

Kate rushed to the hospital.

"Rose, look who's here. Your Auntie Kate." Erica sat in bed with the baby in her arms while Will slept in the green vinyl side chair near the window.

"Splendid name, Rose." Kate stroked Rose's cheeks.

"Splendid. Now that's just a perfect word, Rose Katherine. You'll be so smart, just like your aunt." Erica bent her head down to meet Rose's baby forehead.

Kate's eyes filled. "You named her after me?"

"We just flipped the baby book and took the first name that appeared. Obviously. You are my best friend and now Rose's."

"You're my best friend, too. Come here, little Rose Katherine." Kate took the baby in her arms. She was warm and smelled of sweetness. Baby shampoo. Kate choked back her tears but one landed on Rose's cheek and she didn't flinch. This was a good baby. She felt tenderness, a warm rush through her whole body, sensations that she had heard about, but up until now never fully experienced while holding an infant. Carefully, she lifted Rose back into Erica's arms

"Look at you." Kate cleared her throat. "I knew you'd be comfortable with motherhood right away."

"Yeah, and look at my husband asleep in the chair."

They laughed and Rose sighed. Kate took Rose one last time from Erica and rocked her gently. It felt so good. Her previous lack of maternal feelings for small babies had made her feel unnatural. But she couldn't help it. Babies scared her. So needy. So delicate. She was relieved when motherly types jumped in front of her to snatch up infants, preening with them in their arms as if it was the highest honor in the world. She often thought she might feel differently if the baby were her own and vowed she'd never push her baby on anyone. Rose was different. Rose's peaches and cream cheeks and pursed lips won Kate over.

Will stirred in the chair.

"Tough night, Dad?" Kate teased.

Will threw his head back and let out a tremendous loud yawn. "You have no idea, Auntie Kate."

"Well, I'm going to leave you two to your parenting." She hugged and kissed each member of the new family.

"You look flushed," said Will. "A bit peaked, Katie."

"You look glassy-eyed," Erica added. "Are you sick?"

"Lovesick? What's his name?" Will asked. "Is Detective Dick back on the case?"

The hospital elevator was crowded so she didn't see Doreen Spencer packed in the right corner until they got off at the lobby.

"Mrs. Spencer?" Kate asked.

She was discombobulated on all counts, not the glamour girl Kate remembered from years before. She wore no makeup and her gray-streaked dark hair was pulled into a messy ponytail with much of her hair floating loose. She looked like a traumatized woman who gets interviewed on television after a catastrophic event.

"Huh?" Mrs. Spencer startled.

"I'm Kate. Seamus Finn's daughter? My father and Spence, um, Mr. Spencer, work at the docks together."

"That's right." She was clearly distracted.

"Is everything all right?" Kate asked.

Doreen seemed to want to confide something. "Yeah. Listen, I am in the middle of it here. I just…" She stopped short. "I have to go."

She raced toward the sliding doors at the main entrance. Kate used the bathroom around the corner. When she came out she saw Doreen with her two grown sons, both of whom looked like their father. They walked toward the elevator. Before the doors closed Kate saw them hugging and crying.

Kate's instincts took over. She approached the patient information desk.

"I was wondering if you could tell me what room John Spencer is in?"

"Let's see." The thin, bleach-haired twenty-something scanned the patient list on his computer. His name tag read Lance Sicard, Guest Services. "He's going to be admitted shortly." His fingers trailed over the computer screen. "No clue what room, yet. Still in the ER. Wait. Real time update. He's a Cardiac patient now. Complications. Oh, dear." Dramatically he threw his hand up in the air, as if he were a cop in an old talkie film. "No. No visitors except immediate fam." He tapped his fingers on the desk. "Per this hospital's policy." He leaned on his hands, one spread over the other, "Are you family, perchance?"

"Practically."

He shook his head with more of his dramatic flair. "I'm so sorry."

Visiting hours would be over in fifteen minutes. She needed to act fast.

"Your hair is stunning, Lance. Do you do it yourself?"

He blushed while touching his hair. "I just use peroxide and a conditioner. It's easy."

"I was thinking of bleaching my hair. Could you write down the conditioner you use?"

"Sure," he responded, pronouncing it with a shore inflection, and grabbed a pen from his drawer.

Kate leaned over the counter and read the computer screen.

John Spencer: Cardiac Intensive Care, Ellison 9-14.

"Here you go." The memo paper was folded as if it were an award ballot.

"Thanks for the hair tip!" She walked to the elevator in the Ellison Building and took it to the ninth floor.

Up the corridor a State Police officer stood guard outside one of the rooms. A woman in a doctor's white coat came out of Room 14 with a man dressed in nursing scrubs. As Kate got closer she could hear the doctor say, "Poor guy is pretty beaten up. Pericardial effusion. Lucky we caught it in time. Who would do this to him?"

The nurse chimed in. "To anyone?"

When Kate neared Room 14, the statie on guard never turned

to look at her but simply thrust his chest out in warning at her approach.

"I'm sorry, Miss. No visitors allowed."

"But I'm family," she said.

"How are you related?"

"I'm his niece. Spence is my uncle. Uncle Spence."

"Immediate family only and they're all in there. Good night, Miss."

There was a knock on the door behind him. He took a military step aside as it swung open.

"Dr. Finn?" Madley slid sideways out the door between the two of them. "I couldn't help overhearing on the other side. To be clear, you're telling me that John Spencer is your uncle?"

She peeked through the crack of the door.

"Not you, Detective Madness, I mean Madley. I was telling this officer here."

She could see that Spence had all kinds of medical apparatus hooked up to his body. His eyes were closed and there were streaks of Greentini on his face that had not been fully washed off. She cocked her head at Madley.

"Not by blood, of course."

"I see." Madley was terse. "There is an investigation going on here and you need to leave."

"Why are you being this way? I just want to check on my father's friend."

"Go get some coffee." He dismissed the officer. "I'll watch the door for a bit."

When the officer left, Madley placed his hands on Kate's shoulders. "You need to stay away. This is not a joke. Stop mucking around in what's not your business. Go home."

She shook his hands off her shoulders. "I'm not going home till I get some answers."

"Keep it up and you'll be the one giving answers."

"What the hell are you talking about?"

"At the station. You're impeding an investigation. Now get out of here."

"Real mature, Detective. All this because I wouldn't go out with you."

"Don't flatter yourself so much, Doctor," he said. "You don't know what you're into."

"I'm trying to clear my father's name." Her voice reached a high pitch. "Find Sammy's real killer."

"Newsflash. Your father is the killer."

"Really?" She closed her fists. "Did you notice that Spence has been attacked, the same way Sammy was?"

"Back off, Doctor. Stay out of my way."

"Shh! Keep your voices down." A nurse from the nearby station admonished them.

Kate lowered her voice to a whisper. "Tell me this, will you? Did Spence have any chemicals on him? In his car?"

"Dream on, Doctor. You're barking up the wrong tree questioning me." He pulled his raincoat off and held it over his arms. "Off with you, now. So long. Adios. Be gone."

"I saw him when you opened the door." She saw him flinch. "I know what's going on."

The next morning Kate stormed into Colin's office. He was sitting with McGann.

"Well. This is abrupt." Colin slapped a folder to his desk. McGann retrieved it.

"I'll tell you what's abrupt. There is a man in the hospital named John Spencer. Heard of him? He's in the papers. He was attacked last night, most likely with a chemical, and rushed to the hospital. The case is under investigation."

"What in God's name are you talking about and what does this have to do with me?" Colin stood and motioned for her to sit.

"Thanks, but no." She walked over to the side of his desk and leaned against it.

McGann shook his head. "A regular time bomb."

"I'll handle this." He motioned for McGann to leave, and then sat back down.

Colin and Kate were alone in the office. "Just calm down and tell me what your problem is now."

"Well, it's like this, Colin. I believe it has to do with your henchman. Ed McGann." She picked up a folder from his desk and slapped it back down. "I suspect he's a pusher. Some of the fishermen at Fish Pier have been offered a chemical compound, Greentini, to mask bacteria so the fish pass FDA inspection. Everyone wins. A little more for them. A lot more for Greely Labs."

"Are you sane? You better watch your accusations. I don't know what you're talking about. I can assure you that Ed is beyond re-proach." He hesitated. "I'll discuss your um concerns with him."

"And then what?" She shook her finger in the air. "People are being threatened and attacked."

"Hey, why are you being so hostile? Don't you trust me? I went out on a limb to help your family."

"Did you? For my family or yours? What's going on here?"

"Now you're being paranoid."

"Am I?"

He threw up his hands in a mercy plea. "Just sit down so we can discuss this."

She acquiesced. Somehow, she didn't know why, he knew how to temper her wildness. They sat across from each other. By the time they finished talking she was almost convinced that he knew nothing and that he would get to the bottom of things. She agreed to calm down and trust the investigation to go forward. At least for the rest of the day.

On the Saturday, two weeks after Erica gave birth, she invited Kate to go shopping in Downtown Crossing. Rose needed a white bonnet for her christening day. They parked in the dimly lit garage under the Boston Common and walked up the urine-smelling stairs. No drunks or homeless inside the stairwell in the daytime; just their dried aromatic fluid shadowed the natural concrete.

"Don't touch anything." Kate covered Rose's mouth with the fleece baby blanket sticking out of the diaper bag.

Kate was grateful to get up above ground to the green space, where city workers were stringing festive colored lights onto the trees in anticipation of the holiday season. Across the Common, the gold dome of the State House sparkled in the pale, late fall sunlight. However, the homeless scattered themselves over the park in daylight, some on benches, others on the ground with most of their belongings in dark plastic garbage bags. Kate could never reconcile how a country like the United States could allow their people to live in this kind of impoverishment. Men and women broken and filthy from survival!

One rainy day at least ten years ago, while Kate was shopping with her mother for a dress for the high school science fair, they met a woman with the posture of the Hunchback of Notre Dame trying to cross Tremont Street. Because she couldn't lift her neck to see, she couldn't tell when it was safe to cross. Mom touched the woman's hand and asked if she needed help crossing. She accepted so Kate was instructed to hold the woman's other hand, which felt clammy but surprisingly soft. When they got across the street and Mom saw that the woman's shoelaces were untied, she reflexively bended on one knee to fix them like she did when Kate and Michael were little. Double knots? Kate remembered her mother asking the woman, who nodded. The laces were wet and reeked with the smell of pee. How could her mother stand the smell down there? But the woman was grateful and repeated her good blessings to them while she tried to give them two dollars in nickels and dimes toward a "nice lunch." At first Mom refused but then took two dimes and a nickel to allow the woman her dignity, as she later explained to Kate while they washed their hands in Macy's restroom

Kate snapped her attention back to the present. "Hungry yet?" Kate nodded to Sandwich Queen, a brick-rotunda outdoor cafe.

"Pass on that," Erica responded. "I can't get rid of the visual of what went on in there." She tickled her daughter's cheek. "Not that there's anything wrong with bathhouses turning into cafés."

"Well, those were the days when you could be arrested for being gay!" Kate felt a twinge of defensiveness for her brother.

"I get it. It wouldn't matter if they were heterosexual," Erica said.

"You're so Catholic."

"You can eat there. We won't stop you." Erica headed toward the café.

A female customer who looked to be in her thirties, dressed in jeans, knee-high charcoal-colored boots, and a brown fringed suede jacket, sat cross-legged at one of the outdoor bistro tables, drawing admiring looks from pedestrians.

"She's a spectacle," Erica said.

"Looks familiar," Kate said. "I've seen her before, but not really ever."

"I love when you're so clear. Definitive." Erica nuzzled Rose. "Auntie Kate says she knows the woman, but not quite. What is that?"

"It's called déjà vu. Do you need only facts, mommy dearest?"

"Ouch. Facts do move the conversation forward."

"Look. It's a drug deal." A boy in a hoodie had approached the attractive woman. The young man slid a white envelope across the table. She waited until the boy left and started walking toward them.

"Oh my God." Kate turned back to the garage entrance.

"Where are you going?" Erica yelled. Rose started to cry and attract attention.

Kate motioned to Erica to follow her.

"That's Rhonda. She's the lobsterwoman I've been working with."

"You didn't say she looked like a Brazilian model."

"She's pretty but she doesn't look like that on her boat."

"We should get some of the drugs she just bought, if they make us look like her." Erica soothed Rose and she stopped wailing. "Look. She's gone. Let's just go shopping."

Downtown Crossing bustled with throngs of Saturday shoppers. They walked over to Jack 'n' Jill Nursery Shop in the middle of the theater district, close to Chinatown. Jack 'n' Jill teemed with strollers coming at them from every corner of the shop. Kate's patience wore thin from dodging aggressive parents who used their strollers as an excuse to push through crowds. She believed they were sadists with improper credentials to operate.

Erica picked through the bonnets, asking Kate whether she should choose this one or that one. Kate thought they all looked the same and nodded each time Erica put one on Rose's head. Thoroughly bored with bonnet buying, Kate gawked out the shop's window. Diagonally across the street was Colleen Couture. She could see Colleen through the front window, leaning over at her sewing machine. Her head moved back and forth like Kate's mother's did when she pushed fabric through the machine. The traffic jammed and cleared as the matinee performance was starting at the Opera House. Kate spotted Rhonda walking in the opposite direction of a large crowd and then entering Colleen Couture.

"How about this one?" asked Erica.

"Great. Go for it."

"You didn't even look at it."

"They're all great. Can't go wrong."

"Right! A Bruins cap is a good choice for Rose's entry into the Catholic Church." Erica threw the cap down onto the display counter. "Typical atheist's comment." She nuzzled Rose's nose. "No hockey head for my baby girl."

"Agnostic." Kate corrected. She lost her vantage point on Colleen Couture due to a stalled tourist-filled duck boat. "Look it up in the dictionary. They're different."

"Whatever. One of those A's that lets you forget how you were brought up. I should've taken your Mom shopping instead of you. What's so intriguing out that window?"

Kate turned her attention back outside. The duck boat blocked her view for a bit until the traffic cleared and Kate was able to resume watch. She saw Rhonda leave the shop, heading away from Jack 'n' Jill, but Colleen wasn't at her sewing machine anymore.

After a few moments Colleen came from the back of the shop, slouched down at her machine, and then disappeared as if she had fallen to the floor.

"Wait here for a minute." Kate whipped open the shop's door, which was painted with a mural of Jack and Jill climbing up the hill.

She forced herself to stroll, not run, down the sidewalk to get a better view. She crossed the street, twice avoiding being hit by a yellow cab.

She knocked on the front door. No reply. Then she jiggled the front door, but it was locked. She heard moaning from inside and slid down the alley alongside the shop to the back entrance. The door was unlocked.

"Colleen? Colleen." The moaning was getting softer. "Colleen, are you here?"

"Right . . . here."

She was on the floor, propped up against her sewing machine. Her face was flushed, and a needle hung out of her arm.

Kate called 911.

She pulled the needle out of Colleen's arm and slapped her face to keep her awake. Colleen came to for a second. "You're nice. So pretty."

"Yeah. But you're gorgeous. Come on. Wake up. Stay alive."

"Too tired. Want to sleep." Her chin dropped to her chest.

"No. Don't nod off." Kate shook her. "Stay awake. Damn it."

Colleen's head seesawed back and forth. Kate grabbed it and held it straight. Colleen threw up. The stream missed Kate's face, but splattered on her hands and shirt.

Kate gagged.

"Good. Good. Get it out of you." She rubbed Colleen's back. "Don't worry. Help is coming. They'll be here in a second." She could hear the ambulance in the distance. "You're going to be fine. You'll be good."

"I told her I only wanted a little." She held her thumb and forefinger together in a measured action. "Just a little occasionally to help me work. Helps my creativity. Just once a day. I'm not a junkie or anything." She tipped her head to the right and stared into space.

"They cut it with something bad." Tears streamed down her cheeks.

"I know. I know." She smoothed Colleen's hair. "Who's she?"

"Rhonda." Colleen's voice was raspy and sick-sounding. "She's my friend. She takes care of me." She grunted something inaudible, followed by a demonic scream.

Kate grabbed Colleen's puke-stained blouse and shook her hard. A kaleidoscope of red and blue lights surrounded the store. Kate pulled her up by the sides of her blouse.

Colleen flopped. She ran to open the locked front door.

Two Boston policemen and two male EMTs rushed in. Kate pointed at the needle on the floor next to Colleen. Her breathing had faded. One EMT administered naloxone nasally. The other hooked Colleen to an IV. Her eyes rolled backwards; she was seizing. He opened the IV all the way and rushed her out of the shop on a stretcher.

One of the police officers approached Kate, who was sitting on the floor. "I'm Officer Young. I must say, you handled this beautifully. You saved her life."

"We saved her life." She smiled weakly at him.

He kneeled next to her. "I'll need a statement."

Young took her statement and contact information. Kate told him she worked for Colleen's son, Colin Greely, and gave him Colin's cell phone number. Then the officer was kind, he even offered her a ride home. Before she could respond, Madley ran into the store flashing his badge.

"Detective Madley, MDP. Well, well, well. I should've known you'd be here."

Kate stared up at him. "Shit, Madley, do you ever sleep?"

"MDP?" Officer Young scoffed. "You're out of your neighborhood."

"I was in the nearby and thought I'd stop over. Must keep up with my number one crime scene witness. What's your story this time? You sleep on fabric bolts at the seamstress shop?"

"You're hilarious." She stood up and shook his hand, knowing hers reeked of vomit.

"Don't you smell fresh."

She explained the sequence of events. No fear. No sarcasm. Straight facts.

"This is a wonderful story, Dr. Finn." He winked at her.

He paced, taking sharp corners like a Nazi officer. "Why did you break in?"

"Come again?"

"Did you supply the heroin?" he asked.

"What are you talking about? You and your friend are the druggies. Remember Fourth of July? On your friend's boat?"

Her comment raised eyebrows from the two officers. Officer Young glared at Madley. "It's time for you to be on your way, Detective."

Erica arrived at the door with Rose. "Rich. Is everything okay?"

"Erica. Fine. Yeah. Things here are just fine." He walked over to Erica and Rose. "Isn't she a sweet one?" He tickled Rose's chin. Rose whimpered at his touch.

Erica pulled her away from him and looked at Kate. "What's going on here? Your shirt. It's disgusting."

Madley turned his nose up and nodded in agreement.

"We have to get her home so she can clean up," Erica said.

The officer who had taken Kate's statement handed his notes to Madley, who scanned them. "Standard OD, Detective. The victim was lucky Ms. Finn found her."

"Dr. Finn." Madley corrected him. He read the notes and nodded. "Okay. We're all set here. We'll be in touch. Go on. Get going with your friends."

Kate filled Erica in on the way back to the car. Her voice trembled. "I'm going to have to call Colin and tell him what happened."

Erica was quiet until they walked through the Common. "Will would kill me if I he knew I told you this, but you know how before we were married and took over the bar, I wondered if Will's father had to pay off people to do business? He dabbled a little in some harmless illegal gambling and some other stuff. Will's not like his Dad, but technically we don't own Dingles."

Kate nodded and watched Erica hold Rose tightly against her chest as if to protect her from what she was about to say. "Madley is one of the people who collect from Dingles. When he first came around, I didn't realize what was happening."

"You people wanted me to date that jerk."

"He seemed like a nice guy, at first."

"Hmmm. No."

"Lately, he's been coming around a lot more. High most of the time—all glassy-eyed and fast-talking. He's getting pushy. I heard him threaten Will that if he didn't give him what he wanted, he'd get us shut down."

"He can't do that. He's just a skeley. Well, really, just an ass."

Erica covered Rose's ears. "Language."

Kate apologized.

"When I brought it up to Will, he said not to worry, he'd handle Madley. I'm scared, Kate. He seems like he has a violent streak."

"Everything will be okay. You'll see."

Kate tried to hug her friend and her baby, but Erica pushed her away.

"Not till you shower, puke girl." Erica swung her shopping bag back and forth with one hand and cradled Rose's head with the other while she mimicked Kate. "Quick walk. Claustrophobic in the store. Thanks to your little stroll, Rose has seen her first OD." She readjusted Rose on her shoulder and rocked her. "We need to leave these streets behind us." Kate understood what Erica was saying. She was like a bear with her cub protecting Rose.

Chapter Nineteen

Doug was gowning up when Kate entered the clean area. There was that dirty shoe smell. The poor guy had the brain of a champion and the feet of a homeless man.

"Colin asked me to help you with your work today. He said you've been struggling to get results."

"I have?" She hopped into her clean suit.

"I'm happy to provide you with my expertise for free."

"Still a funny guy, I see. All right. If you must. You can help me populate the fake seas with fake fish." She held the door open for him. "After you, doctor."

"Do you think I'm a primate?" He shook his head. "Lady doctors first." He swung his hand like an orchestra conductor for her to enter.

They approached the groundfish tanks. She instructed him on how to genetically manipulate the haddock and cod.

"I injected these mothers more than two months ago. Look at their offspring. They are not thriving. Even the mothers look weak."

The fish were settled mid-tank, moving slowly. "They're depressed."

"Wouldn't you be?" Doug asked. "Think about it. This is not their natural habitat. They're immigrants. It's generative. The newcomers are filled with transitional stress and homeland vulnerabilities. The second generation adapts more—becoming a bit stronger. And the third? Well that's when the hook is in. No pun intended."

"Doug. That's so obvious. It's genius."

"It's what I am." He pretended to walk on a balance beam, preening, hands out, almost tripping on the turn back.

"Such talent."

"Yeah. Well, science wasn't always my gig."

"Clearly gymnastics wasn't either. But who am I to talk?" She slapped her forehead. "How could I have missed separating the babies? It was glaring at me."

"You have been busy." He winked at her.

"If I can separate the babies into other tanks they'll have a chance to create new communities. Maybe further disease will be isolated and the species will be improved."

"You'll need a bigger boat." Doug spoke wryly. "Get your credit card. We're going shopping."

It took two hours of online research and two Sno Balls each to select the incubators for the babies.

"This calls for dinner." He raised his right eyebrow. "Man cannot survive on Hostess Sno Balls alone."

"It's only four o'clock," she protested.

"What can I say? My stomach thinks I'm a senior citizen."

"Let's do it. Gentleman's choice."

"Fish Shells," he said.

"At Fish Pier?"

"At the Prudential Building. Where the hell else is Fish Shells? You know, it's not a chain."

"Got it." She looked at her watch. "Okay, maybe I could even catch Rob on my father's boat and say hello."

A cold December darkness set in as they walked along Northern Avenue toward Fish Pier.

"Colin wasn't at work," Doug said.

"No?"

Smoky breath floated in front of them when they spoke.

"Did you hear his mom's in the hospital?"

"Uh huh."

"It was in the Metro section of the paper. The guys in shipping and receiving showed it to me. They found her OD'd. Paper didn't say her name, just that a woman was found unconscious at Colleen Couture."

"You guys are gossips."

"She's a seamstress? They say she used to be an exotic dancer." He feigned a pirouette pole dance pose. "Some of the older guys used to go see her."

She could tell he was angling. "It's no secret around here that she was a stripper." She decided to crack the door a bit. "I was the one who found her on Saturday. I was shopping with my friend across the street and saw it happen through her shop window. I called 911."

He shook his head. "That should be good for an immediate

bonus."

"Avarice." She swung her purple hobo bag, and it hit him on the rear end.

"That felt good. I knew you had a thing for me."

"You're kidding, right?" Just the thought of Doug's feet made her gag. She was glad to be outdoors and not in close quarters with him. She knew that if he cleaned up he could be endearing to those who were attracted to his fragile, geeky quality, but not Kate, who liked men who were more rugged and didn't look like they had gluten allergies. Still, Doug was good company. "You're an all-around cool guy."

"But?"

"But. I'm not into anything serious here."

"Colin?"

"What's that supposed to mean?"

"I overheard Norah talking about how you two were spending private time together."

Infuriated, she tried to stay cool. She slowed down and swung her bag evenly back and forth as they neared the Fish Pier. "Doug, have you considered seeing a doctor about your foot problem?"

His face dropped.

"Because bromhidrosis is easily treatable."

"Is it that noticeable?" he asked.

"I don't think I've heard anyone discuss it behind your back. But if I did, I'd probably tell them they were sniffing for something that wasn't there."

"Sorry. I guess I thought I had to try with you. You're pretty."

"Well. Thank you. That's flattering."

"In a Celtic way."

"What the hell is a Celtic way?" she asked.

"You know. Long red hair. Freckles. Kind of short. The works."

"Wow. A complete dissection."

He cracked his knuckles. "To tell you the truth, you're not really my type either."

"Now you're rejecting me? Let's just get some dinner and call it a night, if we can actually get to six o'clock, that is."

The salt and fish aromas from the pier pervaded the air. Truelight sat beside the pier, slapping with the harbor waves. Rob was on the boat hosing her down.

"Why don't you go inside and grab us a table? I want to say hi to Rob."

"How was his catch?" Doug asked when Kate sat down.

"Not bad. Not bad. Quote, unquote. Nice table, Dougie."

"Call me Dougie again and you'll end up in that dumpster." He pointed to a dumpster halfway into one of the building's open bays next to Rob's truck.

They drank two beers each before their food was served.

"Have you ever come to the auction here?" Kate asked.

"No. You?" He had tartar sauce dripping from the sides of his lips.

She wiped her mouth with her napkin in the hope that he would follow her lead but he didn't get the hint. "I grew up here. Practically lived here."

"That's right. Your father."

"It's different now. A lot of it's inside and more techie. But the daily fish auction is still sacred. It's a festival. A feast straight from the sea. You have to go. See the real people. Get here early for the best stuff, daybreak. Folklore is lumpers used to pull the fish right off the boats and weigh it in the scale house."

"Too early for me. I like my beauty rest." He moved his tongue outside the edges of his lips, licking the excess, and to Kate's relief he finally wiped his mouth.

"Who vetted you? Do you even like being around fish?"

"I like eating them. Hey, look how this place started at the turn of the twentieth as a lunch diner for fishermen." He paraphrased from the menu.

"Good stuff." Kate gave Doug a thumbs-up.

Kate looked out the window. The sky had settled into darkness. She saw Rob heading toward his truck and noticed a Mercedes parked next to it in front of the dumpster. She could make out the shadow of a man in a long, dark coat, collar pulled up around his ears, get out of the Mercedes. He approached Rob, who tried to push past him, but the man pushed him up against his truck and held a gun at his head.

"I got to go."

"Where? What did I say wrong? Was it the auction? Okay. Okay. I'll go to the auction. But will you excuse me for a sec? I need to see a man about a fish head." Doug got up and walked to the bathroom.

Kate ran outside.

His voice was demonic, "You will work with us, or you'll end up dead like your friend."

Kate stared in terror.

"Get out of here," Rob screamed over to Kate. "He's insane."

Madley wore black driving gloves and held a gun against Rob's head with one hand, and a container of Greentini in his other, ready to pour the contents on his victim's fear-distorted face. Evidently he reconsidered, because he dropped the container and with his gun directed Rob into the driver's seat of his truck where he pistol whipped him unconscious. He threw the container into the truck, shut the door, then turned to confront Kate, who stood paralyzed.

"Did you come to save your father's lumper?"

She instinctively moved toward Rob to help him but Madley intercepted her and with overpowering force pushed her into his car and locked the door. He tapped the window with his pistol, ran in front of the car and jumped into the driver's seat. Inside the car he reached into his coat pocket and retrieved a vial of white powder and a tiny stainless-steel spoon and snorted.

"Now you're a crackhead?" Kate was shaking.

"Just good old-fashioned coke." He swung his head back in delight. "Job perk. I confiscate and recycle." He measured another spoonful and held it under her nose.

She pulled her head away.

He leaned over and pointed his pistol at her face. "You know what I'm tired of?" His voice was sticky syrup.

She shook her head.

"You. You are a royal nuisance. I'm taking care of it tonight." He sped toward the end of Fish Pier while he sporadically jammed on the brakes. "Heard you're not much of a swimmer; terrified of the water is what I've heard. Yes, siree." He inched the car closer to the water's edge.

Kate was petrified but somehow found her voice. "Not afraid. I just don't like it."

"Right." He snickered at her. "Give me your phone."

She handed her phone over.

Dangling the pistol against the steering wheel with his left hand he took the phone with his right and slammed it against the dashboard and threw it out the window. Then he swung the wheel hard, turned the car around and headed off the pier into the street. "And we'll have a nice quiet ride with no interruptions."

Kate got up the nerve to talk. She'd once read that confronting rapists could distract them and make them stop. She hoped it would work on corrupt skeleys, too.

"Nice car on a skeley salary. Where's your codfish Camry?"

"You think you're so cute. But you got no respect. No boundaries."

"Where are we going?"

"Don't worry. You'll like it there. We have some work for you."

"I'm not doing anything for you."

"Yeah. You will."

"Kidnapping is a federal offense." She was reaching.

"Your word against mine? Ha. Yes, Judge, she was found at the scene the other day sharing a needle with the victim of an overdose and now this. Tried to get her to a safe house but she ran. Heroin. Such a tragic addiction."

"You son of a bitch. I helped Colleen. I've never touched that poison in my life."

"Pity. What was it our friend Pierre said on your morning after? 'Sometimes circumstances are not always what they appear to be.'"

"Our friend?"

They drove through the Callahan Tunnel and took a hard right into East Boston.

He turned onto a rutty, potholed road that led to a large warehouse. A giant dented metal sign on the warehouse read "AgaCulture Traders, LLC." On the side of the building, a few distressed-looking AgaCulture trucks lined the gravel in front of a damaged chain-link fence that dangled from its posts. From the outside, it was not Greely Labs.

He stopped the car, shuffled her into the building, pistol at her back. Inside, Kate heard the familiar symphony of water. While the warehouse was filled with tanks of seafood, it was crude, dirty, and run-down. Workers were not garbed like Greely Labs employees; they were dressed in street clothes and they were all—approximately thirty of them—as far as she could tell, Chinese men.

"Look familiar?" Madley asked.

"Not so much. The place is a pit." She squirmed in discomfort. She tried to hold her breath to stifle the smell of fish carcasses. Not the same smells she was impervious to on her docks.

"I thought rotting fish was your favorite smell." He sniffed her hair. "You got all shiny over at Greely. What happened to the rugged individual I met at Fish Pier so many months ago?"

They passed a tub of fish blood.

"Your friend Sammy never minded the smell. Said it was like the old days. Poor ole boy. He was trying to play us against Greely's buyers to get more bang for his buck, as they say. True story. Sad ending."

"You killed him."

"Me? Be serious."

"Oh. I'm serious."

"You have an imagination, don't you?"

"Did I imagine you trying to kill Rob?"

"A mere warning."

"You bastard. You set my father up. Made me sweat the morning of Sammy's murder. You were gathering evidence in my office for yourself." She thought back to the morning of the murder when Pop's shed door had been tampered with. "It was you. You planted Greentini in our shed." She recalled how her father had blamed the neighborhood kids for messing with the shed door after he had Fort Knoxed it.

"Prove it."

"You're a bad skeley."

"Detective. But to your point, Bostonians don't mind a little crooked from the MDP if it keeps the docks safe. What they hate is the Greely rich. Guys from the neighborhood that make it and flaunt it. Poor Greely. That junkie mother of his will keep him tied up for days." He patted her head. "I don't think he'll be coming for you." He pinched her cheek. "What's Greentini?"

Their eyes met in cold competition.

"You're not even from the neighborhood, are you?"

He whipped his thick dark hair out of his eyes. "Sorry, babe. Cantabrigian. The Port. Where all sweet candy's made." He pulled a roll of Necco Wafers from his pants pocket and rested a wafer on his tongue. "An American classic, dats what I yam."

Kate looked at him in disgust.

"So much for small talk." He yelled to an adjacent glass-windowed office, "Bo."

Unlike the laborers whose clothes were quite tattered—ragged even—Bo was dressed impeccably, as he and Michael had been at Dingles. He meandered over, adjusting his hip belt, which sported his pistol.

"Bo, keep our scientist here in your crosshairs."

"Bo, you're involved in all this?" Kate was incredulous.

Bo seemed agitated but just shrugged. Obtuse. Not the same sensitive poet she'd met at Dingles.

Madley answered for him. "Bo is instrumental to our team." He pulled a glass vial with a red lid out of his pocket and threw it to Bo, who caught the vial midair. Kate saw a sense of relief come over his face. He turned his back and she could hear him snorting.

"You have him jacked up on drugs? Nice."

"Don't worry about Bo. He's a champ. Good stuff, right, guy? Ah, the perks of this job."

Bo turned, his eyes glistening like he had rocketed off the planet. He gave Madley the thumbs-up.

Madley let go of Kate and pushed her forward. "Rumor has it you've done some valuable in-field testing with local lobster. We're trying to ship more lobster and shellfish overseas."

She caught her balance and composed herself. "Let them eat rock lobster."

"The free world loves New England lobster and Chinese adore Seattle geoduck. God those things are vulgar. You eat geoducks, Bo?"

Bo avoided eye contact with Kate. "A delicacy for my people."

Kate shook the stiffness out of her hands and ankles and wondered what kind of people she was dealing with. Bo had been so gentle when they were together with Michael. A poet. Tonight he was packing again and snorting coke. Her dead friend Melissa, a born pacifist, used to get edgy when she wasn't high. One time she held a knife to her brother's throat until he handed over her stash. Drugs plus weapons surely equaled a bad ending. Kate scanned the warehouse. Over to her right, there was a frosted glass door to what she thought was probably an office area.

She turned toward Bo. Maybe she could reason with him. "So, Bo Ming, here you are."

"One and only." He exuded a haughty arrogance. Bo lifted his gun and softly rubbed it under her chin. "Your brother is much better-looking. Too bad he was so dull."

She tilted her head and smiled. "Michael's judgement was off for a minute."

"Funny." He dug the gun deep into her chin. "Nobody cares about a dead scientist."

She backed up and bumped against Madley. Turning to face him, she said, "You really should send Bo to etiquette classes. This work has turned him."

Bo yelled at her. "Not an American wannabe!"

Madley chimed in. "It's okay, Bo. We like you just how you are. She's just cranky that she never really made anything of herself." He looked at Kate. "Let's get going."

He led her to some heaters that looked to be the same as the ones she and Rhonda had planted in the harbor lobster traps. He picked up two and they walked over to the lobster tanks with them. Traps were on the floor stacked next to the tanks. Madley took a laptop out of the cabinet and logged on while they stood face-to-face. "Give me your user name and password to your e-mail at Greely Labs."

"Why?"

"Because I told you to."

She recited her login information and he accessed her e-mail account.

"Give me your boss's e-mail address," he commanded.

She complied.

"Hmm. Reason you won't be at work?" He typed:

Colin,

I've been experiencing some health issues. Woman stuff. Due to a cancellation, I was able to schedule a procedure for tomorrow but I'll need to be out of work over the next week.

Thank you for understanding.

Kate

"How's that?"

"Woman stuff?" She rolled her eyes.

He hit send, disabled the internet access, and handed her the laptop. "Think of this time as an internship."

"Internships are for stupid rich kids." She grabbed the laptop from him.

"Rough! Then again, your father is a murderer."

Kate leapt at him but he grabbed her wrists to restrain her and sat her in a nearby chair.

"Now that you're settled, open the program called Siren. There's data there from our experiments. You need to compare these results to the results you get tonight. Next step, put the lobsters in traps, add the heaters, and sink them. Gloves and utensils, in the cabinet." He pointed at a gray metal storage cabinet. "You'll document time, temperature and response for two hours."

"So now you're a scientist?"

"Forensics taught me a thing or two. Lots of money to be made here. Don't screw it up. My man, Bo, will be watching."

In front of the lobster tank, Bo had set up a makeshift lookout consisting of a six-foot banquet table and an office chair. On the table was his cell phone and pistol. Kate had made a conscious choice to know as little about firearms as possible; what she did know was that she had seen Bo load his gun and pull down a latch which she assumed was the safety. She'd learned this from TV crime dramas. "The safety slipped" or "He thought the safety was on," but of course the safety wasn't on and the character was dead.

She had the sudden urge to use the ladies' room.

"Bo. I need to use the bathroom."

He waved his gun. "C'mon. I'll show you."

The bathroom consisted of a toilet with dark copper water stains running down the inside of the bowl and a matching sink with its own graphic designs of filth. The floor was wet, not mopped in months. Toilet paper was strewn on the wet floor. What was left of a clean roll sat on the floor next to the toilet.

"Only the finest," she said.

"Yeah. We keep guests in stylin'."

"Styling. Bo. It's styling."

"I said that."

"No, Bo. You said 'in stylin'."

He cocked his head at her and pointed his gun into the bathroom.

She fumbled around in the bathroom, touching as little as possible. The smells of the warehouse and bathroom made her dry-heave. She surveyed the bathroom for any kind of an escape. A tile in the ceiling, a hole in the floor, a window. There was no exit. Her body trembled. Vertigo set in. A feeling of nausea arose and again she dry-heaved. After a few moments, she pulled herself together and made a vow to herself to stay hyper-vigilant so she could get herself out of this nightmare, and soon.

Bo banged on the door.

"Hurry up, Princess. You have work."

"Almost done."

For the first time since grammar school, Kate blessed herself and said a silent prayer.

God, I know I haven't been your best fan for a long time, not even sure if you exist. If you do I could use some intercession. Please, just get me out of here?

Another bang on the door. "Let's go, sister."

She opened the door. "Give a woman some space, will you?"

"You complain too much."

Whether it was the prayer or her confidence that she could whip through the work and maybe they would release her, Kate felt stronger.

"Can I go home tonight?"

"Sounds like no." He was still playing with his gun.

"Phallic syndrome?"

He lunged toward her and retreated.

She shrunk in fear worried that he was psychotic from coke withdrawal.

Kate ignored him as much as possible and focused on work to deny her reality. She put lobsters in the tanks and analyzed the data from their files. From time to time she'd look up and notice workers walking back and forth out of the frosted glass office door and around the plant. And then she saw Madley and Pierre walking together. How bizarre! No wonder Madley referred to Pierre as our friend.

When had they colluded? Maybe the whole time. She thought back to dinner at the Pour Over House and their banter. And the morning on Fish Pier after she and Pierre had slept in her office. Madley had toyed with him good, except she was the one who had been played.

Tonight, Madley's posture looked rigid and intense as Pierre seemed to be admonishing him. She wondered if Madley was in trouble for kidnapping her. But in trouble from whom? Pierre? But then Madley patted Pierre on the back, clearly a reassuring gesture. Pierre turned to look at Kate, shrugged his shoulders and appeared to loosen up. Madley laughed and motioned like he was air-snorting coke and Pierre nodded in apparent acceptance. Another coke-head? Haley had confided in Kate how edgy Pierre had been. The two men disappeared into the office.

It felt like hours before she saw the two men leave AgaCulture together, laughing and heckling each other but neither one ever looking toward her. It felt like several more hours when Bo yelled over from his guard table.

"Clean up for the night, Princess. I'll show you your room."

Kate cleaned the lobster tongs, tore off the gloves, and washed her hands in the sink. She looked over at Bo, who received a brown paper bag from one of the workers.

Bo motioned Kate to his satellite office, where he'd laid out a ham and cheese submarine sandwich with chips and a Coke. It was one o'clock, six hours since she had last eaten. She wolfed down the sub. Since she'd been running on adrenalin, she hadn't realized how famished she was. Later, Bo led her into the back of the building where there was an expansive display of large three-level wooden storage racks serving as bunk beds for workers who were crammed together and still dressed in their work clothes. Each level appeared to house four to five workers and each worker had their own blanket. They watched her as Bo led her to a small windowless room beyond their quarters. One of the men blinked his kind eyes slowly at her as she walked by; this gave Kate inexplicable hope so she returned his gesture, which quelled her fear for a moment before it resumed with more intensity. She was feeling claustrophobic.

"I like how you treat your workers," she said.

"My uncle's better to our people than your Uncle Sam. Better than your people sleeping in the street. No blankets, no food, no work."

He struck a nerve. She thought of all those who slept on park benches and under bridges. An image of the smelly bag lady she and Mom had helped cross the street flashed through her mind. She couldn't find the words to challenge him anymore. He led her into her quarters. A whirlpool of chilly air accosted her. She fought back tears. It was rough, with a sense of evil pervading it. Surely no MilPort Hotel. About a five-by-eight space with a mattress slung carelessly on the floor, a pillow and two military-style wool blankets strewn across it. Bo pointed to a black plastic garbage bag against the wall.

"We got you necessities. You can take a shower tomorrow. Sleep tight, Princess." And with that he closed the door. A padlock clicked and locked, and footsteps faded away.

Inside the plastic bag she found all-new articles: one pair of black sweatpants, a white long-sleeved tee, two pairs of white socks, a pair of size 12 jeans, which she decided must have been bought by a man who hadn't seen her. She'd have to peg them. Also in her bounty was Right Guard deodorant—so manly—and a box of thirty tampons—how thoughtful of them. Although, a box of ten might indicate an early release.

After she changed into the sweats and tee, she lay on the bed thinking about the day. Surreal! How did she get here? Little good her prayer did. God or whatever that force was had rung void years ago when she prayed to him during hard times. Instead, she'd found solace in her fantasy angelfish with soft green wings and purple eyes, floating above the sewer steam heading down to Newbury Street to shop. The vision of her childhood imaginary creatures comforted her as she stared up at the one bare light bulb on the ceiling and pretended that the scratching and squeaking she heard was not rats.

Chapter Twenty

Morning came with a harsh bang on her door and a loud, "Shine and rise, time to go fishing."

She yelled back, "You mean rise and shine. Hey, virtuoso, how about that shower you promised?"

"Shine and rise flows better. You'll shower tonight. You got a lot catching up."

Bo unlocked the door. "Good sleep?"

"Yeah. Princess and the Pea style."

"Back to your lobster trap," he said.

"Bo's witty. Comedian and poet." But she wasn't laughing. Fraught. These guys intended to kill her.

"Continental dining just for you." A McDonald's breakfast sat on Bo's table: Coffee, juice, and an egg sandwich.

My new dining room, she thought. Kate finished her breakfast.

"Before you start your work, the head office wants to speak with you."

Bo led her over to the office. The facility was in full swing with

stations downstairs and more upstairs. Each station had four workers; two netted product out of the tanks and the other two loaded
it into Styrofoam coolers. In total there looked to be about forty
laborers across the plant. Inside the office there were three desks
and a door to an interior office. In the outer office, Pierre and
Madley were seated on their desks, chatting with each other. A large
canary-yellow pocketbook sat on top of the third desk. The frosted
glass door to the interior office was closed but she could see what
looked like figures of a man and a woman and hear a soft drone of
conversation.

Pierre spoke first.

"You're looking good this morning."

"How wonderful to see you." She shook his hand. "I saw Haley.
She's good. Very good. Must have been marriage holding her down."

"Yeah? Not biting," he said.

"We talked about that awful night I spent with you. She thanked
me for it. One less night she'd have to spend with you."

"Still caustic as ever. Good luck with that." But Kate saw Pierre
cringe, which gave her a drop of satisfaction.

"So, you boys were already partners the morning after Pierre
crashed over?"

"What do you think, Red?" Madley asked. "Did you move your
cot to Greely's?"

"The location of my cot is none of your business."

"Got her Irish up," Madley taunted.

The men laughed.

Kate knew she might be exacerbating her situation with Pierre,

Madley, and Bo, but she long ago recognized that she was a lot like her father, who ran off at the mouth when threatened. It was a form of self-defense, bordering on self-destruction. Before she could formulate a clever response to Pierre and Madley, the inner office door opened.

"Welcome, Kate." Rhonda motioned for her to come in.

Kate shook her head, trying to hold her ground.

"Please. Close the door." It wasn't a request.

Kate entered the office and closed the door behind her. A distinguished-looking Chinese man in a tailored black suit sat behind a large mahogany desk. The same man who showed up at Dingles when Kate had met Bo. Bo's uncle. He wore square navy-blue-framed glasses and smiled at Kate.

"Hello, Kate. I'm Li Ming." His voice was refined.

"I know who you are." Kate looked around the room, trying to avoid eye contact with either Ming or Rhonda. "Quite a venture you're running here." She sucked her right cheek in and chewed on it.

He opened his arms in gesture of abundance. "You like?"

"The place is a pit." She finally looked at Rhonda. "I thought you were at least halfway decent."

"Harsh and in front of Mister Ming."

"Mister MYOB, the kind of friend you keep to yourself?"

"Mister Ming is a good money guy. Trusts me with operations. He's into lobsterwomen." She crossed her legs.

"Nice boots. Is it your branding?"

Rhonda played with the buckle on the side of her black leather boots. "Irish knit sweaters. What's the story with those sweaters? Each family had their own drop stitch so when someone died at sea, they could trace them? Don't worry. We'll spare your family—burn you."

"You were the one who pirated our traps."

"Mister Ming's traps." She smiled at him. "That's the problem with you, Kate. You get ahead of yourself."

"Poser! You made it sound like you were the last of the great breed."

"You're so blind. I could've told you anything and you would have lapped it up. You kept getting in the way. I told you to get lost, but you were a rodent. Kept coming back till extermination day."

"You cut the traps to make it look like you were a victim? The guys at Cardinal Medeiros said you were a lightweight. Nothing but a part-timer. A hobbyist."

"I don't give a crap what they say. Do you know how hard it is to be a woman in this business? I got sick of hustling years ago. Why should all you nerds have the glory?"

"Share the glory, I say," Kate said.

"Girls." Mr. Ming pointed his finger at them. "We have work to do. No fighting."

"One more question," Kate said.

Ming nodded.

"Where did the Greentini come from?"

At first, he stared at her without expression. "Greentini? Ah. I get it. The cocktail. Greentini." He held his belly. "So funny."

"I'm often hilarious," Kate said. "I saw McGann give it to the guys at Fish Pier. How did you get it from him?"

"My recipe." Ming pounded his chest. "I was a chemist back in my country. Chinese look for reasons not to import American seafood. They say there's too much bacteria. You Americans are at their mercy—risk losing their market like you lost the beef trade for a bit. I found, let's say, an alternative avenue to ship our seafood masked with, as you call it, Greentini. I get everything through the channels. Import, export." His cynical, high-pitched laugh caught Kate off guard.

"That's a hoot, considering your country grows fish in feces," Kate said.

Ming shook his head. "Boston. Hub of parochialism. Little do you know, my country is the entire international market. Not Chinese. Not American. My chem solution masks many sins. With my plan, we'll take over your entire New England area, and beyond and beyond and beyond." At each "beyond" he pointed his finger at the oceans and seas map on the wall. Kate noticed it was drawn with the same fine hand as the map Rhonda drew for her own boat.

Kate sensed a certain madness about Ming and at the same time realized his genius. "Have you seen Greely Labs?" Kate asked. "State of the art."

"Too much overhead. Labor here is practically free. But we take care of our people. House them and feed them." He straightened papers on his desk. "Send some money back to their families. Two shifts, twelve hours each. Greely and the like can't compete with this kind of human force. Even with their robotic equipment."

"How did Sammy and Spence end up with your recipe?" Kate

asked.

Ming rolled his eyes. "The fisherman. A fickle sort. He's in. He's out. He wants money. Suddenly his conscience won't allow it. Dangerous. Can't afford such inconsistencies while we ramp up."

"How did Sammy get involved?"

"Got it from Pierre. Pierre's worked for AgaCulture all along. He handed my juice out to a few local guys like Sammy. Dolts. At first, they were pouring it on like ketchup. You Americans always overdoing. Less is more. That way there's no trace. No buildup on the fish."

Kate was already aware that her equipment could not have deciphered the solution on Sammy's catch, and now she was slightly relieved to hear that there was no way she could have seen the Greentini on the surface of the fish while working at the FDA.

"We wanted to see if it passed your FDA tests. Clearly it did." Ming took a long breath. "But then McGann wanted in. Pierre said he hung around everywhere. Wanted to know all about Rhonda, too. Creepy guy. Like a stalker."

Kate couldn't argue that point. She remembered that McGann had sent her to Cardinal Medeiros and told her to talk to Rhonda but not to mention his name. What was his deal, anyhow? If she didn't make it out in one piece, she'd never find out. She decided to ask the real question. The one that had nagged her all along.

"What did you add to the ammonium perchlorate to turn it green?"

Ming looked at Kate for a long time before he answered. "My dear, a truly successful business has one primary trade secret, which the enterprise will never reveal."

He collected his laptop off his desk and put it in his briefcase.

"Now I need to get home. Ling and I are off to Zurich tonight." He pulled Rhonda to him, patted her behind, kissed her hard on the lips, and walked out.

Rhonda gently bowed and placed her hands in a formal martial arts salute after Ming left.

"A bit of a dramatist?" Kate quipped.

Rhonda sneered at her. Kate had once read that there was a light around decent people, an aura of energy. Today Rhonda had no light; the layers around her were concentrically dense. She bred bottomless darkness.

"Good family man." Kate coughed. "Ling? His wife?"

"Ling's lovely. We've become friends."

"I bet. What about your friend Colleen Greely? Or were you just her connection?"

"Shame about Colleen."

"That's how you treat friends?" Kate asked.

Rhonda kicked the desk. "You're one to talk. I am a friend to Colleen. Her son barely gives her the time of day. She just needs a little mother's helper, once in a while."

"Once a day is more like it."

"Eh." She opened the palms of her hands. "Some people drink coffee. Whatever."

"What do you want from me? You got this. Release me."

"You heard Mister Ming. Your kind is dangerous snooping around."

"What's the worry?" Kate asked. "Like you said, there's no story here."

"Yes. But like stories, everyone comes to an end at some point," Rhonda said.

Kate stared at Rhonda, searching her eyes for some glimmer of humanity. She knew they planned to kill her. "Colin. Is that what this is about? You can't let the past go, can you?"

"Greely is in my rearview mirror." She leaned into Kate's face. "But, boy, did we have the real thing. Not like you. You little twit. You nuzzle up to whatever guy is in the room."

Kate held her hand up in an oath-taking position. "In my defense, only one at a time. You, Pierre, and Mister Ming." She held up three fingers. "What's the old saying? Don't shit where you work. And certainly not twice."

Rhonda laughed. "Eye on the prize."

"I get it. You need to prove you're smart."

"I like money. Now don't just sit here staring at me. What are you, a toddler? Get back to work and go easy on Bo." She turned away from Kate and rummaged through the credenza.

Kate scuffled out of the office past Pierre and Madley.

Madley teased her. "Watch out for BoBo. He's a little trigger-happy."

But before the door closed, she heard Pierre say to Madley, "Ming said to take care of this soon. Opaque. Not like the last one."

Chills ran through Kate as she darted eyes around the room for an escape route.

Bo picked up her tail and followed her back to work.

She ranted all the way back. "Are they paying you well to live this life, Bo? They got you all drugged up. You work for people who kill. Did you have an insane childhood filled with poverty and abuse? God knows you were properly educated. What about all that talk about being a poet?"

He shrugged. "Just a job."

"Just your job. Really? My father had a good job until you guys came along. This isn't about money. You chose this. You want power."

Bo exploded. "I choose nothing. My parents were taken in the night. My sister was raped and thrown into the slave trade. My uncle rescued me."

Kate appealed to Bo's ego. She believed persuading him was her only hope of getting out alive. "The first time I met you, you seemed stronger, more in charge. One of those who pulled themselves up by the bootstraps and seized their own way. All that talk about your parents and poetry." She shook her head. "Now you're just someone else's soldier."

"Enough." Bo signaled to his firearm. "I'll never be a poet and I'm not in love with your brother."

They reached the lobster tanks station. She was afraid. How could her brother have not seen these signs in Bo? But she knew she'd missed them in Pierre as well. She supposed Bo had reasons for how he had turned out. He was traumatized, trigger-happy, and apparently unable to love whom he wanted while living under his uncle's rule. Not to mention his coke habit enabled by Madley.

Things were clear but it was too late. Madley definitely put her father in jail after he planted Greentini in Pop's shed the morning of his arrest. Knowing this now wouldn't matter; she knew she was a dead woman.

The next two mornings, Bo repeated the same process for Kate: Knock and unlock, McDonald's breakfast, and the promise of a shower, soon. During bio-breaks, she cleaned up using the bathroom sink but felt rancid inside and out. She refrained from all conversations with Bo. She stared through him when he tried to engage her.

On the third day of her interment she was becoming blank-eyed.

"Rough night?" Bo sounded oddly concerned.

"I'll be fine," she responded.

He had a pained look on his face before he asked, "How is Michael?"

"Better off." She'd lost any sense of compassion for Bo.

"I deserved that," he conceded, to Kate's surprise. "I know you don't realize it, but I'm trapped here, too. I can't let Uncle Li down after all he's done. He has me watched, you know. Pierre's one of his soldiers; called Uncle to tell him I was at Dingles with Michael. Uncle doesn't want me with Michael or any other man. Says it's mental illness. He's traditional. Pressures me to conform." His voice cracked. "Chose a wife for me to marry and have a family."

Kate squelched any urge to have the slightest bit of empathy for her captor. "You can break away."

He shook his head, "He'll turn me over to Immigration. Anyhow, I can't let him down. My wedding is in two weeks." He pointed his gun between her shoulder blades and led her to her workstation.

In the middle of the day Kate fell asleep leaning at her laptop station, dreaming of an ice cream smorgasbord with toppings of all kinds: chocolate jimmies, rainbow jimmies, M&Ms, Skittles, chopped walnuts, and coconut. Coconut, little tiny Sno Balls. What a marketing idea. If they didn't kill her, she could pitch her product idea of little tiny Sno Balls to Hostess. In her dream, she prepared a hot fudge sundae with all her favorite toppings. Just when she was about to take her first bite, she was jostled awake by the sound of rain pounding on the roof. It was a fierce storm, vibrating the building and sounding like hooves running on metal. At that moment, the doors to the warehouse flew wide open.

A man yelled, "Immigration and Customs Enforcement. Line up."

Workers screamed: "ICE!" Some cried.

Bo grabbed Kate by the arm and put his gun to her back. "Don't move." He pushed her out into the center of the warehouse. A team of armed agents dressed in full regalia rounded up the workers.

A robust agent directed the Chinese workers to separate. He motioned with his hands for them to stand to the right of him if they had papers and to the left if they didn't. Kate saw their looks of terror as they all stepped to the left. Bo dug the gun into her back between her shoulders.

Madley came out of the office holding his skeley badge. "What can I do to help?"

"Get the girl away from the kid over there," said an agent. "We're here for her. The rest is a bonus."

Madley walked toward them and Bo stuck the gun to the back of Kate's head.

"I'll use it," Bo said. "Let the workers go."

"Hey there, cowboy." Madley motioned to Bo. "Put the gun down."

"You promised you'd protect all the people because you're a cop. No one deported!"

The large immigration agent turned to Madley, "What's he saying?"

"Chinglish," Madley retorted.

Kate was shaking. She wanted to scream out that Madley wanted her dead, but every instinct in her knew that Bo would kill her if she made a move. He was protecting his people.

"Clearly, he's psychotic." Madley backed away from Kate and Bo.

"Step aside, Detective." The robust agent motioned to three other agents, who raised their guns.

Bo jabbed the gun harder and Kate lost her breath. "Tell them to put their guns down. Let them go," Bo yelled again.

The head agent nodded. "Okay. Okay."

Shots came from behind. The impact pushed Kate to the floor. Her flesh burnt from inside. Colored dots. Blackness.

Kate was looking down on the scene in an out-of-body experience when the EMTs wheeled her out. She could see the IV held up by a female EMT and shards of light from the police cars. Someone ran up to her and touched her head. "Don't worry, Kate. You're going to be okay." It was McGann. And then there was noise from an incoming helicopter and the sensation of being lifted.

Chapter Twenty–One

Mom was sitting beside her bed. Michael sat across from her looking out the window, its shelf filled with flowers. Her throat was parched. She tried to ask her mother where she was, but nothing came out.

"Beth Israel Deaconess. They air-lifted you here two days ago, honey." Tears exploded from her eyes. "After you were shot."

Kate could feel her temples getting wet from her own tears.

Michael moved over to the bed and wiped her cheeks with his hand. Kate tried to say thank you but nothing came out.

"We were so worried. We called everywhere. As soon as Rob woke up that night, he reported what happened on the docks. Your co-worker Doug was trying to help." She started to weep. "You always call to tell me you won't be home. Well, one night maybe not, but definitely two."

Her continual chattering was making Kate agitated. Slowly, she managed to eke out a dry whisper, "Is Rob okay?"

"Yes, honey. He's fine. Don't worry. You need to rest." Mom

patted her hand. "Go back to sleep now."

And Kate went out again.

A man and a woman in scrubs stood at the foot of her bed discussing her chart. They looked like doctors and sounded like they were yelling up from a deep well. Kate could make out some of the man's words, the left shoulder, nine millimeters, and the bullet didn't pierce any vital organs or major blood vessels. No extensive bone or soft tissue loss. Concussion from the fall induced added shock. The woman said, debridement was minimal because the bullet entered in best possible scenario considering it was fired from a short distance. Missed her heart by less than an inch.

She tried to move her left side but a kind of supernatural force pushed her down. She faded back to sleep.

The sun shone through her window and it reminded her of sleeping in her office at Fish Pier.

"Well." The speaker cast a shadow over her bed. "You certainly look better than the first day I saw you."

"Thanks. I forget your name."

"Understandable. Reverend Aaker. But you can call me Jan. You've earned it."

She smiled at him, motioned to him with her right hand for him to sit. "Oh, God." Her hand burned from the IV needle. She scrunched her face in agony, not holding back curses. "Sorry, Reverend, Jan."

"I've been calling His name for you, too."

"Why are you here?"

"I rotate with other clergy to provide a spiritual presence for patients."

"Lucky for you I came up in the lottery."

"I'm not on duty, now. Just wanted to check on you. You were in tough shape two days ago."

"I'm in and out. Really tired."

He held a prayer book in his hand. "I wondered if I could say a prayer with you."

"Oh boy. Not really that type." She flashed back to the bathroom at AgaCulture when she had asked God to help her out. She guessed he had, in some screwed-up way. She reconsidered. "Okay. Let's do it."

The Reverend Aaker recited Psalm 23: "The Lord is my shepherd. ..."

"That's nice, Reverend. You know, I did say a prayer for the first time in years when I was entombed at AgaCulture, but I didn't ask for this."

"Our prayers may not be answered as we ask. Often later it becomes clear why things happen a particular way. And often, if we don't choose bitterness, our suffering permits us to become softer, humbler, more vulnerable. Better people."

"You're such a kind man. Maybe it's the morphine but you have a halo all around you. You seem like a holy man. I'm sorry about your wife."

JOANNE CAROTA

"Maddie? She's well. We're taking an Arizona trip with the grandkids. Staying at a dude ranch."

"Wow. I just assumed after the . . ."

"The what? Some nosy news reporters trying to hurt us. We're stronger than that. Maddie's the best wife and mother I know. I love her. So what! She likes to dance. She loves people of all ages. Sometimes I go with her, but I can't always keep up. We're not Puritans, after all."

"Did you study in Paris or something? You're so liberal. Are there more of you out there?"

"A few of us clergy have risen from the Dark Ages." He smiled a gentle smile. "I was impressed with how you wanted to save your father." He placed the prayer book on the nightstand.

She nodded in deference. "Thank you."

He started out the door, seemed to reconsider and turned back. "Your father did argue with Sammy Robbins the morning of the murder. It was on your father's boat, Truelight. The skeley showed up after your father left. He and Sammy took off on Milady."

"Rich Madley?"

"He's under indictment. Watch the news today."

"Bad skeley."

"Yes. I was going to testify to that, too. When Madley came to interrogate me, I didn't know who I could trust. He took my statement out of context and ran with it."

"Now I'm the jerk. Kind of sicced the paparazzi on you."

"You love your father."

After Aaker left, Kate flipped on Channel Five. The story broke at noon. An attractive blonde woman reported from outside the Boston Police Department's headquarters:

"Massachusetts Dock Police Detective Richard Madley was arrested yesterday at his South End apartment. This morning he appeared in US District Court in Boston, and will be held without bail. He is being indicted as the result of an investigation by the Federal Bureau of Investigation, and the Food and Drug Administration with assistance from the Massachusetts Dock Police, Mass State Police, Boston Police Department, and Immigration and Customs Enforcement, ICE, who were the primary responders on the scene. Also arrested on the scene and charged are Rhonda Conway, Pierre Gosselin, and Li Ming. The charges involve murder, kidnapping, unlawful employment of illegal aliens, violation of international trade laws, and possession and trafficking of Class A, B, and C substances. Madley maintains his innocence."

An electric shiver ran through Kate's body when an image of Madley in his signature raincoat appeared on the screen. The reporter continued: "When asked for a statement he said, 'The fact that a defendant has been charged with a crime is merely an accusation and the defendant is presumed innocent until proven guilty.' After further questioning Madley added, 'Circumstances are not always what they appear.' The Commonwealth has indicated that they will also press charges. Back to you in the newsroom."

"Typical. Cambridgeport rat," Kate muttered and changed the channel. NECN showed a clip of Tony Monero speaking as he left the US District Court: "This is a clear case of discrimination. My client, Mr. Ming, is an upstanding businessman in the Chinese-American community. His nephew was killed. There will be justice."

"Monero. What a chump! Pop was absolutely right about that guy." Michael had entered the room and stood at the side of her bed. She didn't turn toward him.

"Really? You're going to rub Monero in my face now?" Her legs agitated under the sheets. "Too bad you were so off about Bo."

After a long pause, she clicked off the TV and turned to see Michael's watery eyes. Immediate compassion shot through her heart for her brother.

"I'm so sorry this happened to you, Sis."

"You know how to pick them."

He leaned over and kissed her head.

Tranquility embraced her spirit. She felt a new calm, a deep stillness.

"What did Pop say about your Bo-friend trying to kill me?"

"He's glad the guy's dead, because he'd kill him himself with his bare hands. You know Pop."

She raised the bed and pulled her hospital gown together to cover her chest. "Exactly what does he know about you and Bo?"

His right leg twitched. "I told him." He looked up at the ceiling.

"Can you still be my brother?"

It broke the tension.

"He handled it. Jail's mellowed him in that area."

"From what I hear it's a party for guys of the other persuasion. You don't think Pop . . .?"

"Shut the hell up. You can joke about anything."

"It's my gift."

"I have to get back to work."

"I get it." She squeezed his hand. "Hey. If it makes you feel any better, Bo stood up for his fellow workers. Kind of honorable. Maybe that's the part that he touched in you."

"Thanks, sis. But I can assure you, that's not the part he touched."

"Choose wisely next time." She turned the television back on. "That's all I got for you."

"Can I do anything for you?"

She looked down at her johnny. "Tell Mom to bring me a decent nightgown."

Eight days after she was shot the hospital released her. The doctor said he had kept her longer than most patients with such wounds because she had contracted bronchitis. Nothing antibiotics couldn't cure, he said. She was to rest at home for the remainder of the week and begin physical therapy the next to help regain more fluid movement on her left side.

At home Mom made Kate all her favorite meals. They watched movies together. She had forgotten what a compassionate nurse her mother could be. She knitted while Kate caught up on her marine biology journals.

On a daily basis, Doug e-mailed her to keep her up to speed on their first-generation groundfish incubator. Erica, Will, and Rose stopped by and brought candy and flowers. The best visit of all was when Kevin came over to give them excellent news—Pop would be released. The DA had conceded that there was virtually no viable evidence left to convict him.

On Kate's second day home, Colin stopped by with flowers. Mom excused herself, saying she had some errands to run.

Kate sat in her father's chair and Colin came in and kissed her on the head. He sat on the couch across from her.

"How's your mom?" she asked.

"She's in treatment. Again. This time it will stick. She says that every time."

"We all have our stuff."

"Well, she's got more than most," he said. "Insists she's not an addict, just a casual user."

"It was the one thing she was clear about when I found her. 'Just once a day.' "

"It's an old story. Your story's more interesting." He leaned over and smoothed her hair with his hand. "You are brave. Practically Wonder Woman."

"Thanks. I get this to show for it." She lifted her sling.

"No cracking lobster tonight."

"Ugh. Lately, lobster's been a cruel lover." She got up slowly and sat next to him on the couch.

He put his arm around her. "I lit a candle for you every day at Our Lady of Good Voyage."

Kate thought back to the day of the fish auction. The day Louie and Pop and his friends stood up to thugs and Michael ran to the old chapel and how Pop was tender with Michael and how they lit candles, including one for Mom. "Wow. I used to go to the old one with my Pop sometimes. Loved the murals of the fishermen. You go to church?"

"God, ya." He was solemn. "It's always been my sanity. You met my mother."

She laughed. "Ironic that you are the honorable man in all this."

"Well, you know. It's what I do."

"But, there's still that thing."

"What thing is that, Doctor?"

"You thought my father was guilty."

"I said even if he . . . never mind. He's innocent. I beg your pardon."

"Thank you." She smiled. "Hey, I think I saw McGann going into AgaCulture before I went unconscious. He was nice to me."

"He's a Fed, special agent. Been working undercover for two years trying to nail these guys. Buddied up to Pierre. Put the heat on him around the clock. Even let me use his cool suite at MilPort when he was on travel. Have to give it up now." He lowered his head and shook it with regret. "Freaking place was beautiful."

"Damn." She nudged him. "Back to that crappy house of yours. Wait a minute, you seduced me in another man's suite? You said it was yours!"

"Yeah. Sorry. White lie. Anyhow, Agent McGann says the Bureau and various agencies are indebted to you. Catching the bad guys. The whole deal."

"He must have been the one who wrote the report to help get

my father off." She shook her head in amazement. "He likes me." She felt a warmness in her chest.

"Very much. Says you are hellfire. In a good way, of course."

"Of course," Kate added.

"He was just doing his job. Used the Labs for a cover."

"And Norah?"

"She really doesn't like you. Hopes you're going to take as much time as you need to get fully healed. Quote unquote."

Kate laughed hard and it didn't hurt. He leaned over and they kissed.

"That's enough for tonight." He rubbed her thighs, moving his hands up to her hip. She could see he was aroused. "Oh God. You got to get your rest. And I must, well, get out of here before you drive me crazy."

She teased him by kissing him again and again.

"You'll need a medical note to go any further." He held her right hand to his chest with both hands. "I miss you. Get well."

"I miss you, too," she said.

He rose and backed away from the couch. "Good instincts."

"What?"

"You never did warm up to Madley."

"You're right. First impressions."

"Hey. I told you I wasn't a monster." He blew her a kiss.

Chapter Twenty-Two

Pop was released a week before Christmas. Judge O'Hara granted the motion filed by the District Attorney's Office to dismiss charges based on lack of evidence and new evidence incriminating Rich Madley for the murder of Sammy Robbins.

In the courtroom the bailiff removed Pop's cuffs as Kate, Michael and Mom looked on. Mom rushed to him as he shook his wrists—a free man. They held each other for a long time. He'd lost more weight and stooped a little, but he was grinning. Then he hugged Kate on her right side. "Look at you. Look what you've done for me."

"I took a bullet for you, Pop."

He hugged Michael, shook Kevin's hand and patted him on the back. "I couldn't ask for a better family and friend. Now let's get the Christ out of here."

"I made a nice meal for you."

"Not that shitty beef stew, I hope."

Christmas morning arrived with two inches of snow. Just enough to make a splash, but not ruin Christmas. Kate was recovering well, had even stopped wearing her shoulder sling. The Finn house was filled with the warmth of Christmases that Kate had felt as a child. Their house was a home again.

At nine-thirty, the four Finns drove over to Fish Pier with a wreath. The Finn family walked down the docks past Truelight; the other fishermen and their families were already there along with Father Murphy. They clapped and took turns shaking Pop's hand. Rob Fitzpatrick offered him a hit off his flask decorated with holly, but he waved them off. "Not yet. I got unfinished business here. Father, would you start?"

Neptune, god of the sea, watched over them from his perch on the stone conference building as they lowered their eyes and Father Murphy led them in prayer. During the recitation of the Our Father, a white Dodge truck pulled up to the docks. John Spencer, his wife, and their two boys walked over to the group. Spence used a cane and his gait was quite slow. Pop nodded to him and Spence reciprocated.

After the prayer, the men formed a sacred Fisherman Ring with the wreath in the middle. It was ten o'clock and the Uilleann pipes blasted from the pier's speakers, right on schedule. The families formed a second ring that enclosed the fishermen. Seamus pulled a piece of paper from his coat pocket and called Kate into the inner ring beside him. He recited a prayer to Saint Andrew in Sammy's honor, then he handed her the wreath. Kate threw the wreath off the dock where she had found Sammy dead. Boston Harbor's current pulled it out to sea.

Rob started to hum it first and it built to a crescendo with everyone singing Sammy's favorite song, Three Dog Night's "Joy to the World," with full emphasis on, "fishes in the deep blue sea." Afterward, the group whistled and applauded and in the distance a foghorn blew.

"What do you say?" Rob held his flask in the air. "A round for Sammy behind Yanks?"

"Count me in," said Father Murphy.

The rest of the men followed with, "I'm in."

Mom had her hands on her hips, "We'll never have Christmas dinner."

Michael slipped his arm through hers. "Let him go, Mom. I'll keep an eye on him."

"You're going, too? We've got guests coming."

"Don't sweat." Michael kissed Mom on her head. "We'll be there."

They sat waiting at the kitchen table covered with a white lace tablecloth and Belleek place settings that only came out for holidays. Finally, the back door opened. Pop was in full "Danny Boy" serenade.

Michael cautioned him in the back hallway. "Pop. Straighten up. Mom's going to be mad."

"Nah. She knows. Just a man and his son having a couple of drinks together."

"Holy crap, Pop." Michael giggled. "I can't believe we went up to Mrs. Burke's door to wish her a Merry Christmas. And you gave her a nip." He was barely getting the words out, through his giggling. "And she said, 'What the cripes am I going to do with an airplane bottle of booze?'"

Their laughter reverberated.

"Mrs. Burke. She's good people."

Kate cringed at Pop's platinum praise phrase.

He stumbled into the kitchen singing his finale and gently led Mom out of her chair, twirling her in their Celtic waltz. She threw her head back laughing. "At least you don't smell like fish and beer. Just beer." The dance finished and they kissed deeply, leaving the entire dinner crowd breathless.

The following silence jangled Kate's nerves. Colin made the first move. He stood and shook Pop's hand.

"Pleasure to meet you, sir."

Pop stood erect, chest puffed.

"Same here, Colin. My daughter says you have treated her well. I'll take her word for it." He slouched into his chair and shook his head. "Colin Greely. At my table. Who'd ever think?"

"Seamus." Mom cocked her head toward Colleen.

He made it out of his chair to shake hands with her.

"I remember you. The Sizzling Seamstress. God. You were amazing."

"Just Colleen these days." She shook his hand and patted it.

"Nice to see you, Seamus."

"No. You were incredible. A legend. Even better than that there Saucy Sally. Hey, what ever happened to her?" He continued to stand over Colleen.

"Finished school. Started a law practice." Colleen took a sip of her water. "I still see her. Smart girl."

"Yeah, Ma. She's a genius. She didn't even pass the bar and she was taking clients illegally. Got shut down."

"La-di-da. Listen to my son. Such a snob. Can she help it she if didn't want to waste time studying for a stupid test when she already had the skills?"

"Brilliant logic." Colin didn't let up.

She admonished Colin with her eyes and shimmied back and forth. "Not everyone is in bed with the law. Besides, you are one to talk, quitting college. You did okay for yourself."

Colin placed his hand over his heart and mouthed to Kate, "She's exasperating."

Colleen turned back to Kate's father. "Sorry about my son's interruption. I taught him better than that. You were saying, Seamus?"

"When you think about it, what better practice to become a good lawyer, eh? Listening to drunken men spill their guts for a drink. Hell." He wobbled to his chair and sat down. "Yes, siree. We'd get off our boats and practically run to the Combat Zone to catch your afternoon show." He stood up again and bowed to Colleen. "Welcome to my homes." He slurred. "We're honored to have such a celebrity as yourself."

"Thank you, Seamus," Colleen gently nodded.

Mom cleared her throat. "Time for grace."

Kate couldn't believe Pop's cavalier attitude. He was going to be in so much trouble the next day.

He sat down, folded his hands on his belly and rocked back in his chair. "This was all before I was married, of course." He pulled the chair back to the floor and leaned in toward Colin. "Colin, you're a good catch. How come you never married?" He pointed to his son. "Are you and, ah, Michael here on the same page?"

Michael rolled his eyes.

"I guess I just hadn't found the right girl, yet." He looked over at Kate and smiled.

Pop recited grace. "Thank you for these gifts which we are about to receive through Christ our Lord. Amen." And then he toasted with his water glass, "Go raibh maith agat!" The rest of the family translated, "May you have goodness." He made it through dinner and fell asleep in his chair. The rest of them sat in the kitchen and talked late into the night.

At the end of the winter, the surgeons at Beth Israel Deaconess gave Kate the green light to go back to work. She still had pain in her shoulder and chest, but her mobility was about eighty percent. She'd spent most of the winter at Colin's house. They went out for dinner a couple of times during the week and on weekends. One evening while they sat drinking wine in front of the fire in Colin's study, she confessed that she didn't want to go back to work for him.

"I almost died working for you. No pun intended."

"No pun necessary. Because it's actually kind of true. What will you do?"

"I've thought about lecturing. But I love research. Besides, we still haven't fully figured out Ming's Greentini compound."

"That's your takeaway from all this?" Colin laughed.

"Could be a matter of national security."

"Don't get ahead of yourself."

She hesitated before speaking. "I've been thinking about moving. Dr. Zion used to say he always has a place for me at Nobska Fisheries. Pierre's gone so it will be a fresh start."

"You'd go back to the Cape?"

"We could still see each other here some weekends. And you could come down to see me in Falmouth. With the money I've saved, I can buy a small place."

Colin was quiet.

"I can lecture and research there. It's the perfect situation. I might be able to work with you on new joint projects if any come up and Dr. Zion wants me to, just not the crap you had me doing. Blah." She stuck her tongue out.

"Okay. Okay. I get it. You hate for-profit. If this is what you want, we can make it work. It's only an hour-and-a-half drive."

"Exactly. You can stay at my place for a change."

"Can you make anything besides cryo Sno Balls?"

"Doubtful. But there are a few restaurants in Woods Hole."

Kate ran back and forth to the house loading her car. Mom had packed her a cooler of food, even though Kate had explained to her that she'd be staying at the Knotty Sea Inn for the first month and going out to eat for every meal. But when she went upstairs to check her room one last time, her mother had shoved the cooler into her car. She pretended not to notice. It was her mother's way of coping with goodbye. In fact, they all refused to say goodbye. Michael left early for the Financial District. Pop went fishing on Truelight. Mom worked the crosswalk in the morning as usual. And Kate promised to come home the next weekend for a visit. It was their way. If they could avoid the sloppiness of emotion, they would.

With the car fully loaded, Kate slammed the hatchback shut and that's when she noticed them—a mother walking to the school crosswalk with her little girl. Bent arm held high, her tiny fist clenched a water-filled plastic bag containing a goldfish. The fish glimmered in the sunshine.

"Look, Mommy. He has wings. I bet he can fly."

"Remember, Daddy said to be careful with him, Catie. Goldfish are very delicate."

Kate drove slowly to the corner and watched as her own Mom kneeled, gushing over Catie's fish before she stopped traffic to let them cross.

"First love," Kate said out loud as she blinked back tears.

Epilogue

When she got to the Knotty Sea, her room was ready. She walked down to Eel Pond to admire the boats. Then she drove toward Nobska Fisheries. The water on the beach below was filled with whitecaps from the offshore breeze. She turned into the road near the Nobska lighthouse. The smooth pebbles pillowed her ride.

The parking lot was packed. She parked in a visitor's spot, reconsidered and moved to the staff section. At the familiar double doors she buzzed the alarm. A woman's voice came over the intercom.

"May I help you?"

"I'm here to see Dr. Zion."

"Is he expecting you?"

Kate hesitated.

"Tell him Doctor Finn is here to see him."

"Please wait in the lobby and I'll send him down."

The door buzzed open.

Dr. Zion met her in the waiting room.

"I'm here to replace you."

"What took you so long?"

He led her through the inner door.

About the Author

Joanne Carota teaches writing at the University of Massachusetts Lowell. Joanne is a graduate of the Solstice MFA Program and holds an MA in Writing and Literature from Rivier University. In January 2018, she received The Sterling Watson Fellowship to attend Writers in Paradise, and has attended Green Mountain Writers and NOEPE. She's been published in *The Subtopian, Solstice Literary Magazine*, *Pink Panther*, *Merrimack Journal*, *Chelmsford Independent*, *Middlesex Beat*, and *Andover Townsman*. A lover of family, friends, reading, travel, movies, and fine food, she lives with her husband nearby their adult children in Massachusetts.

Made in the USA
Middletown, DE
19 January 2020